'... You designed that boat and the boat cracked up, and you killed your brother and Henry's a cripple. Well, don't think I'm going to sit around and do nothing about it ... You saw Henry coming and you took his money and built him a deathtrap.' The line went dead.

I put my end down quietly and tried to catch my breath. My legs felt rubbery. She's right, I thought; it is my fault. If the boat did crack up, I killed them.

SAM LLEWELLYN

Dead Reckoning

SPHERE BOOKS LIMITED

SPHERE BOOKS LTD

Penguin Books Ltd, 27 Wrights Lane, London W8 5TZ (Publishing and Editorial)
and Harmondsworth, Middlesex, England (Distribution and Warehouse)
Viking Penguin Inc., 40 West 23rd Street, New York, New York 10010, USA
Penguin Books Australia Ltd, Ringwood, Victoria, Australia
Penguin Books Canada Ltd, 2801 John Street, Markham, Ontario, Canada L3R 1B4
Penguin Books (NZ) Ltd, 182–190 Wairau Road, Auckland 10, New Zealand

First published in Great Britain by Michael Joseph Ltd 1987
Published by Sphere Books Ltd 1988

Printed and bound in Great Britain by
Richard Clay Ltd, Bungay, Suffolk
Set in Times

Chapter One

I woke suddenly in the dark. The clock said 4.03, and the wind was moaning round the slates. Behind it there was a lower, duller roaring. It was then that I knew why I was awake.

As I rolled out of the warm bed I started to shiver. Woollen underwear, jeans, oiled-wool jersey, thick oiled socks. Downstairs into the kitchen, last night's dishes piled in the sink. A look at the kettle; no comfort there, no time for coffee, because I was already in the porch, hauling on calf-length boots, yellow rubber with non-slip soles, yellow oilskin trousers and coat, woolly hat and sou'wester over the top.

Outside the front porch the wind hit me like a wet sack. It nudged at me, clearing my head, as I ran down Quay Street and into Fore Street. Tarmac and shopfronts gleamed with rain under yellow streetlamps. It could have been any small town in England at four o'clock in the morning, except for the smell of the wind, which was salty, and the drubbing roar that grew louder as I scuttled across Fore Street and down to the Front. And what had woken me up.

It was bad; I had learned to judge how bad during twenty-five years of watching Fore Street. On a calm day in July, Fore Street looked like a travel poster: Come to Sunny Pulteney, white houses stacked up the hill above a blue sea fringed with lacy foam. Now the lace was angry clouds of spray that hissed across the formal beds of tulips

1

and a car that some idiot had left on the inland side of the road. Head down, I ran towards the corrugated iron structure two hundred yards to the left, under the shelter of the Customs House.

A salt-rotted Cortina whipped past, fans of spray hissing from its tyres. I kept running. In front of the corrugated iron was a bright white light. It lit two men as they got out of the car and ran through the doorway. I was a minute behind them, blinking under the hard lights that illuminated the white upperworks and navy-blue hull of the *Edith Agutter*.

'Last one,' said Chiefy Barnes, the coxswain, large eyebrows knitting under the rim of his sou'wester.

'What have we got?' I said, struggling with the braces of the RNLI-issue wet-gear. It had taken me four minutes since the maroon.

'Yacht,' said Chiefy. 'The Teeth.' He turned away. 'Starting engines.'

In the bowels of the boat, the twin diesels coughed, turned over, and started sweetly on the first revolution of the flywheel. I wanted coffee. I did not like yacht jobs. Too many of my friends were mixed up with yachts.

'Doors open,' said Chiefy. 'Stations.'

The wind's drubbing turned to howling, and the far end of the shed changed from wood to rain and wind. I clipped on my lifeline. The lights went out.

'Let go,' said Chiefy.

There was a dull chunk as the wedges came away. The lifeboat started to move. As she passed the doors the wind staggered her. Beneath her keel the carriage rumbled briefly for that moment of weightlessness, twenty tons of machine and twelve men doing exactly what gravity asked; then the pressure in the knee joints as the boat hit the water in a giant flower of spray, shook herself, and began to move.

I went below to try for some coffee. George was jammed in his corner, muttering at the radio. It smelt of paraffin and bilge down here; the *Edith Agutter* was an

2

old boat, overdue for replacement. She was named after my grandmother, and my grandmother had been dead for forty years.

Jerry gave me a mug of coffee and I drank. It was sweet and scalding.

George said, 'Transmissions ceased.'

It did not sound good. It felt bad, too, from the lurching corkscrews of the old boat as she wound her way among the swells. An hour later, when we got there, it looked even worse. I was on deck by then; we all were.

The wind whipped sheets of water across the cockpit. Through the spinning circle of the windshield the waves were black in the growing dawn, except where the Teeth chewed them to a horrible creamy froth that extended a mile along the southern horizon, broken here and there by black fangs. They looked bad that morning, the Teeth.

'Not a bloody hope,' said Jerry. He glanced at me and looked quickly away again.

Chiefy massaged the twin throttle levers, and we crept closer, into the fringe of the broken water, where the spume blew like shaving-foam. I found myself swallowing nothing, dry-mouthed. Chiefy's face was mildly interested; I knew from past experience that he would be humming monotonously. I also knew that if anyone could get to whatever was happening in the middle of those rocks, Chiefy could.

Foot by foot, feeling her way, the *Edith Agutter* closed in. The movement of the deck became arbitrary and jerky. Heavy spray rattled on the plate-glass and streamed wobbling down.

'There she is,' said Jerry.

It was not difficult to see her, once you knew what to look for. The difficulty had been looking for something that looked like a ship. This was a slab of white stuff, like a giant eggshell rolling among the granite chunks, lifting a stub that became a broken mast trailing a web of rigging.

'There'll be nobody in that lot,' said Chiefy.

As always, he was right.

3

We watched the sluggish roll of the shattered hull, and I listened to my heart beating very hard and very slowly.

'Maybe there's a raft,' said Jerry. But he knew as well as anyone else that if there had been a raft it would have been blown onto the stones too, and its inmates would have had about as much chance as if they had gone swimming in a concrete mixer.

'Better wait for the tide,' said Chiefy.

He brought the *Edith* round in a wide, slow arc that took her out of the robbly backwash and into the rhythm of the swell. Then he started a steady cruise to leeward of the reef.

It was calmer in here, and the wind was dropping for the dawn lull. To seaward, a fog of spray hung above the reef like a curtain.

As usual, it was Chiefy who saw it first.

Out of the curtain of spray floated a yellow survival raft, a little rubber tent over an air-filled tube with a rubber floor. The deck heeled under my boots as Chiefy shoved the throttles forward, and we took positions. I was on the starboard bow, so it was me that caught it with the boathook. Two of the inflated sections were punctured, and it was nearly awash. We walked it back to the waist. The boat's side was level with the tent's door, but the shadows made it hard to see in. I did not have to see in, though. I knew.

We brought out two bodies. The first one had been lying face down in a foot of water, and would have drowned if he had not already died of a fractured skull. The second one was still alive, which was a miracle. We brought him out on a stretcher, very gently. He was semi-conscious, but his legs flopped limply, because he had a broken back.

Once they were below, we called up the choppers for the injured man and set out for home.

'She'll come off that ledge and go down,' said Chiefy. 'No point waiting for the tide.' He was speaking to me, and me alone. I knew why.

4

The yacht on the Teeth, which would sink at high tide, was called *Aesthete*. I had conceived and designed her myself. And the dead man was called Hugo Agutter. He was my younger brother.

Chapter Two

There is an odd quietness that comes over Pulteney when the lifeboat is in after a bad night. At first it is apprehensive; the *Edith Agutter*'s predecessor is scattered among the crevices and tide rips of the Western Teeth. Then the apprehension changes to suspense, as the chopper hacks its way overhead when it has picked up the bodies. And the suspense gives way to a sort of miserable calm once the word has gone around: one dead, one broken back. The dead man from the town, the broken back a yachter. The word travels fast: from a shower where a tired lifeboatman is soaping off the salt before he starts his day's work; to his wife, frying fish fingers for breakfast; from his wife to the milkman, from the milkman to the postman, and so through the narrow streets of white houses where the holiday people and the yachters live; up to the council estate tucked over the back of Naylor's Hill, and down to the old warehouses by the harbour where the sailmakers and yacht designers are starting their day. And eventually, once the village knows, the news spreads outwards to the rest of the country.

I went down to the garage. My rusty BMW sneezed at me, and started. Grey rain drifted onto the windscreen and the cobbles and the window-boxes my neighbours liked to set against the whitewashed granite of their holiday homes.

It was a road Hugo had known well. He and I had learned

6

to ride bicycles on it, in the days before Pulteney became a yachters' haven. In those days, the traffic had been Yeo's lorry for the fish that came off the boats that unloaded in the harbour every morning. But in those days, there had been fish to be caught in the Western Approaches. In those days, there had been no need for the signs banning cars from the village street. I drove past Maginnis' window. In those days, the window had been made of wood, with panes that distorted the dusty sweets inside. Now it was plate-glass – a memorial to Hugo's first attempt at teaching himself to drive. I had been his instructor, and I vividly remembered sitting in a pile of newspapers, shrimping nets and sherbert fountains, laughing hysterically as bricks rained on the car roof from the lintel of the devastated window.

The new houses on the edge of the village came up and fell behind. Out here the roads were wider and faster. I felt the tears rise for poor old Hugo. But he was past crying for; it was Sally who was in trouble.

She had got engaged to Hugo while I was at Southampton, doing a Naval Architecture course. Ridiculously early, the parents all said. Hugo loved to win; I think that had been it. But it had worked, and they had been very happy. Yes, very happy.

Until this morning.

Hugo's house – Sally's house, I should say – was long and low, grey granite tucked under a hill of wind-thrashed oaks. The gates were open; they had never been closed, as far as I remembered. But the house looked closed, its windows blind and wet in the drizzle. There was only Sally's Peugeot van, parked untidily by the front door.

Sally herself came to meet me. She was dressed as usual in a blue jersey and jeans that were unfashionably tight but showed her long and beautiful legs. She had a good face: Egyptian, with a slab of black hair on either side, hollows under finely-modelled cheekbones, and a wide red mouth. Her eyes were long, and beneath their thick black lashes, astonishingly green. She was pale, her face

7

sunk back over the bones. She had not yet started to cry; perhaps she did not yet know. But as I came closer, I noticed that her eyes had a dazzled look and her head moved not with its usual grace but with a slow, awkward swing. When her eyes fixed on me, they were suddenly full of pain.

'Let's go inside,' I said.

We went in. The house was full of her junk, Chinese and London art-gallery. An Elizabeth Frink bird stood on the hall table, crowned with a yachting cap. Hugo's.

'Amy rang,' she said. 'Henry's got a broken back.'

'I know,' I said. I was going to continue, but she interrupted.

'And you came out here to tell me. Well thanks, Charlie, but I already know.'

I put her in a chair. The muscles at the corners of her jaw were knotted. She would not want sympathy.

'Charlie,' she said, 'why don't you go and make yourself some breakfast.'

The kitchen was big and bright, with an oilcloth-covered table and paintings above the dresser. The paintings were mostly of boats; there was an Alan Lownes of steam drifters and an Alfred Wallis of St Ives harbour with schooners. I was tired, my stomach sick and acid. I dropped eggs into a frying-pan, thinking of the times we had come home after sailing all night, me and Hugo, and had breakfast in this room, with the salt still on us. Sally's voice murmured on the telephone in the next room. It was scarcely possible to comprehend that Hugo would be away for ever.

Sally came back in as the coffee boiled up in the percolator. She had herself under control again.

'I'll look after . . . things,' I said.

She laid her hand on mine, cold and dry. Then she left.

I finished my coffee. The sun came out and I watched the blackbirds hopping after the worms on the lawn and the heaving of the rhododendrons in the wind. The telephone rang. I picked it up.

8

It was a woman's voice, brittle and full of raw nerves.

'Sally?' it said. 'Darling, if there's anything I can do to help – '

'I'm afraid Sally's not here,' I said.

'Who's that?'

'Charlie Agutter.'

'Oh.' There was a pause. I knew the voice. It belonged to Amy Charlton, wife of Henry with the broken back. 'I suppose you were on the lifeboat,' she said.

'Yes.'

'Well, Henry's conscious,' she said, tightly. 'But he's paralysed.'

'I'm sorry.'

'And so you bloody well should be,' said Amy, her voice rising suddenly. 'Last night, I had a perfectly good husband. This morning, they're taking him up to Stoke Mandeville and you know what that means. He'll never walk again and I'll have to spend the rest of my life changing his damn nappies.'

'They're very good at spinal injuries,' I said, as gently as I could.

'Don't tell me who's good at what, Mr bloody yacht-designing Agutter. You designed that boat and the boat cracked up, and you killed your brother and Henry's a cripple. Well, don't think I'm going to sit around and do nothing about it. You Pulteney bastards, you're all pirates. You saw Henry coming and you took his money and built him a deathtrap.' The line went dead.

I put my end down quietly and tried to catch my breath. My legs felt rubbery. She's right, I thought; it is my fault. If the boat did crack up, I killed them.

Then my eyes went to the colour photograph above the telephone: an ocean racer, decks cluttered with sails and ropes and people. *V.Ex*, winner, One Ton Cup, the ultimate testing-ground for state-of-the-art sea sledges. Designer, Charlie Agutter. Designer of good boats, that won races. Not deathtraps. There were more reasons for hitting rocks than your boat cracking up.

9

Chapter Three

Fifteen years ago, Pulteney was what is known as a nice little fishing village. It had a long, windy beach, from which wise people did not bathe, and a horseshoe-shaped harbour jam-packed with wooden fishing-boats. Its situation, in the unfavoured part of the South Coast between Bridport and Torquay, meant that the crowds left it alone.

Then everything changed. The cause of the change was the death of Lord Cerne and the subsequent sale of Bollard Row, a picturesque slum above a cobbled alley too narrow for cars. The purchaser had been a 25-year-old Deptford scrap dealer called Frank Millstone. Though young, Millstone had a vision of the future which included himself as feudal entrepreneur. Under the hands of his builders and interior decorators, Bollard Row became a little epic of seaside quaintness. Soon after, he had brought a load of yachting journalists into the harbour aboard his fifty-foot catamaran, pointing out its advantages as a yacht haven. The journalists saw the advantages, through a fog of Millstone's Bollinger. The Pulteney boom was on.

More streets came on the market, and the people who had lived in them for years moved to the council estate over the hill. The new owners of their homes were also the owners of the sleek yachts which had taken the place of the fishing-boats in the harbour. Spearman's boatyard, long one of Pulteney's main employers, moved to new premises and doubled its workforce.

10

One of the few houses in Pulteney that Millstone was unable to get his hands on was ours. It was a white Georgian town house, long and low, with two floors and a huge bow-window. It clung to the hill, overlooking the harbour. It had been built in 1817 by my great-great-grandfather, an extremely lazy man who had spent most of his life in the bow-window with a telescope, spying on the shipping. It was one of those houses that, while it is by no means beautiful, is exactly right in every detail, and it had inspired in successive generations of Agutters a love amounting almost to obsession. Millstone had also been affected by its spell. He had lost no time in making an offer for it, and the Agutters had lost no time in refusing.

Despite our resistance to Frank Millstone, the Agutters did pretty well out of the Pulteney boom. My father owned a decaying line of coasters, one of which he had driven himself. The line's assets were four 1,000-ton rustbuckets and a warehouse down by the quay.

The ships were sold to a Greek coal merchant, and the warehouse was converted into offices for companies who wished to bask in the glamour of the new Pulteney.

One summer, I drew a boat for a merchant banker whom I had met in the new Yacht Club Millstone had built on the site of a net shed by the harbour, and he sailed it into the Captain's Cup team. That year, the British team had come second, which was encouraging, as the Captain's Cup is one of the four most important yacht series in the Northern Hemisphere. Pulteney was now feeding racing-boats into the offshore racing circuit in Australia and the US as well as Europe, and I was doing a good share of the designing.

My mother had died while I was at university, and my father and I lived one in each half of the house. My father's only condition in this arrangement had been that he was to have the side with the bow-window, since he was now of an age where an armchair and a telescope on a busy harbour were the only amusements left.

In this bow-window he spent most of his days, his legs

11

wrapped in a loud tartan rug, ministered to by the bulging but extremely efficient Nurse Bollom. Nurse Bollom lived in a hot, scrubbed room in the attic, and I had learned not to mind the fact that she disapproved of me intensely.

I parked the BMW on the quay beside the office door and went into my office past Ernie, the draughtsman.

My workroom occupied much of the ground floor of the warehouse. It was a large, bare room, with a huge blow-up of *V.Ex* on the whitewashed wall, a computer on a black desk, and a drawing-board lit by a vast window overlooking the stone horns of the harbour. It normally dwarfed people who weren't used to its echoing spaces. But Frank Millstone went a long way towards filling it.

He was an enormous man, with an enormous face and little blue eyes in nests of wrinkles that made him look as if he was permanently on the point of breaking into a big grin. He was wearing a navy blue pea-jacket and a pair of faded blue O.M. Watts trousers. If you had seen him rolling down Quay Street, you might have taken him for a jolly nautical tramp.

You would have been wrong.

Frank bought and sold money and commodities on a huge scale. He was also Life President of the Pulteney Yacht Club and a keen buyer of racing-boats. Two years previously, he had won the Half-Ton Cup with *Pallas*, designed by one of my principal competitors, Joe Grimaldi. This year, he had designs on the Captain's Cup team. The series of offshore races that served as trials for the Cup were due to start in June. Three months previously, he had said that he wanted Charlie Agutter to design him a contender. Whether or not I liked Millstone, that had been good news.

'Charlie,' he said. 'How are you?'

'Fine.' Frank was not a man to confide in about a lost brother, or even a lost night's sleep.

'How's my boat?'

12

'Going for finishing on Monday.'

His eyes twinkled in their nests of wrinkles like twin refrigerators in need of defrosting. 'Yes. Charlie, I'm coming straight to the point. I'm worried about the rudder.'

I thought about my talk with Amy, and goose-pimples pricked my skin. 'What's wrong with the rudder?'

'It's not a normal rudder.'

What he was trying to say was that the rudder was a thing I had designed myself, using research lifted from the Royal Navy and NASA. Most rudders slowed a boat down when they steered her. Not this one: theoretically, it should make her faster.

'Charlie, Hugo's boat had one of your new rudders. I think we want a normal rudder,' said Frank.

'There was nothing wrong with the rudder,' I said.

'I said I would like a normal rudder,' said Frank.

It was only now that I realised that what we had here was not the standard client-designer debate. This was the professional relationship teetering on a knife-edge, aggravated by Frank's suspicion of me as Old Pulteney, and my suspicion of him as New Pulteney.

I said, 'Hold on –'

'Will you change that rudder?' said Frank.

'No, I bloody well will not,' I said. 'Now, why don't you tell me your problem?'

'I suggest you go and talk to Henry in hospital,' he said.

'You have been speaking to Amy.'

'Perhaps.'

'It's not like you to listen to gossip, Frank.'

He got up. His eyes were definitely not smiling. 'Go and talk to Henry,' he said. 'And please stop work for the moment. I've suspended payment.'

'What?' I said. I couldn't believe my ears.

'We'll wait for the salvage report,' he said, and rolled heavily out.

I sat there for a moment, feeling as if I had swallowed a big cold cannonball. If Millstone and Amy had the idea

13

that the boat had a design fault, it would not be long before the rest of the world got it too – which would be a disaster.

Contrary to popular belief, yacht designers do not make a lot of money, unless they are very successful. I was on the way up, but I was not at the top. I was designing Frank's boat as a contractor, overseeing the building myself and taking my fee out of the price I had quoted him at the beginning. It was an unusual arrangement, but it was attractive to owners because it put the risk firmly on me. It was not the only risk I had to take.

In order to get to the top, I needed to get some boats of my design into the Captain's Cup. The trials for the Cup were now some four weeks away, and invitations to compete had been issued by the National Offshore Racing Federation to thirty likely entrants. Some of these entrants had been training for months. Others had not yet got boats. What they had in common was that they were very rich and very competitive, and prepared to spend six- and seven-figure sums to make sure their boats got into the three-boat team.

The fact that they were very rich meant that a lot of people listened to them, very closely. If I was getting on the wrong side of my owners, I was in deep career trouble. I had sunk a lot into getting into the Captain's Cup. In fact, I had sunk everything I had, and more besides, and I was broke. I also had my father to support, together with Nurse Bollom, not to mention my own boat, *Nautilus*.

I sat at my desk and tried to think. It was not easy, because my brain was operating in the thick fog that always descends when I am very tired. All I could decide was that the sooner we got *Aesthete* off the bottom and into a yard, the better.

Outside the window, the wind was wailing in the halyards of the moored boats. It was being a bloody awful April, and with a wind like that there was no chance of salvaging the wreck from the middle of the Teeth. But I

14

have never been good at sitting still and waiting, so I picked up the telephone and dialled Neville Spearman.

There had been Spearmans in Pulteney for longer than there had been Agutters. Spearmans ran trips round the bay, set lobster-pots, worked in supermarkets and ran estate agencies. Neville was easily the most successful Spearman. He had played the Pulteney boom very cleverly, expanding a yard that used to turn out good, heavy fishing-boats into one equipped to build state-of-the-art racing-yachts. He was a gloomy old devil, though, who always managed to give the impression that the Pulteney boom was too good to last, and that he expected a general collapse imminently. But he combined this quality with a shrewd perception of what side his bread was buttered, so as long as things were going well, he could be relied on. The telephone rang for a long time. Finally, he answered. I could hear the whine of sanders in the background.

'Morning,' he said.

'Have you got that salvage barge in the water?'

He got my drift immediately. 'Yes. But not in this weather. Charlie, I was about to ring you.'

'Yes?' Chilly winds of disaster drifted from the receiver.

'Sir Alec Breen was on the blower. He's asked me to stop work on *Windjammer* till . . . things are cleared up. He's writing you a letter.'

'Is it the rudder?' I said.

'He seems to think so.'

'You told him you thought they're okay? That NASA and the Royal Navy are using the materials?'

'Do me a favour,' he said. 'You know what owners are like.'

'I'll find out what really happened,' I said.

'That would be nice. Then we could all do some bloody work.'

'Book that barge to me as soon as we get a calm day.'

'Will do,' said Spearman.

Sir Alec Breen was another of my clients. We were a

15

week into finishing a one-tonner of my design at Spearman's yard. She was a nice boat and another strong Captain's Cup possibility, and Breen had come to me only after some hot competition. Boat designers like me are as much slaves to public opinion as pop stars. The difference is that our public is smaller, consisting of the couple of hundred men who can afford to spend a quarter of a million pounds on a boat every three or four years.

Under the right circumstances, Breen was my favourite kind of owner. He was no more addicted to sailing fast boats than he was to synchronized swimming. What he enjoyed was organization. Presumably he was not getting enough of it in his everyday life, most of which he spent running the chain of a hundred and twelve gravel-pits that brought him in an income reckoned by City analysts to be between three and five million pounds a year. Having organized a designer and builder for his boats, Breen liked to organize a crew, then sit back and wait to see his name in the papers. He was seldom disappointed.

He had a reputation as a cold fish. I rather liked him. He was small, with a slight Northern accent, heavy-lidded eyes and a perpetual cigar. He was one of those people who will sit in the corner of a room, unnoticed until he opens his mouth – at which point it is apparent that he is the focus of everything that is happening in that room. The first time I had gone to see him, he had taken me on a tour of one of his gravel-pits, and identified seventeen different fossils, with an evident appreciation of the excellent organization of the evolutionary process.

One of the things he admired about evolution was the principle of the survival of the fittest. For Breen was one of the most competitive people I have ever met, both in business and in the small world of offshore racing, which was where my problem lay. Breen was not a sentimentalist about his employees. If they didn't deliver, out they went, and he was not shy of advertising the fact. In the boardrooms, clubs and other expensive places where the owners of offshore racers meet and talk, the word would

16

be out that Agutter had problems. Disaster is the favourite topic in such places, and Agutter would be the disaster of the week, this week.

I tried to call him. He was not available, which was no surprise. If Breen was writing a letter, Breen was writing a letter.

I was tired, I felt sick, and I wanted to go to bed. But it was too early. I decided I needed air. I was at the door when the telephone rang again.

'Charlie,' said the voice. It was the voice I had been going for a walk to avoid.

'Archer,' I said. 'Can I help?'

'In a way,' said the other voice. It was level and sounded slightly amused, but that didn't mean anything. 'I heard about *Aesthete*. I'm very sorry about Hugo.' He paused. 'Are we still sailing tomorrow? Because we should talk.'

'Of course,' I said, and rang off.

Jack Archer was the design manager of Padmore and Bayliss. P and B produced eight hundred yachts a year, and I had just negotiated the contract to design a complete new range for them: seven models, from racers down to bilge keel cruisers. It was a lovely job, and not the least lovely part was the royalty P and B had agreed to pay me on each boat.

One-off racing-boats establish a designer's reputation, provided they win. But they do not pay the milk-bill. It is the fleet-boats that pay off big, and fleet contracts are like hen's teeth. I had sweated nails going after this one, and I was very, very worried about what Archer was going to say when we had our little chat tomorrow.

'Hell,' I said. I took the phone off the hook and marched out the side door of my office.

Chiefy was in his usual corner at the Mermaid, with a glass of rum in his hand and a pint of bitter at his elbow. He was usually there after the lifeboat had been out.

17

Ashore, he was smaller than you would have guessed if you had only seen him at the wheel of the *Edith*. He was an ordinary-looking man, baldish, with bushy grey eyebrows and square brown hands. It was only the eyes that gave him away, blue and very sharp, with a distance in them that went beyond the smoke-mottled walls of the Mermaid and onto horizons saw-toothed with big seas.

'Have a drink, boy,' he said.

I accepted a pint of bitter.

'Won't light no fires with that,' said Chiefy, reprovingly.

'I've just been out to Sally,' I said.

Chiefy nodded. 'It weren't Hugo at the helm.'

The same thought had occurred to me. Hugo was a beautiful helmsman and he knew Pulteney backwards. If he had been at the wheel, he would never have gone anywhere near the Teeth on a night like last night.

'Unless something did go unseemly on that there boat of yours.' Chiefy's idea of a good boat was the *Ark Royal*, reinforced wherever possible with lengths of railway line. 'Not what I calls seaworthy,' said Chiefy. 'Not properly. None of your bloody racing-boats. Look at Edward Beith.'

I was getting tired of people telling me my boats were unseaworthy. 'Why don't you shut up?' I said.

Chiefy darted a glance at me. His eye was less sharp than usual; he was far gone in rum. He had loved Hugo, too. 'Beith didn't look too happy when I saw him at Spearman's yesterday. Trouble with *Crystal*, I reckon.'

Ed Beith was more Old Pulteney. He, Hugo and I had been friends since before we could walk. Pulteney regattas, in the days before the big money had arrived, had been contests between Beith and his crew and the Agutter boys. We had sailed 505s, very hard. We had smoked illicit Capstan Full Strengths in Chiefy's net shed. We had pursued girls, among them Sally. In short, we had had a gang.

When Ed's father died, he had inherited the farm, inland from Pulteney. It had once run all the way to the

18

cliffs, but Millstone had bought the cliffside bits cheap, by setting-up a cousin of Ed's. The cousin had begged the land from him to give him a start in sheep-farming. Ed had sold it to him cheap and Millstone had paid off the cousin and built chalet bungalows.

It was a gesture typical of Ed, who, outside a racing-boat, was incapable of subterfuge. He had a lot of land, but he was known to be in hock to the bank. His forty-foot sloop *Crystal* would not be helping. She was a fast boat, but her hull was made of a heat-bonded composite of resin and aramid paper that didn't like staying together. There were rumours that he was finding her expensive to run.

'Did you talk to him?'

'He said to tell you to drop in,' said Chiefy. 'Well, I'm off. You ought to check that bloody rudder of yours, though. I've heard a lot of nasty talk about it.'

'No checking anything till we can pull up *Aesthete*. But I'm off to see Henry Charlton in Stoke Mandeville, just in case he remembers anything.'

'You'd better have a lie-down first,' said Chiefy. 'It's a bloody long way.' His rock-hard hand clapped me on the shoulder. 'And when you've finished popping about, we can have a drink about Hugo.'

'I'd like that.'

I finished my pint and trudged up the steep cobbles, thinking: I'd better ring Hugo and talk about *Crystal*, see if there was anything we could do. Then I remembered that Hugo was dead.

Chapter Four

At the house I wearily made the bed and did the washing-up. Then I poured myself a Famous Grouse, put a John Coltrane record on the turntable and moved round in a dreary trance, straightening the pictures. I stopped in front of the little glass case which held my bronze medal from the Montreal Olympics, trying to remember the surge of power that I had felt there, the confidence that nothing could go wrong from now on. The glass reflected a thin face, fair hair sticking out in harrassed spikes above low cheekbones and sunken cheeks, the eyes sunk into gloomy pits above deep pouches. Not the face of an Olympic medal winner, but of a man under suspicion of professional incompetence which had caused the death of his brother.

'Ugh,' I said. The face in the mirror's glass bore no resemblance to the Charlie Agutter seen by readers of the *Yachtsman*, or the viewers of the BBC yachting programmes. That Agutter was a bronzed, fit optimist. Grey pessimists, like the one in the glass, did not have successful careers.

'Ugh,' I said again. I turned off the stereo, tipped the whisky down the sink, and took a shower. Then I got the BMW out of the garage and started inland, trailing flakes of rust.

It was twelve miles to the A303, and from there on it was a matter of keeping foot to floor until the outskirts of London.

I had rung the hospital. They had said that Henry was conscious, and able to talk. As I pushed the BMW through the traffic, I tried not to worry about what he was going to say. He did not like me, I knew; and, to tell the truth, I didn't much like him. He always managed to give the impression that the world had been invented expressly for his convenience, and that his fellow beings were there to do his bidding or, alternatively, to be beaten in competition. I don't think I have ever met a man who needed to win as desperately as Henry. He was by turns rude and patronising to Chiefy, and had behaved towards Hugo as if Hugo was his invention.

It was dead on two o'clock as I came to Stoke Mandeville Hospital. Apprehensively, I followed a bright nurse along sunny corridors floored with green linoleum.

'He'll be pleased to see you, I expect,' she said. 'Only five minutes, though.'

He had a room to himself. His face looked big and red against the pillow and the white plaster of paris that encased his upper chest. My eyes strayed to the mound of his body under the blankets. In most bodies, there is a sort of tension. In Henry's, there was none. He was like a sack. Only his eyes moved, glazed and bloodshot.

'Henry,' I said. 'I came to say how sorry I am about all this.'

'Thanks,' said Henry, in a blurred voice.

'What happened?'

'I hit my head. Can't move.' He sounded drugged. It seemed unlikely that the hospital would have told him the full extent of the damage.

'The race,' I said. 'Can you manage to think about it?'

'Who won?' said Henry.

'Beeston.'

'Sod,' said Henry. His eyes cleared for a moment. 'What are you doing here?'

'I want to know how . . . what happened,' I said slowly. There was no sense in pretending to Henry that we liked each other.

21

'Tell you,' said Henry. 'Had the Teeth to leeward. Doing nicely, opening the Quay Light.' He frowned. 'The steering went. No helm, wouldn't answer. Don't remember. How's Hugo?'

The nurse came in. 'Now then, Mr Charlton, we'd better get you ready for the doctor.'

'How's Hugo?' said Henry, again.

'Never mind Hugo,' said the nurse.

'That's it,' said Henry suddenly, in a loud clear voice. 'It was Charlie Agutter's bloody rudder. It broke.'

My stomach clenched like a fist.

'Charlie – bloody – Agutter,' he said again, in a voice hideous with scorn and anger. Then the tears began to roll down the big, red face.

The nurse said, 'You'd better go now,' and I backed away, watching her put the screens round and hearing dimly her cheerful chatter. Life went on, said the chatter; Doctor Amin was ever so nice, Bernie in the next ward was in a wheelchair now, wasn't that nice?

I said, 'Sorry,' but nobody heard me. Then I turned round and left the hospital.

I drove home like a robot.

Hugo ran one of the world's most technically advanced sail lofts. He had just taken delivery of a new computerised cutting-machine, and he had made *Aesthete* a new mainsail. He and Henry had gone off to try out the mainsail in the Boulogne Bracer, an early season Pulteney race. It was sailed as a two-hander and had been designed as a trial for long-distance racing. Nowadays, it was used by the Pulteney owners to test new gear and helmsmen before the season started in earnest. The Bracer took yachts up-Channel to within sight of Cap Gris-Nez and back again to Pulteney Quay. The start is on the morning tide and the boats come in two days later. This time, they had gone up-Channel on a dead run with a force five westerly behind them. The westerly had then backed southwesterly and freshened to force six, eight later. This

22

was convenient, since it meant they did not have to come home with the wind dead against them, tacking hard with a tired crew.

The main problem with a sou'westerly would be the Teeth.

The approach to Pulteney is nice and easy. All you have to do, assuming you know where you are, is to stay eight and a half miles offshore until you open the harbour – or, at night, until you are due south of the harbour light. This brings you along the southern fringes of the Teeth, which run like a wall parallel with the coast. Then you pay off for the light. Races are won by good navigators, who shave it close even on a night like last night. It is reasonably safe, provided your steering-gear holds out: but then you would hardly give a second thought to your steering-gear, because holding out is exactly what it is built for. If the gear failed in a southwesterly wind, of course, the tendency would be for you to be pushed to leeward – north-east, towards the rocks.

I winced, imagining it. Rain and wind howling up from Biscay. Heavily reefed mainsail and storm jib, the deck heeled steeply towards the roaring white shadow a few hundred yards to the northward. Henry braced at the wheel, his mind working at the problem of shaving between wind direction and the reef. And then, suddenly, the wheel slack in his hand and the yacht slewed head to wind, everything flapping and roaring, and the wind pressing her back into the teeth of the rocks . . .

It was unimaginable. But it had happened. I thought of the life raft, and what had come out of it. And now the tears ran in earnest.

It was nine o'clock when I got home. The sun was hanging over Beggarman's Cliff, pulling a trail of orange blotches across the bay. Far to seaward, the Teeth blew plumes of mist that the sun turned to gold.

My feet seemed impossibly heavy as I staggered up the crooked stairs. I washed my face, fell onto the bed, and went to sleep.

23

Chapter Five

The telephone was ringing. My mouth felt as if it had been swilled out with glue. I grabbed the receiver.

'Charlie,' said a smooth, cheerful voice. 'Archer here. Just ringing to see we're still all right.'

'All right?' I said muzzily.

'For this morning.'

'Oh.' I could picture him, pink and scrubbed, anxious to do the right thing. Archer was a great one for doing the right thing. 'Of course,' I said.

'Ten o'clock all right?'

'Ten o'clock.'

I put the telephone down, swung my feet out of bed and sat looking at them. Bloody Archer. Must keep up appearances, though.

The stairs seemed hard to negotiate, and the power lead would not fit into the kettle. Two spoonfuls of instant coffee in a little water improved things. The world began to tick. I dressed in canvas trousers, oiled jersey and Docksiders, and went down to the office. There was about three times the usual amount of mail. Perhaps it was from people who wanted me to build new boats. Then again, perhaps it wasn't.

There was one letter I did open because I had been expecting it and I wanted to get it over with. The envelope bore the Consolidated logo. There were no surprises. It was from Sir Alec Breen, and it said that, while he realised that in ocean racing accidents did happen,

24

pending full investigation of the *Aesthete* wreck he was sure I would understand that he could not continue with the project currently in hand at Spearman's yard. Had I any comments to make?

I had. I dialled his number. The secretary who had told me yesterday that he had been unavailable put me through.

'Yes,' said Breen.

'I got your letter,' I said. 'I don't think you're being fair.'

'Oh?' said Breen.

'You're assuming the boat's unseaworthy before you've any evidence,' I said.

'True,' said Breen. There was a pause: I could imagine him taking the cigar out of his mouth. 'I'm allowed to.'

'But is that a fair assumption?'

Breen paused again, the pause of a man so powerful he did not give a damn about leaving embarrassing silences. 'I don't have to be fair,' he said. 'I just make assumptions, never mind whether they're fair or not.'

I played my final card. 'If we stop work now, you won't have a boat for the Captain's Cup trials. We've only got four weeks.'

'You salvage that boat, and we'll see,' said Breen. 'There's always next year. Well, Charlie, nice chat. Bye, now.'

He put the telephone down.

He was right. He could wait. I was the one who was in a hurry. I had to get a boat in the Captain's Cup to impress Padmore and Bayliss and the rest of them. That would be why Archer was so keen for a sail.

I looked at my watch. Ten to ten. Time to forget about bankruptcy and poor old Hugo, and put on a nice grin and go and be the life and soul of the joyride.

Jack Archer had arranged for my boat *Nautilus* to feature on *Age of Sail*, a TV programme dealing with classic

25

yachts. All I had to do was provide a crew, look noble at the helm, and bask in the free publicity, though I was by no means clear what good publicity would do a yacht designer with no yachts to design.

The TV crew were waiting on the quay outside. I pointed out *Nautilus*, her long bottle-green hull blade-like and elegant among the more plebeian boats lying against the quay. The director started setting up long shots, and I leaned against my office wall and waited for the day's guests.

The first to arrive was Johnny Forsyth. Johnny was tall and thin, his leathery jowls pocked with old acne scars. He was not quite Old Pulteney, but he was not quite New Pulteney either. He had been in the Special Boat Service, from which he had emerged resolved to spend the rest of his life as a marine painter. With this in mind, he had moved with his wife to Pulteney perhaps five years before the Millstone invasion.

It soon became apparent that Forsyth was better at building and sailing boats than at painting them. In fact, he was a brilliant racing tactician, if a little aggressive. During the season, he picked up fees as a consultant to various offshore racing campaigns. For the rest of the year, he freelanced – doing a little broking, designing the odd boat and doing detail work and rebuilds for Neville Spearman at the yard. His wife ran the restaurant at a pub called the Lobster Pot, near Spearman's yard on the Coast road. Frankly, she was not much of a cook. But she rubbed along, and Johnny rubbed along, and they were nice people. Personally, I always found him a little puzzling. He could do a lot of things, and if he had done one at a time he could have done very well. But as it was, he never rose beyond a sort of mediocrity, punctuated with flashes of brilliance.

This morning he said, 'Sorry about Hugo.'

'Can you come to the funeral?' I said.

'Sure.' He clapped me on the shoulder. 'What's happening this morning?'

26

I told him. 'Scotto's aboard. And Georgia.'

'Ah,' said Forsyth, with his lipless grin. 'Sweet Georgia, the chocolate charmer. I'll pop across and give them a hand.'

I looked after him, reflecting that Georgia, who came from Trinidad, might not have enjoyed the description. Johnny was full of little awkwardnesses.

Now that Forsyth had gone, another man got up from a bollard. He was slim, too beautifully dressed in a blazer and flannels, with a tan too brown and even to be genuine.

'Hi there,' he said, with what he probably thought was a boyish grin. 'Hector Pollitt, *Yachtsman*, and you're Charlie Agutter. Have you got a spare minute?'

I looked down the quay. A Mercedes had drawn up in the car park and a stocky figure was picking its way over the tarry rubble that separated it from the quay. 'No,' I said.

Pollitt's eyes followed mine, and lit up. 'That's Jack Archer!' he said. 'You're building a boat for him?'

'Not for him personally.'

'Ah,' said Pollitt. 'Contract job, is it? For P and B? Listen, could we have a comment from you on the *Aesthete* tragedy?'

'Hugo was my brother,' I said. 'I'm very upset and I'm not about to discuss my private life with the trade press.'

'Ah . . . Yes . . . Of course, we're all very sad . . . you designed *Aesthete*, didn't you?' He knew damn well I had. 'There's a rumour that they had trouble with the helm.'

'Who told you that?'

'Oh, you know, scuttlebutt. But my readers would like to know.'

'Naturally, I'll be on the salvage barge, as and when we pick up *Aesthete*. I'll be in a better position to make a statement at that time.'

'Of course you will,' said Pollitt, nodding brightly. He did not put away his notebook. 'Good morning, Mr Archer.'

27

Archer was solid, brown and economical. He had won an early STAR – Single-handed Trans-Atlantic Race. He had rapidly earned a reputation as a hard man and a formidable helmsman and he was much in demand on the international offshore racing circuit. But nowadays he mixed his racing with Padmore and Bayliss. He professed to dislike the commercialisation of Grand Prix racing. When he wasn't putting contracts on hold, I liked him.

He gave Pollitt a practised smile and shook me by the hand. His handshake was warm, dry and hard.

I said, 'Shall we go straight out to the boat?'

Pollitt said, 'Is this a professional visit, Mr Archer?'

Archer smiled at him. He had to sell five hundred boats a year, so he smiled at a lot of journalists. 'What exactly do you mean?' he said.

'In Cowes they're saying that you're talking series design with Charlie.'

'Do they really?' I said. What I meant was different. The only way of salvaging my P and B contract was to keep it dead quiet until I could prove *Aesthete* had gone down from natural causes.

'I have a tremendous admiration for Charlie's work,' said Archer.

'How about the rumours about *Aesthete*?' Pollitt winked at me, as if we were having a little laugh instead of trying to wreck my livelihood for the sake of his story.

'I've heard them. But grown-up people don't listen to rumours, do they? Nice to see you, Hector.'

Hector persisted. 'But you believe them enough not to sign the contract.' He simpered at me apologetically, then said, 'Would you have another designer in mind, if this . . . fell through?'

I found myself itching to clout him. Archer smiled and shook his head, and said, 'We ought to get going.'

Pollitt said, 'Of course,' and walked away.

'Look out,' said Archer. 'Here comes another.'

This time it was the Yachting Correspondent of the

28

Morning Post. We ran along the quay and down the steps to *Nautilus'* deck.

'Phew,' said Archer, and grinned. His grin was boyish and attractive, and good for at least a hundred sales a year to Padmore and Bayliss.

Nautilus was a converted twelve-metre and the light of my life. Hugo and I had found her fifteen years previously, on a mud bank near Burnham. Rebuilding her with Hugo had taught me more than any naval architecture course. As well as paint and timber and screws, we had given her part of our souls. Now she was a poem in dark green with a gold stripe, and the beauty of her was almost as good as seeing my brother again. Almost.

We slipped the mooring and went past the quay head under sail. I felt the familiar tug of the water on the wheel, and squinted up at the tower of the mainsail. Every time I came aboard *Nautilus* it was like coming home.

'Okay,' said the TV director. 'Now, Mr Agutter . . . er . . . Charlie, if you could tell us who's who?'

I introduced him to Forsyth, and also to Scotto and Georgia. Scotto was an amiable blond gorilla from Christchurch, N.Z., who worked around Pulteney as a freelance boatnigger or paid hand, which meant that he spent a lot of time on *Nautilus*. Georgia, his girlfriend, had worked her way across the Atlantic from Trinidad, and was as handy on a boat as Scotto.

'Right,' said the presenter. 'Let's do it.'

He asked me a lot of questions, and I answered them without thinking about them, because my eyes kept moving about the boat, and my mind was saying: that was the bit of deck Hugo was going to put in next week, and that was the Turk's head Hugo had tied last time we sailed up to the Skagerrak.

When he had finished with his questions, he went away to ask the crew questions about what sailing on a twelve-metre meant to them, or something. Archer came alongside me at the wheel.

He said, 'Charlie, you are not going to like what I am going to tell you.' I looked across at him. His blue eyes were worried in his fair-minded brown face, but his chin was stuck out, as if he had decided to do something and he was not going to be deterred.

'What,' I said.

'We've decided to review our contract situation,' he said.

'You mean cancel it.' *Nautilus*' great white wing of sail dipped in a puff, and I brought her up delicately, delicately, till the luff shivered like a maiden's thigh.

'Don't make it awkward,' said Archer. 'We're holding it up pending enquiries into the *Aesthete* wreck.' He spat it out as if to say, there, that's it, let's leave it.

I did not want to leave it. 'You've been listening to rumours,' I said. 'Archer, you're a friend. What have you been hearing?'

'They're saying the rudder dropped off,' Archer said. 'They're saying that you won't have a boat in the Captain's Cup trials this year.'

'I thought grown-up people didn't listen to rumours,' I said bitterly. *Nautilus* dived into a wave with a comfortable sploosh.

Archer's blue eyes were definitely worried, now. 'Look,' he said. 'If those rumours cost us two sales, they've cost us fifty thousand quid. And they could lose us two hundred sales. See?'

'So you're dropping the contract.'

'Delaying it. If you can convince us and the press that *Aesthete* was not a design problem, and if you can get a boat or two through even as far as the Captain's Cup trials, we'll all be happy. I can't say fairer than that.'

'Cruel but fair,' I said, ironically.

Archer said, 'Don't be bloody childish, Charlie. We're bending over backwards.'

'Sure,' I said, and began to pass the wheel through my hands. 'I think we'll go home now.'

The director said, 'Another twenty minutes, till the light changes?'

'Get stuffed,' I said.

Scotto eased sheets, and *Nautilus'* razor nose settled on the tiered houses of Pulteney. I knew I was behaving like a madman. But now there was no Hugo and no work, I was suspended over an abyss with no visible means of support.

Except my friends, I thought. Scotto and Georgia were looking worried, and Johnny Forsyth's pock-marked face was bent to the TV director, explaining something. Explaining that I was a little jumpy, death in the family, poor fella? Or possibly doing a little hustling for a spot on the box himself.

It was always hard to tell what your friends were up to, in the sportsmanlike world of offshore racing.

Chapter Six

Nurse Bollom rang down when I got home. 'Your father's a bit better,' she said briskly.

I went up the stairs to his part of the house.

'Barnes was here,' he said. 'Told me about yer brother.' His eyes were pinkish blue and bright. 'Yer mother would have bin terribly upset, poor gel.' He paused. 'Poor chap.' He raised his thin shoulders in a heavy sigh. 'Let's have a drink.' He filled two tumblers from the bottle under his rug and gave me one. 'I remember you two little beggars the day you sank that Admiral who came to open the Regatta. Pinched his bungs, didn't you?' He shook his head. 'Good chap, Hugo. Damn sad.' A tear formed at the corner of his eye and fell into his whisky. He drained the glass, and watched me as I did likewise, like a priest overseeing a fiery sacrament. The subject was closed.

I forced myself to tell him about the problems with Archer, concentrating with an effort. He shook his head at the mention of the name.

'Archer!' he said. 'Used to be damn good when sailing was sailing. Pity to hear he's gone professional.' I waited dully. The routine was a familiar one. ''Course, when I was a lad there was none of this money rubbish,' he said. 'You sailed because you ruddy well wanted to sail. Nobody gave me any money when I built *Petrel*.' He had sailed single-handed in *Petrel* from San Francisco to Yokohama in 1926. 'And racing used to be fun then, as ye know. Now it's all thugs on the deck and lawyers in the

32

cockpit. And ye can't recognize those things as boats.'

'What things?'

'Those things.' My heart sank as his bony liver-spotted hand rose in its familiar groping gesture. He was slipping again. 'Those silver-paper canoes ye call boats. I hear one of your plastic rudders fell off.'

'Who told you that?'

'Can't remember. Someone. In my day we made rudders out of oak and bound 'em with iron. Stands to reason. Where's your brother anyway? Haven't seen him for a while.' I squeezed hard at the arm of the chair. 'If it was me, I wouldn't give my brother a duff rudder. He's dead, someone said.'

I sat there in a small personal hell as he lapsed back into his muddle, where history was tied in knots and the only fixed point was that he had someone he could trust to pay the nurse and look after him.

If things carried on as they were, I had a nasty feeling that my father's trust might be none too well placed.

I spent most of the afternoon in the office – not that there was a lot to do. But I sat at my drawing-board and tried to make a set of lines for a motor-sailer that now would probably never be built by Padmore and Bayliss. And when I had had enough of that, I gazed out of the window and watched Chiefy red-leading rust spots on the pot winch of his lobster-boat, anchored between the stone horns of the harbour. It would be a lot simpler to set lobster-pots.

The telephone rang. It was Sally. Her voice sounded as if she had a scarf wrapped hard round her neck.

'It's Henry,' she said. I waited. 'At the hospital. The doctor told him he'd be paralysed from the chest down. He –' Her voice disintegrated into something between a croak and a sob. I heard her take a deep breath. 'He put a plastic bag over his head and killed himself,' she said.

Out there, in the whip of the breeze, Chiefy's lips

moved, and I knew he was singing as he chipped away the brown rust.

'I'm coming over,' I said.

There was a Subaru pick-up in the drive. I walked in without knocking. A murmur of voices came from the drawing-room, and Hugo's hat was gone from the head of the Frink bird. His coats were gone from the hook by the door, too. I was looking at the place where they had been when Sally's voice came from over my shoulder.

'Has anybody found anything?' She had been crying.

'Not yet. Too much sea.'

'I suppose there is. Poor Charlie, it must be hell.'

'Don't worry about me,' I said fatuously.

A smile broke through, making her cheeks small and round and giving her momentarily the face of a little girl. 'It's better than worrying about me. I hear they think it's the steering. Come on in. Ed Beith's here.'

'Horrible about Henry. How's Amy taking it?'

Sally shrugged. 'Raging. You know Amy. Only – ' She hesitated.

'Yes?'

'Well, she might . . . God, what a horrible thing to say. But she and Henry weren't getting on at all well. I think she might even be secretly relieved.'

I thought back to my conversation with Amy. Changing his damn nappies, she had said. 'You might be right.'

Sally shivered, and I could see that she was close to tears again. 'Come on. Drink.'

It was good to be in the same room as Sally and Ed again, though it made the gap left by Hugo's absence all the more painful.

Ed was a large man with crinkly hair, dressed as usual in a dirty boiler suit. He was sitting on the sofa, clutching a glass of whisky. None of us could think of anything to say. In the end, I asked him about his problems with his

34

boat *Crystal*. He said that she was fine, but he did not sound altogether convinced.

'But Frank Millstone wants to buy her,' he said.

'I'm not surprised,' I said. 'She's fast.'

'If she stays together,' he said. 'That bloody hull keeps coming apart.'

'So sell her,' I said.

'I don't much fancy selling anything at all to Millstone,' he said. 'Not after that land business.'

He seemed to want the subject changed. So I told Sally about Millstone and Breen, though not about Jack Archer's big contract.

'Bastards,' she said. 'They can't.'

'They have.'

'What you need,' said Ed, 'is a PR trip. A junket. Take them out in some other boat with one of these rudders and convince them.'

It was about the first positive suggestion anybody had made since the lifeboat had come back. It lightened the gloom perceptibly.

I laughed. 'Ed wants me to convince them that Agutter's boats are fine, so Millstone will leave him alone.'

'Well . . . yes,' said Ed. 'Why don't you borrow *Ae* off Billy Protheroe?'

'Call him now,' said Sally, infected with the sudden purpose in the room. 'Go on.'

Ae was *Aesthete*'s sister ship. She had come out of the same mould, and she was the only other yacht in the world that had *Aesthete*'s revolutionary rudder technology. She was a very fast boat, and Billy Protheroe was confidently expected to sail her in the Irish Captain's Cup team.

'What will it prove?' I said. 'The rudder won't cave in to order.'

'It will prove you're not worried,' said Sally. 'Anyway, I'd like a weekend in Kinsale.' She smiled, and the smile squeezed two tears out, one on either side of her small, straight nose. 'The funeral's tomorrow.'

35

So, as much to keep from thinking about funerals as anything else, I rang Billy Protheroe at his house in the dirty green hills behind Kinsale, and asked if we could borrow his boat for Saturday. Protheroe was a bloodstock dealer and loved a little gamble. The idea appealed to him greatly.

After that, all I had to do was charter an aeroplane. Then I had to issue the invitations, and hope that I had enough money left over to buy petrol to get me to the airport.

Chapter Seven

In films, it rains at funerals. At Pulteney, it blows. That is why the tombstones in the graveyard on top of the cliffs are propped up with piles of stones, and the church itself hides in a hollow, behind a bank of azaleas and rhododendron. The azaleas were just coming into flower, yellow against the green of the leaves, the day Hugo was buried. I stood and watched, numb, feeling the ache that the coffin's weight had produced in my shoulder, as the earth rattled on the lid. The grave was in a little forest of Agutter headstones, in a corner near the grave of two Frenchmen blown off the French 74-gunner *Cinna* during the Napoleonic Wars.

There was a big crowd, but nobody looked at the stones. The inhabitants of Pulteney knew them off by heart, and the yachters do not care much for things like tombstones. Chiefy, who had been carrying the coffin too, said afterwards that he did not reckon many of the yachters had come out of respect for the dead; it was because they wanted to make certain sure that the town's best helmsman was nailed under six feet of earth.

They had also come to gossip. I was catching a lot of meaningful glances from out of the corner of my eye. I found I was beginning to get angry, because this was Hugo's funeral and all these yachters were using it as a cocktail party.

Neville Spearman, owner of the yard, sidled up to me

37

afterwards, looking, as always, haggard and a little shifty.

'Sorry about . . . all this,' he said. 'Look, Charlie, I had a word with Alec Breen and Frank Millstone, and they're making time to pop over to Ireland with you.'

'That's very kind of you,' I said.

'Oh, no,' said Neville. 'Self-preservation, mate. I don't want to lose the work for the yard.'

'Thanks anyway, Neville,' I said.

He shrugged gloomily, and shuffled away into the crowd spilling from the lych-gate. I stood there for a moment, watching people failing to catch my eye, feeling tired and hollow.

'Hi, Charlie,' said a voice behind me. It was Hector Pollitt, the journalist, grinning, his expensive teeth white against his expensive tan. 'How's things?'

My irritation bubbled up and spilled over. 'How d'you think?'

He shook his head. 'Bad business.'

'Yes. Now, if you'll excuse me?'

Sally was hemmed in by men in expensive sailing clothes. She caught my eye, and I saw the whites of hers. Pollitt persisted.

'I hear you're off to Ireland for the weekend.'

'True,' I said.

'Would you mind if I came along for the ride?' He stood there grinning at me. You little bastard, I thought. He knew and I knew that what I was looking at was not Hector Pollitt, but a gun levelled at my head. Nothing I proved to my planeload of customers would do me any good if Hector Pollitt was not convinced.

'No,' I said, with a smile that hurt my face. 'Welcome aboard, Hector.' Then I walked quickly away, to stop myself beating his head against a tombstone.

I found Sally with my father, in the middle of a press of people. Sally was crying. She was not making a sound and her face was quite composed, but the tears were pouring out of her long green eyes, down her cheeks and splashing off her chin onto her grey silk double-breasted jacket. My

38

father, crouched in his wheelchair wearing a blue serge suit, looked completely lost. He was staring at a yachter standing in front of him and saying in a distant, reflective voice, 'What an enormous arse!'

I took them away. We were meant to go and drink tea at Sally's house, with the rest. But we left the tea ladies to dish out the tea, collected Ed Beith and Chiefy and some other very old friends, and went back to my house, where we sat out of the breeze in the sun, and drank whisky till we all wept.

During the days that followed, the wind continued to blow and the seas to roar among the Teeth. The telephone in my office remained silent, except for journalists looking for quotes on what they now referred to as the *Aesthete* disaster. My father had taken a violent turn after the funeral, and his confused roarings were making the house miserable. Furthermore, I knew that Nurse Bollam needed paying, and that I was good for about two more months' salary. The trip to Kinsale, which had started by resembling an unpleasant duty, was beginning to look like a holiday in the sun.

I arranged to pick Sally up on the Saturday morning at eight-thirty. A thin drizzle was hissing in from the sea, and the met. report spoke of Atlantic lows. But she waved cheerfully from the doorstep, and jumped into the car with a happy anticipation that was a joy to look at. At the funeral, she had looked grey and ghostly; this morning, she looked as fresh as a glass of orange juice. Her amazing skin was shining, her eyes gleamed, and her short dark hair was crisp and bright against her neck.

'So,' she said, 'what's the timetable?'

'Rendezvous Plymouth airport, 10 a.m., for coffee and dirty looks. Personnel: Archer, Breen, Millstone, Pollitt, first class. Steerage: you, me, Gloria, Scotto. Lunch Protheroe, so he can get the gossip. Sail, subjecting boat to cruel and unusual punishment.'

39

'What do you mean?'

'As tour guide, one likes to keep a little something up one's sleeve.'

'All right. Next, please.'

'Drinks and dinner with my friend Protheroe, bloodstock man and owner of *Ae*.'

'Must we?'

'Public relations,' I said. 'Protheroe's keen on the new rudder. He'll make the others jealous and there's nothing as convincing as jealousy.'

'Oh,' she said. 'In that case.'

The rest of the journey passed in sprightly vein, despite the drizzle that continued to fall and the grim suburbs of Plymouth that climb the hill to the airport. We got out of the car in an extremely good mood. Unfortunately, the mood did not survive the atmosphere of the private waiting-room I had engaged.

The First Class and the Steerage were already there. Frank was talking to Archer and Pollitt.

Breen looked up from the corner where he was making notes on a copy of the *Financial Times* with a gold pen. He was small and thick-set with a shock of wavy grey hair and his inevitable Romeo y Julieta.

'Charlie!' he called, and came forward and shook my hand in his chubby, dry hand. As he shook, I could feel myself being pushed backwards into a corner. Breen never did anything without a reason.

When he had me in the corner he took his cigar out of his mouth and fixed me with a cold eye.

'Charlie, I must tell you I needed some persuading to come along,' he said. 'Let's sit down.' We sat. That made us both the same height. 'I've come because I think you're good, and I want you to get through this bad patch, and I believe in supporting talent. As long,' he said, 'as it delivers. Okay?' He smiled and clapped me on the back. 'That's all,' he said, and walked back to his *FT*. I went over and ordered coffee.

Pollitt grinned.

40

Archer said, 'Morning, Charlie,' and bent his diplomat's ear back to what Pollitt was saying.

Millstone shook hands with his unnecessarily powerful grip and said in a soft, confidential voice, 'Word in your ear, Charlie. What are you up to, then?' The eyes were blue chips in the nests of wrinkles, and his mouth an unfeeling slot full of teeth.

'Up to?'

'We were sorry not to see you after the funeral.'

'Were you?' I said. I had no idea what he was getting at.

'Yes,' he said. 'Very sorry. You know, in a way death is a . . . community occasion. And in a community like Pulteney, close-knit as it were, we've got to all pull together.'

'Have we?' I could feel myself getting angry.

'Yes. We all liked Hugo,' said Frank. 'We all wanted to . . . rally round. But you weren't there. Amy Charlton had lost Henry, after all. But you persuaded Sally to go home with you.'

'Frank,' I said. 'Hugo was Sally's husband and my brother. Don't you think you should mind your own bloody business?'

'Pulteney is my business,' he said. 'Where would it be without me?'

'Money can buy houses. Some houses. But it can't buy people, Frank,' I said. And as soon as I said it, I knew I had gone too far. Millstone fixed me with those icy eyes, and his enormous torso swelled and shrank, swelled and shrank, as he took two deep breaths. Then he turned and went to the coffee tray and poured himself a cup and drank it in one gulp.

Public relations, I thought. Agutter, you stupid bastard.

'This way, please,' said the stewardess.

On the plane, Sally gripped my hand. 'You look terrible,' she said. 'What's happened?' I told her. 'Pretentious oaf,' she said. 'Pay no attention.'

The Twin Otter accelerated down the runway and jumped into the air. We bumped up to five thousand feet,

41

and I calmed down. When we were at our cruising altitude I went to the table, where the First Class were sitting, and said, 'Before we get to the other end, has anyone got any questions?'

'A little detail on *Ae*, please,' said Breen.

'*Aesthete*'s sister ship. Same number of hours afloat, same layout and equipment, including steering gear. I want you, as owners – '

'Potential owners,' said Frank Millstone, with a sullen shifting of his great body in the seat.

' – as potential owners, to see for yourselves how the system works. Naturally, Hector will be telling his readers about it, too.'

'For better or worse,' said Pollitt, and giggled.

Chapter Eight

Returning to a yacht you have built yourself is an odd sensation. It was high water, and *Ae* was tied up alongside the quay, a huge grey plastic willow-leaf against the dirty green of the Kinsale water. The deck of an offshore racer is almost flat. Aft is the trench, a long waist-deep slot in the deck with a companionway at its forward end, flanked by the big barrels of the winches that control sails, halyards and runners. Below is a cabin, with the most minimal galley that can be got away with under the International Offshore Rule, radio and navigating gear, ten pipe cots made of nylon webbing on aluminium tubing, a lot of sailbags and nothing else. Give or take a winch, most offshore racing-boats have a pretty similar layout.

Sally was very quiet as we went below, stored our gear, and came up again. *Ae* was *Aesthete*'s double; she was being reminded of things best left.

Protheroe had come down to see us off and, incidentally, to give his wandering hands a walk over Georgia. He was a long, gloomy-looking man, with a convivial red nose and a cold eye.

Standing on the dock with his hands in his pockets, he said, 'Well, I'd say you know your way round. Don't break her, now. We had the steering checked the day before yesterday at Hegarty's yard.' He climbed the iron ladder up to the quay.

The engine whirred, and *Ae* turned slowly. Then she

43

got the ebb under her nose, came round, and started towards the open sea. Her halyards slapped the metal of her mast. The wind tried to get under her bow and swing her. She lurched a little in the wavelets it made on the tide. It took a cold twenty minutes to get to the channel end buoy. The wind-speed and direction indicator read 26 knots, S.W. It drove low grey squalls of cloud over the humpback of the Old Head of Kinsale three miles away, and streaked the dirty grey Atlantic with lines of foam.

Scotto looped the halyards onto the cabin winches and heaved up main and genoa. I gave the helm to Archer. Above, the unsheeted sails roared. I wound her genoa sheet onto the winch and took up the slack. The sail rippled hugely. I cranked the winch, Scotto heaved on the mainsheet, and Archer eased the wheel a fraction to starboard. The wind snapped into the sails from over the starboard bow. *Ae* dug her port rail into the grey Atlantic and surged forward.

Frank Millstone's big face was already red and blue with cold. He dived below and came back wearing yellow wet-gear. The others already had theirs on. *Ae*'s sharp bow met the first of the Atlantic waves from the open water beyond the lighthouse which stands at the tip of the Old Head. Spray whizzed astern, and I heard Sally laugh.

Ae was as close to the wind as she would go. The lighthouse was coming up abeam.

'I'll take her,' I said to Archer. He stepped aside.

'Hold tight,' I said.

And for the next hour I took *Ae* and knocked hell out of her. First, we went a couple of miles out to sea. Then, by way of crescendo, we came in under the Old Head. There is a heavy tide-race off the Old Head, and today the wind was setting against the tide, raising a fierce short sea. Scotto and I flung *Ae* at it, and she took it like a railway engine running over a beach of boulders. She crashed into the waves, and the water flew in sheets, and the passengers shut their eyes and hung on. Finally, well past the Head, I turned her quarter to sea and Scotto flew

44

the big spinnaker. A gleam of sun pierced the overcast sky and lit the green-and-orange belly of the sail. Glittering fans of water swept from under the flare of her bow and turned to rainbows in the sun as she tobogganed down the face of a wave. The log needle swept up and round to eighteen knots.

Sally's face broke into a sudden, dazzling smile. She dug Hector in the ribs and said, 'Write that down.'

Hector leaned over the side and vomited. Frank Millstone shook his head, smiling; his eyes were no warmer. Archer caught my eye and winked. The next wave came under the stern.

'I haven't finished,' I said. 'Scotto, fly us the number four genny.'

Spray from the next wave squirted from under the bow as Scotto wrestled with the billowing sail. The spinnaker came down. Beyond it, the clouds were separating, revealing ragged-edged patches of blue. The anemometer read twenty-five knots. As I turned the wheel and laid *Ae* on the wind, the iron-taut rigging began to scream. Down went the lee rail, and the water began to arrive aboard – not the fine, hissing spray of the downwind leg, but blustering lumps of Atlantic as *Ae* stuck her nose into the tide-race. The lighthouse came up over the bow.

'Action replay,' I said. 'That lighthouse is the Teeth. Round we go.'

Millstone, Breen and Archer were torn between watching me and watching the foaming cliffs of the Old Head two hundred yards away. They knew that *Ae* was doing exactly what *Aesthete* had been doing a few seconds before the end. Pollitt must have realised, too, because he was sick again. And Sally – well, I didn't look at Sally. She had a good imagination, and it would be working on Hugo.

Ae plunged into the waves, kicking. The lighthouse was close abeam now.

'Easy,' I said.

A big wave came under the boat; I felt her go up. The

45

wind battered at us, the anemometer needle swinging to thirty knots. We were so close to the Head that I could see the individual tufts of bladder-wrack. Hector turned away and retched over the side again.

'She takes it nicely,' I said. 'No problem.'

'This is bloody stupid,' said Millstone. 'There wouldn't be, would there? Can we go home now?'

Breen said mildly, 'I'm finding this most interesting.' His Romeo y Julieta had gone out, doused by a wave. His eyes and the cigar end stared at me, three disconcerting black holes.

The lighthouse was past the sightline scored on the deck.

'Paying off – ' I said.

I never finished the sentence. *Ae* toppled sideways off the slope of the big wave, landing in a cushion of spray. The wheel kicked hard. There was a slight jolting sensation. Then everything happened at once.

The sails began to flap and drum, and the nose swept up and round, head to wind. *Ae* rolled forty-five degrees back on herself. Pollitt slumped to the cockpit floor and I saw Millstone's mouth, wide with surprise, as it went underwater and came back up again, spluttering. Breen was halfway up on one knee as we went, and the lurch knocked him over. There was a vicious crack as his head hit a winch and I saw Scotto grab his ankle, wrapping his own leg round a stanchion with an extraordinary octopus-like movement, as the side went under. Georgia's arms embraced a winch and she stuck to it, eyes tight shut. Archer staggered, caught himself, and came back on his feet like a tennis-player preparing for the next shot. Sally had grabbed my waist, and the wind whipped her hair back into my eyes.

I could hear a sort of dim roaring that was not the sea; human voices, panicking. But I could not do anything. Millstone's face loomed before mine, red-eyed and blue-veined, yelling. *Ae* rolled back on herself, then to leeward again. But there was nothing I could do except spin the

46

wheel, port then starboard, and think: some bloody PR trip.

Millstone's face came up again. This time, I could hear what he said. 'What are you doing?' he bellowed.

I answered him so the others could hear. 'It's the steering,' I said. 'It seems to have failed.'

Chapter Nine

For a split second, there was complete silence, as it sank in. I heard Archer say quietly, 'Christ.' Then Millstone started to shout, and so did Pollitt, and the clamour gained a new and sharper edge as their eyes shifted from the boat. What they were looking at was the high black cliff fifty yards downwind. They were measuring the time it would take us to hit it. And they were coming to conclusions.

Pollitt, on his knees, started to yell. So did Millstone. I shouted, 'Shut up!' and hit the engine starter-button. Nothing happened.

Archer and the other three were already moving into position.

'Everybody quiet,' I said. 'Archer, mainsheet.' I willed my fingers not to freeze on the wheel. The noise of wave on cliff was a dull, stunning rumble. But the heart started beating again, as it does, and the knees strengthened.

We were in half a gale, on a lee shore. Overhead, the sails, unsheeted, walloped at the wind. Hector was still staring at me, silent now, the colour of putty. So was Frank Millstone. I felt frightened and responsible and very silly. At that moment, I have to say that I did not much care if the cliffs got me. But there were the others and in particular Sally, who was crouched over Sir Alec. But there was no time to worry about how I felt, or how anybody felt.

I yelled up to Scotto, 'Back the jib!'

48

He understood, retrieved the flailing sheet and hauled in. The nose came off the wind. Archer was hauling on his mainsheet, and as the nose came off the main filled.

'Bring the jib across when I say,' I shouted to Scotto. 'Frank, crank the engine! Sally, flares! Georgia, radio!'

It is by no means difficult to sail a boat without a rudder, if you know the boat well. The secret lies in the fact that the mainsail, being aft of the keel, tends to pivot the boat into the wind while the jib, being forward of the keel, tends to pivot it away from the wind. It is an exercise that most dinghy sailors can perform, in harbour in a light breeze. In a force six and a sea that has travelled all the way across the Atlantic for the express purpose of slamming itself into the cliffs of the Old Head, it is not so easy. But I stood there and shouted orders to Scotto and Archer, while Georgia and Sally dragged Breen down to the cabin, followed by Millstone. The motion eased as soon as the sails were full; pitching and yawing, *Ae* began to creep ahead. But by this time the cliffs were a mere forty-five yards away, and we were in the fringes of the white water from the backwash.

High on the cliffs, I could see the tiny figure of a man, looking down. He waved. I waved back, praying that he would get the message. But he stayed and watched the fascinating spectacle of the little yacht floundering in the boiling foam. Then Sally came up with the flares, and the first red comet whizzed into the sky. Still the man stood.

The cliffs of the west coast of the Old Head run northwest for perhaps half a mile before they fall away northward. If we could make that half-mile without being pulped on the cliffs, we would have plenty of clear water between us and the shore.

Millstone appeared at the hatch. 'Bloody thing won't start,' he roared.

I could hear Georgia below, giving the boat's name and position. And I could imagine the news spreading from the aerial at the transom: steering failure on yacht *Ae* after a similar accident a week previously on her sister

49

ship; designer Charlie Agutter claims no problem with steering-gear; it'll be better for old Agutter if he hits the cliffs and doesn't get home. But there was no point worrying about that, for the moment.

'Can you take her, Archer?' I said. 'I want to go below and have a look.'

'Sure,' said Archer, squinting at the sails, then at the cliffs. We had made perhaps two hundred yards. But the cliffs were only forty yards away now. 'Mend it if you can, old boy.' Even now, he managed to exude reassurance.

'I will.'

The steering-gear was housed under the cockpit sole. I grabbed a torch and wriggled in. It was a very simple mechanical steering-gear, steel wires running from the wheel across pulleys to the rudder stock. Protheroe had not been fibbing when he said he had had it checked. It was gleaming with grease, and it looked exactly as it had when I had passed it out of the yard the previous autumn. I followed it through to where the stock of the rudder disappeared through the yacht's bottom.

It was in excellent shape, which was a disaster, because the novel parts of the system were outside the hull – as far away as China in this sea. And it was that part of it that had gone wrong. The full implications didn't bear thinking about, but I thought about them anyway for perhaps five seconds, lying in that greasy, little plastic coffin. Then I wriggled out into the cabin.

Sally was bending over Breen, who had lost his menace and now looked small, white and sick. She glanced up at me. Her skin was like paper and there were tears on her face. She said, 'He's all right. Concussion, I think. Charlie, I am sorry.'

'The lifeboat's on its way,' said Georgia, from the radio.

I smiled at Sally, with difficulty. It was typical of her that she had not mentioned what she was thinking: this was just what had happened to Hugo.

As I came through the hatch, I was deafened by the

50

shriek of the wind and the thunder of the waves at the foot of the cliff. We were thirty yards off now, and as I stood up I saw the wave that had passed under us turn white ten yards to starboard and collapse in a smother of foam.

Millstone had been watching it, too. He shouted, 'Why don't we anchor?'

'Because if the hook doesn't hold, we'll pile up.'

Millstone said, furiously, 'You crazy bastard, I never thought you'd bring her in this close.'

'Unlash the life raft,' I said. 'Get it ready to go.' I put my head down the hatch and said, 'On deck, all of you.'

The man on the cliff above had been joined by others. They were no longer waving; they were watching, motionless. There was nothing they could do. No rocket-lines: nothing. And we had two hundred yards to sail to the point and the wind was blasting out of the southwest. The masthead lurched crazily against the sky, which was now as blue as blue; and *Ae* sailed on, staggering, but moving forward.

Archer said, 'I think we'll make it,' conversationally, as if discussing a walk in the park. And it looked as if we would, just, if we could keep her on her heading. When I lined mast and forestay against the point we had to round, I saw that we were about ten yards clear.

'Keep her sailing,' I said, unnecessarily.

Then it happened.

The tiny figures on the clifftop disappeared behind a rock, and I remember thinking: there must be an overhang. Then everything flapped and *Ae* came onto an even keel as the wind bounced downwards, rocked her back to windward, and knocked her sails empty. In the tiny silence that ensued, Scotto's voice said, 'Whoops!' A wave shoved the stern shorewards, pointing the nose up towards the wind.

'Back your sail, Scotto,' I said, equally quietly.

Then the wind came back with a roar. Scotto scrambled forward like a giant ape and grabbed the leech of the sail in his vast hands. Millstone's mouth yelled curses from his

51

doughy face. *Ae*'s nose came round and we were sailing again. But she had lost ground. Now the nose pointed not at the open sea, but at a big, black cliff with a tangle of foam-lashed boulders at its foot.

I got her sailing again. The wake bubbled from her stern, mixing with the white foam. The cliff raced up to meet us. We would hit bang on the point . . .

Bang on the point.

The stern lifted under the next wave. The wave broke as soon as it had passed under her bottom. The next one would take us with it.

'Let go genoa!' I shouted to Scotto.

As he let go, I joined Archer on the mainsheet, giving it a final crank that brought *Ae*'s nose hard onto the wind in a lurching luff that carried her over the top of the wave. But the rock was on us now. Scotto crouched in the pulpit with the spinnaker pole, the cliffs reeling round his head. I found I wanted to laugh. Crazy idiot, I thought; did he think he could fend off forty-nine feet of surfing boat with that thing?

We were so close that I could actually smell the weed and see individual winkles. Someone, probably Millstone, was bellowing in the far distance about life rafts. It was too late for life rafts. The backwash from the last wave swirled in the ten-foot gap between the boat and the rock. I drew breath, to have air in my lungs when the moment came. The next wave, the fatal one, hunched ugly grey shoulders to seaward.

The backwash pushed us off. The gap widened to forty feet.

I yelled, 'Genoa, Scotto!'

Scotto heaved in the sheet and *Ae* shot past the headland with six feet to spare. As we passed, there was a dreadful crash and a jolt that knocked me flying. Then the land fell away and we had a hundred beautiful yards of clear water to starboard and everyone was talking at once because the lifeboat was round the point and cruising down to take us in tow.

52

I talked and laughed with the rest of them, light-headed with relief.

Scotto and Archer banged each other on the back.

'Brilliant,' I said. 'Nicely done.'

Chapter Ten

When I went below, Sir Alec was on a bunk. He was pale, but his eyes were open, and the tautness had come back into him. He didn't say anything, but those eyes rolled over at me like gun barrels. Sally was dabbing at the side of his head with a wet rag, and his wavy, grey hair was plastered to his skull. She looked at me and then down at my feet, pointedly. I had already seen it: a couple of inches of water over the cabin sole. The pump handle was clipped to the bulkhead where the head would have been if there had been a head. The waves boomed in the hollow cavities of the stripped-out hull as I slotted in the handle and began pumping.

The rhythm was lulling, a metronome for the thoughts; the thoughts were not. Hugo, Henry, *Aesthete*, *Ae*, Millstone, Archer, Alec Breen. Round and round the names went, marching to the beat of the pump. The water level stayed constant.

Breen said, 'Well, Charlie, this looks like the finish, eh?' Then he moved slowly and ponderously onto the deck; I could hear him being sick. And Sally unclipped another pump handle and pumped too, with her knee touching mine.

'I'm sorry,' she said.

'Can't be helped,' I said. But it could have been helped. Somehow. The names kept marching. And, as they marched, there rose before my eyes the structural engineers' reports on the rudders. And the conviction

54

grew in me that something was not right. In fact, something was very, very wrong.

Protheroe was waiting on the quay, dressed in a tweed suit and a Lock's felt hat, sad-eyed and impassive, every inch the bloodstock man. The others waited in a soggy group, watching as he came up to me. His eye was cold as a gull's. I steeled myself.

'What's happened?' he said.

'Rudder failure.' There was a pause; he nodded, and I could read in that nod what he thought of new-fangled rudders that failed. 'I want to take her round to Hegarty's at Crosshaven for a full inspection.'

'And it's not just the rudder, I hear.' His voice was cold and deliberate, but there was a hiss in it. He was very angry. I couldn't blame him.

'No. We hit a rock. The keel bolts are sprung.'

'Ah.' Protheroe fingered his chin. 'Sounds like it'll cost the odd quid.'

'That's down to me.'

'Ah,' said Protheroe. 'Well, now. Your lot'll be wanting to get back, and I'll take them, so.'

They started to climb into the minibus. They all made way for Breen. Frank Millstone was issuing loud instructions to someone to turn on the damned heater, and Hector Pollitt was muttering into a portable dictaphone.

For the first time since I had known him, Archer seemed embarrassed. He came and planted himself in front of me, and seemed about to say something, and to stop himself at the last minute. In the end, he clapped me on the shoulder and said, 'Sorry,' and climbed in. Scotto winked and Georgia came and squeezed my hand. It was all very awkward and embarrassing – not unlike a funeral. My funeral.

Sally hung back.

'Come on,' said Frank Millstone irritably from the bus.

She took my arm. I looked down at her and she smiled at me out of her long, shadowed eyes. The pressure of her hand on my arm was the warmest thing I have ever felt.

55

Hector Pollitt stared at us, his face inward-looking and calculating until he caught me looking back. Then he put on his false smile and waved.

'Hurry up! I'm freezing,' said Frank Millstone.

Sally held my arm for a moment longer. Then she said quietly, 'I can't face that lot tonight. I'll hire a car and bring your stuff to Crosshaven. The Marine Bar.' Then she went over to the minibus.

The sun had come out now, and the shadows of herring-gulls flicked across her as she walked across the stones of the quay. Hector Pollitt put out a hand to help her into the bus. The doors slammed, and streets swallowed the noise of its engine. I turned away, thinking of Pollitt's Judas grin.

It looked like Charlie Agutter might be in need of industrial retraining.

They put a motor pump aboard *Ae* and we towed her round to Crosshaven behind a fishing-boat. At Hegarty's, they pulled her out on the crane and wheeled her into the shed.

Billy Hegarty, who ran the yard, was an old friend, a small man like an exceptionally well-dressed gnome. When I asked if I could take a look at the boat, he said, 'Well, I don't know about that,' and avoided my eye.

Billy had easily built a dozen boats for me. Now his small, rumpled face was more than usually creased, and I could guess why.

'You've heard the rumours then, Billy?'

'I have.'

'And old Protheroe's worried I might be fingering this and that to hide the evidence.'

'That's about the size of it, now.'

'So he rang you to say not to let me in.'

'Right.'

'Okay.' I couldn't ask Billy to go against Protheroe. Protheroe was a ruthless bastard, and he was worth good

56

money to Billy. 'Well, I'd say I'll just have to lump it.'

The cracks in Billy's face deepened. 'Jesus, Charlie,' he said in disgust. ''Tis a bad business, so.' He lit a Sweet Afton and puffed at it like a steam engine. Finally, he said, 'I'm away to the wife's sister's wedding. Protheroe's coming too. It's above in Bandon, and we'll be away in a half-hour.'

'Well now,' I said, understanding that loyalty to me had triumphed over loyalty to Protheroe. 'Look out for yourself, Billy.'

'And the same to you. The fella'll come and let out the guard dog in a couple of hours.' He handed me a Yale key. Then with a level glare from his dark blue eyes, he marched away to his car.

It was six o'clock. Dinghies were scudding in the harbour, and gulls wheeled over the Marine Bar's dustbins. I turned away, as if to walk along the beach. When I was in dead ground behind a thicket of gorse and old oil drums, I doubled back.

I came up on the blind side of the sheds. The door of Shed C said PRIVATE – NO ADMITTANCE. My feet rang on the concrete inside. *Ae* sat like a big, silver whale on the cradles, gleaming in the pale light from the perspex sections in the roof. I stopped. The shed was cool and quiet as a cave; the only sound was the drip of water from her hull.

I walked across to her, and pushed the rudder. It rotated free on the stock, which did not move – which should have been impossible.

My rudders are moveable-silhouette aerofoils. When the helmsman turns the wheel, the first five degrees of movement turns a cam inside the rudder, which distorts the flexible surface of the side of the rudder opposite to the one in which he has turned the wheel. This reduces the water pressure on that side, producing lift, so the stern half of the boat is actually sucked in that direction; the bow, of course, turns in the direction intended. Each time a helmsman steers with a conventional rudder he baffles

57

the water and obstructs the boat, slowing it down. With my system, the baffling effect is enormously reduced – with the result that my boats are faster and demand less muscle-power from the helmsman.

I lugged across a step-ladder, borrowed a toolbox from one of the workbenches and went to work.

The rudder is an aerofoil of foam and carbon fibre. It fits snugly onto the stock that bears the cams, held in place by a pair of flush-head bolts.

The bolts were in place, their tops gleaming in the late sun from the rooflights.

I attacked them with a big screwdriver, removed the fin and laid it carefully on the concrete floor. Then I returned to the shaft. What I saw froze me solid.

The titanium bolts locking the cams cost twenty pounds each. Perhaps that was why someone had taken them out and replaced them with ordinary quarter-inch aluminium bolts.

All the aluminium bolts had broken, allowing the rudder-stock free play in the cams. That was why the steering had gone. It was amazing it had lasted as long as it did.

Carefully, I replaced the shattered bolts in their holes, hoisted the rudder blade back into position and fastened the top bolts. Then I let myself out of the back of the shed, drew the door behind me, skirted back to the beach and walked slowly towards the Marine Bar.

Around me, the steep banks of the harbour were green in the late sun, and gulls screamed. I walked through them in a trance. Sabotage. A word from the Second World War. Not one generally used in connection with sailing races.

I pushed at the frosted glass door and entered the stale tobacco fug of the Marine Bar. Sally was waiting in the window, beside a pile of seabags. She took one look at my face, ordered a hot whisky, and moved herself to a chair beside the coal fire. I realised that I was still wet, and freezing cold.

She said, 'What happened?'

58

'Somebody sabotaged the rudder,' I said. Her glass stopped dead, halfway from the table to her mouth. I watched her face go still and pale as it sank in.

'Does that mean someone sabotaged *Aesthete*?'

'It might, mightn't it?'

'So Hugo was murdered? And Henry?'

'It would amount to that,' I said. 'Not that it would be a very clever way of doing it. Unreliable.'

She nodded.

'Two boats,' I said. 'Both with my new rudder. Both with steering failure. What does it add up to?'

'Someone doesn't like your rudder.'

'Which is bloody stupid.'

'Or somebody doesn't like you.'

'Which is likelier.' I meditated for a moment. 'Because it doesn't matter that it was only the rudder that went. What they'll be saying is that my boats won't take a hammering. And once word gets round . . .' I laughed, without being amused. 'It's already got round. You heard Breen. I'm finished.'

'Until you show someone those bolts.'

I drew strength from her level green eyes. 'I can't get the bolts,' I said. 'Billy Hegarty would be crucified if anyone knew he'd let me in. And the dog's on duty by now, so I can't go back.'

'So,' she said. 'Someone's killed Hugo and Henry and is trying to wreck your reputation. But you're not allowed to tell anyone.' She finished her drink. 'Who'd do a thing like this?'

'It's either an incompetent murderer, or someone who hates my guts on general principles, or someone who doesn't want me in the Captain's Cup team, or someone who thinks I don't deserve to design for Padmore and Bayliss . . . Hell's teeth, this is offshore racing. You can't help making enemies.'

'*Aesthete* could have been an accident.'

'It could have been,' I said. Neither of us believed a word of it.

59

'Will you go to the police?'

I finished my whisky. 'No,' I said.

'What, then?'

'I'm going to get one of my boats into the Captain's Cup team,' I said. 'And I'm going to find out who's behind all this.'

'I hired a car,' said Sally. 'And I booked us in to the Shamrock, in Kinsale. I thought you wouldn't want to see Protheroe.'

'Telepathic,' I said. 'But I want to ring Protheroe first.'

Irish telephone boxes always make me laugh with their emergency services instructions: dial 999 for Gardai, ambulance or clergy. I grinned into the telephone as the ringing tone sounded; then I realised that it was the first time I had been amused by anything for days. An answering machine asked me to leave a message after the tone. I told it my whereabouts and went back to Sally.

News of the accident had evidently gone round Kinsale like a bush fire. Even the receptionist at the Shamrock commiserated as we signed the register.

'Fierce bad luck,' he said, and told us about his life, which had been spent following offshore racing. 'Sorry for your trouble,' he said to Sally, in the time-honoured formula of the Irish funeral.

We dined at Ballymaloe. It was hard to feel as if we were living under the shadow of sabotage and murder, with lobster and Pouilly Fumé on the table and Sally on the far side of it. We had an almost light-hearted evening. Partly, it was the removal of uncertainty. But partly, it was something else; something I did not feel like admitting to myself, because it made me feel disloyal to Hugo; but something that Sally felt too, because on the way back to the hotel she wound her fingers into mine, and we walked very close from the carpark to the lobby. It was the need for mutual comfort, I told myself after I had kissed her goodnight outside her room. The world had shown itself big, cold and deadly, and humans will crowd up for warmth. That was all.

Next morning, the telephone rang at eight. It was Protheroe.

'I had your message,' he said.

'I'd like to be there when they strip down the rudder for you.' I could feel a new confidence in my voice.

'Of course,' said Protheroe, mildly. 'The fella from Lloyd's wants to see too. He's coming in to Cork at 11.30 and I'm picking him up after Mass, God help me. So will we say half-twelve?'

Chapter Eleven

It was a lovely morning. The wooded shores of Crosshaven had their feet in the water as the hired car snaked along the lane above the harbour, and the sun was turning the oaks a brilliant green.

It was cool in Billy's big corrugated iron shed and the high roof blurred the voices of the three men standing round *Ae*'s stern. There was Protheroe and Billy Hegarty and André Martin, the man from Lloyd's. I had met him before, when I had been trying to convince the underwriters that my rudders were an insurable proposition. He was smooth and rotund, with upward-slanting eyes that never held any expression. He had been hard to convince, I remembered. Still, that was his job. There shouldn't be any trouble this morning.

After we had exchanged greetings, Martin took charge.

'So you think it's sabotage,' he said. 'We've taken the liberty of examining the parts that show.'

I shrugged. 'Fine.'

'So now we'll dismantle the rudder itself.' He peered at the retaining bolts. 'I take it we're agreed that there are no marks of violence here?'

We looked after him. There were no scratches on the retaining bolts. Whoever had sabotaged the rudder had been careful, and so had I last night.

'Billy?'

Billy Hegarty took out the retaining bolts and lowered the rudder blade. We closed in to examine the shaft. Billy put up his hand and pulled out a fragment of a bolt. 'Them's the fellas went,' he said.

'Well?' said Martin. 'Have you anything to say, Mr Agutter?'

I stared at the broken pieces of metal in Billy's hand. 'Impossible,' I croaked, from a dry throat. For the bolts that last night had been made of aluminium had somehow, unbelievably, changed. Now the splintered fragments in the calloused palm of Billy's hand had the bright, satiny sheen of titanium. 'Impossible,' I said again.

''Fraid not,' said Martin. 'Mr Agutter, I think that, pending tests of these bolts, you should tell your clients that Lloyd's are refusing a certificate to craft fitted with this type of rudder. And the same will, I suspect, go for the International Offshore Rating authorities.'

Protheroe fixed me with his gull's eye. He said, 'You've let me down, boy,' turned and walked away beside Martin. I knew that was the last I would see of Protheroe, client. The shed door closed with a tinny slam. I sat down suddenly on a crate.

After a decent interval, Billy said, 'They shouldn't have gone, not titanium bolts.'

'They didn't,' I said. I told him what I had found the previous night. 'So somebody must have had them out and put them in a vice and smashed 'em, and switched the bits back last night after I'd gone. Did you see anyone?'

'Sure I was at the wedding.' Billy's dark blue eyes shifted away from mine. I could see he only half believed me.

'You mentioned a guard dog.'

'Ah, when I came in this morning the bloody thing was asleep.'

'Where is it now?'

'I couldn't say.'

We walked round to the back of the shed. A large alsatian was lying in the sun, sleeping. Billy went up to it and prodded it with his foot. It opened an eye, then went back to sleep.

63

'Funny,' said Billy. 'Normally he'd have the leg off you.' He prodded it again, harder, and shook it for a bit. This time, the dog did not even open an eye.

'Was there a watchman on?' I said.

'There was. But he does spend all the night in the Marine, below.'

'Great,' I said, with irony.

'Which isn't so stupid when you think there's only the one road,' said Billy. 'If there'd be a car or a man he wouldn't recognise, he'd be out of there like a shot.'

'Could we ask him?' I said.

'Sure he'll be on his bed,' said Hegarty. 'But I'll ring him.' He walked across to the wall phone above the littered workbench and spoke at length. Finally he came back. 'There was nobody,' he said.

'It's what they call an inside job, then?'

Billy made a face. 'I bloody well hope not,' he said. 'There's something wrong with that dog, though.'

'Yes.' I looked down at my feet, bowed under a grey weight of gloom. 'If you could do a stress test on the bolts, and a dope test on the dog? And you'd better mend the boat and send me the bill.'

Billy nodded.

'And you might ask around a bit among your men, you know.'

'I will,' said Billy. His wrinkles conveyed worry and distaste. 'But they're good lads.'

'See what you come up with,' I said. 'I've got to get back to England. I'll be back, though. Soon.'

We shook hands. I walked slowly back to the car, looked at the OS map, then drove among the tiny lanes to the top of the cliff to the west of Crosshaven. It was a forlorn hope – the nearest approach to Crosshaven by road without actually passing through the village.

The beach path started here. The wind bent the plumes from the tall chimneys of Whitegate oil refinery across the water. The ground was soft in the parking space at the end of the lane; a couple of disused coastguard houses crouched among blackish-green gorse bushes. I stooped, looking in the peaty, black mud. There were footmarks, not too blurred, small, a woman's probably, with domed hobnails. They led down to the beach and back. On the beach, they were lost in soft sand. I walked back to one of the houses and knocked on the door, then tried the other. They were empty, waiting for the season. Their black panes watched me impassively as I got back into the car and drove away.

I told Sally. She took it in silence. Last night had turned leaden. We were both occupied with our own thoughts and the silence continued as I carried her bags down and went to pay the bill.

The ocean racing receptionist was on duty. I had no desire to discuss yesterday's events, but he had.

'And I heard about that other trouble you had, in England, with Mr Charlton getting killed and all. The poor woman,' said the receptionist. 'But I'd say she's a brave one.'

'What on earth are you talking about?' I said.

'Mrs Charlton. Oh, she looked great this morning. I followed it in the English papers.'

'Amy . . . Mrs Charlton was here?'

'Surely you saw her?'

'No.'

'Well now. She's just after checking out herself.'

'Is she really?' I said. What the hell had Amy been doing here? Then I thought about footprints and said, 'What was she wearing on her feet?'

'On her feet?' said the receptionist.

'Yes.' I felt a complete idiot.

'Wellingtons. Green ones. Them ones with the studs,' said the receptionist, frowning. 'I'd say you'd meet at the airport. That'll be nice, won't it?'

But we did not meet.

I told the Protheroe party to go back without me. I did

65

not feel I could face them for the moment. Before Sally and I caught the afternoon flight, I checked at the information desk that Amy was not on any of the rest of the day's passenger lists. Perhaps she had gone by boat, or by Dublin.

All the way home, Amy's green wellingtons marched through my thoughts.

No, I kept telling myself: it was absurd, far too much like a real coincidence. I wished I had had time to hang about in Ireland, and make some serious inquiries. But time was passing, and the Captain's Cup trials were looming close, and I had to do something about getting in there.

As everyone knows, the Captain's Cup is much more important than little niggles about sabotage and murder.

Chapter Twelve

I dropped Sally at home that evening. Halfway back along the high-banked lane to Pulteney is the turning to Brundage, where Henry Charlton had lived. A hundred yards past it, I slammed on the brakes, reversed, and took the Brundage road. I had to talk to Amy. It was going to be nasty, so I wanted to get it over with.

She lived in a converted water-mill. The gates were shut and there were no cars on the smoothly-raked gravel of the drive. I crunched across the gravel and knocked on the door. The housekeeper, fat and solemn, said Mrs Charlton wouldn't be back until late tonight, poor thing. I told her to say I'd called, and went home.

My father was making a mess of a soft-boiled egg, watching *Songs of Praise* with every evidence of enjoyment. I wanted to talk to somebody; but he was obviously not on form. So I went through to my own quarters, decided not to drink any whisky, and rang Georgia.

She came at about eight, with shopping bags, looking like an Indian temple sculpture in paint-spattered jeans and an old blue guernsey. We sat at the walnut table eating fried chicken she had cooked.

I said, 'Tell me what happened in Ireland after we left.'

'We went back to Protheroe's. Protheroe had to go out, but we sat around, had a few drinks, you know. It wasn't a very jolly party.'

'Did anyone go out?'

67

'Are you kidding? Nowhere to go. Anyway, old Breen was feeling pretty bad. Well, we all were.'

'So you just hung around and went to bed.'

'We played poker,' she said. 'Archer was hassling me a bit. He always does, me and anyone else who happens to be female. It's real flattering.' She made a face.

'Really,' I said. 'Archer? He's always seemed so, well, statesmanlike.'

'Anyway, I went to bed soon after that, and Scotto came too. The other guys stayed up late. Then this morning nobody said much at breakfast and we all came home in that plane.'

'And as far as you know nobody went out last night?'

'Not in a car, anyway. I was sleeping at the front of the house.'

'You're sure?'

'Yes. Because I heard Hector Pollitt coming back in.'

'Back in?'

'He got out of the bus in Kinsale. Said he had people to see. He came back in a taxi, after midnight.'

'Did he,' I said. 'Did he really?'

Georgia was looking at me very hard. 'Charlie, what is all this about?'

'Oh, nothing. What were they talking about, in the house?'

'You, mostly. They kind of went over your career and, well, I guess reappraised you is the right word.'

I nodded. I was thinking about Pollitt. Him and Amy, on the loose in Kinsale. But why would either of them have wanted to sabotage *Ae*?

After Georgia had left, I went to bed and lay staring at the ceiling. Amy in her green gumboots still marched round the inside of my head. But this time she was with Hector Pollitt, dressed in wet clothes and slinking about in the dark. I worried at the events of the day. And slowly but surely, the cast grew. Why had Millstone said, 'I never thought you'd bring her in this close'? And Archer. He never said much, but there was sometimes a coldness that

68

came across his face and made him look capable of just about anything. Even Sally could have done it; she'd had the opportunity . . . But at this rate, I'd be believing that I'd done it myself.

The telephone woke me at eight o'clock the next morning. It was Amy. I felt muzzy in the head, ill-equipped to deal with her.

'What do you want?' she said.

'I wanted to talk to you.'

'That's what you're doing now. Could you hurry it up? I've got more important things to do.'

Sleep was still drugging me and I couldn't think of the tactful way to ask what I wanted to ask, so I asked it anyway. 'Look, Amy, I want to know what you were doing in Kinsale.'

I heard her breath zip between her teeth. I could imagine her face, tight and foxy. 'What on earth are you talking about?'

'You were in Kinsale,' I said.

'Who says?'

'I do.'

'Mind your own bloody business.'

'Amy, I'm trying to find out what happened to *Aesthete*.'

'I thought we all knew. Particularly you,' she said. 'Have you seen the *Daily Post*?'

'What's that got to do with it?'

'Read it and see. Oh, they're going to see to you properly, you bastard.' The receiver went down, no doubt with a crash. I put my end back slowly. I could still hear the raw edge of hatred in her voice. Amy seemed very keen on the wreck of Agutter's career. Keen enough to sabotage my boats?

Apprehensively, I dressed and slunk out.

*

69

I knew it was bad from the way old George Maginnis looked at me in the shop. But I had not imagined how bad it could be.

The *Daily Post* had headlined it ESCAPE FROM DEATH BOAT NO. 2 and went on to give heavily-slanted biographies of me and my guests for the day. Sir Alec Breen and Frank Millstone were by way of being public figures, and the *Post* treated them with its normal toad-eating deference. They had no such scruples about me. They pointed out that the wreck confirmed suspicions that my new rudders (which they managed to make sound subtly unsporting) were a danger to the public. They also pointed out that their reporter, in pursuing me, had discovered that I had checked in to the Shamrock Hotel with a woman named Mrs Agutter. I was known to be unmarried. The story was echoed with varying degrees of stridency by most of the other newspapers, some of which also carried a quote from Protheroe saying that he never wanted to see me again except in court, where he planned to sue me for my last cent. As far as I could see, the only glimmer of light was that, by the time the court got around to awarding damages, I'd be bankrupt anyway. Hugo had always thought what newspapers wrote was a huge joke. I missed him badly, because I found I was taking them very seriously indeed.

The telephone rang steadily as I worked my way through the pile of newsprint. Mostly it was reporters. I managed to divert them by pretending I was somebody else. The last call, however, was from a voice that sounded heavier than the normal Fleet Street model.

'I'd like to speak with Mr Charles Agutter,' it said.

'Who's that calling?'

'Detective Inspector Nelligan, Plymouth CID.'

'In connection with what?'

'I think I'd better speak to Mr Agutter.'

'You are.'

'Ah.' There was a pause. 'Could I pop over?'

'If you like.'

70

'In ten minutes,' said the voice. 'If that's convenient.' He did not sound at all bothered whether it was convenient or not.

'By all means,' I said, and he rang off.

I called my solicitor, and told him to buy the newspapers and see if he could find anything that was actually libellous. He expressed horror, mixed with eagerness as the sums involved sank in. I went through to see my father, who was watching the test card on the television and picking his nose. He didn't recognise me. Nurse Bollom said he had been very bad.

'He messed himself this morning,' she said.

'It's not unusual.'

She pursed her pillar-box red lips. 'Er, Mr Agutter,' she said. 'Have you any idea when my cheque might be coming through?'

'I'm sorry,' I said. 'Completely overlooked it.'

She administered a measured dose of red-smudged teeth from over her starched bosom and fragments of powder fluttered on her small moustache. 'Not at all,' she said. 'I know you have a lot on your mind.' There was a copy of the *Daily Post* on the table, next to her coffee cup.

I wrote her a cheque for an enormous sum of money, and left. As I entered my part of the house, the telephone was ringing again. I took it off the hook, and put four cushions on top of it. It was twelve o'clock. I do not normally drink at lunchtime, but I thought that a morning like this would have been enough to make Job drink at lunchtime. So I opened a beer and sat with it, reading the newspapers again and trying not to be sick.

Ten minutes later, the doorbell rang. I opened the door to a small, slender man with eyes hidden under a low brow-ridge.

'Nelligan, CID,' he said. 'Nice place you've got here.' He glanced round the garden, with its tulips and early geraniums shining in the sun, and twitched his little moustache appreciatively at the scent of the honeysuckle. I invited him in, and he sat down.

71

'Do you mind if I smoke?' he said. I did, but I didn't want to start on the wrong foot by telling him so. So he lit a John Player Special and glanced furtively about him. 'Nice paintings,' he said.

'Have a beer,' I said. He was meant to say not while he was on duty, but actually he accepted.

'Nice beer,' he said, looking at the tin of Budweiser I gave him. 'I like that American beer.'

'Good,' I said, wishing he would stop acting like a house clearer's appraiser. 'Now, what's the problem?'

'Problem? Oh, I see.' He had a slight West Country accent. 'Well, we had a rather funny telephone call, from one of those newspapers in London. They asked would we comment on the fact that . . . well, it's rather personal.'

'Say it anyway,' I said. A chill had descended on the room. Something dreadful was about to happen.

'What they said was you'd been staying the night in a hotel in Ireland with the widow of your brother, recently deceased in a boating accident.'

'True,' I said. Then, seeing what he was leading up to, 'In separate rooms.'

'I am told there was a connecting door.'

'Who told you this?' I said, thinking: Amy.

He smiled and shook his head. 'Sorry.'

'So what did you tell them?' I said.

'No comment. I mean that was what we told them. But the thing is, is it true? About Mrs Agutter, I mean.'

'No,' I said. 'It is a shameful bloody lie.'

He nodded. 'But . . . well, pardon my asking, are you sure you weren't having an affair with her?'

'Quite sure.'

'Not before the . . . er . . . accident with the boat?'

'No.' I was beginning to get angry. But getting angry would be unprofitable.

'So this was in the nature of a . . . er . . . one night stand?'

Profitable or not, I lost my temper. 'If all you can do is

72

sit there and make insulting suggestions, you can bloody well get out.'

He made no effort to move, but stroked his small moustache and had the grace to look faintly embarrassed.

'Yes. Well, you've been very frank, Mr Agutter. We'll want to look at that boat when she comes up. Because, of course, this opens new lines of thought for us.'

'If you will excuse me, I've got better things to do than –'

'Help the police with their enquiries? Yes, well. Sailing yachts is a rough sport, isn't it? Accidents happen. Just say you'd been having an affair with Mrs Agutter before your brother's death. Then you could have a motive for, well, causing the accident.' He raised his small, soft hands as I got out of my seat. 'No, no. Don't get upset, Mr Agutter. But you do see that we have to follow everything up? Because it looked like an accident at first. But now, of course, it could be murder.'

'Listen,' I said wearily. 'I've just been shipwrecked in Ireland, exactly the way my brother was shipwrecked in England. I was on the boat at the time. Do you think I'd murder myself? If I were you, instead of coming up here making comic suggestions I'd go and look for whoever it is that's trying to wreck my career, bankrupt me by sabotaging my boats, and frame me for bloody murder. Have you got that into your thick head?'

'Language,' said Nelligan, mildly. 'You said sabotage. Have you got proof?'

'No,' I said. 'But I'll get it.' My ears were ringing with fury.

'Well,' said Nelligan. 'I'll look forward to seeing it, Mr Agutter. Meanwhile, don't disappear, will you?'

He squashed his cigarette out with great concentration and walked out into the wind that had not stopped blowing since the black night of *Aesthete*'s wreck.

73

Chapter Thirteen

I went down to the office that afternoon, and tried to work on the lines of the Padmore and Bayliss motor-sailer. But I was so restless I could hardly stay in my seat. Unless I started to take positive steps to get into the Captain's Cup, working on the Padmore boats was a waste of time.

After half an hour, I gave up and picked up the telephone and rang the Shamrock Hotel. I got hold of the knowledgeable receptionist and asked if Mrs Charlton had had any visitors on Saturday. The receptionist said she had not, none that he'd seen anyway. She had gone out to dinner and come back alone. I put the receiver down. Well, she might have been dining with Pollitt. But what would that prove? It was too much to hope for that Pollitt's late arrival at Protheroe's should be linked with Amy's gumboot prints on the cliff top. If, indeed, it was Amy who had made those footprints.

My next call was to Spearman's. I got hold of Neville. He sounded even more depressed than usual.

'That boat of Alec Breen's,' I said.

'Yes.' He was always wary. This time, he sounded actively suspicious.

'It must be using up shed space.'

'Yes, it bloody well is,' he said. 'Are you going to give me the go-ahead with it? I've got a queue of stuff that needs building.'

'I'd like you to finish her.'

74

'Good idea.' I knew what was coming next. There was a long pause, during which I could imagine him screwing up his face and running his hand over his dark-socketed eyes. 'We've known each other a hell of a long time, and of course I admire your work and everything, but, well, who's paying?'

This was the tricky bit. 'Neville,' I said. 'As you say, we have known each other for about thirty years. And thank you for your kind remarks about my work. Would you consider doing it on spec? Breen'll come round. If he doesn't, we'll sell her to someone else.'

I could hear him breathing into the receiver. Finally he spoke. 'Charlie,' he said. 'Let me tell you the facts of life. Number one, you won't get that boat finished in time for the Captain's Cup trials. Number two, nothing personal, but your name has gone actively poisonous, cocky. Finishing that boat without a definite commission is throwing away money, because she won't sell. Even if she's a good boat, you're too late. I'll do you a favour. She can stay in the shed for another week. But after that she's on the heap. Okay?'

'A week,' I said.

'Good luck,' said Neville, and rang off.

I made a list of possible buyers, and sat looking at it, trying to crank myself up to start selling. It was like standing barefoot at the bottom of Everest. Also, Neville was right. She'd missed the bus for the Captain's Cup.

I was just picking up the telephone again when Ernie, the draughtsman, stuck his head round the door and said, 'Sally rang. Said she'll see you at the cocktail party tonight. Mr Beith's going with her.'

I was pleased to hear from Sally, but perhaps a little disappointed to hear that Ed was taking her to the party. The memory of that moment of closeness in Kinsale had been popping up quite frequently these last few days. But of course, it could never lead anywhere. At the moment, both of us were probably best off around old friends like Ed.

75

Nonetheless, I indulged in a little private swearing. If anything was needed to put the lid on a lousy day, it was the Cocktail Party. It is the official beginning of the Pulteney sailing season. It takes place in the white clapboard clubhouse, with its terrace built out over the harbour, and an appearance is *de rigueur* for serious competitors. I had to assume I was a serious competitor, even without a boat.

I spent the afternoon failing to make a sale. At six, I climbed into a blazer and an RORC tie, took a deep breath, and walked across to the Yacht Club.

A few of the younger drinkers were braving the breeze fluttering the flags on the mast above the balcony. Older salts were already tucked up near the bar. Several pairs of eyes rested on me for a second too long, then swivelled pointedly away. I went out onto the balcony, leaned on the railing and contemplated *Nautilus*, green and glossy against the blue evening sky. The wind seemed to be moderating. I gulped my whisky, and thought about myself and *Nautilus* and Hugo. All of us built for racing, and none of us going to race again, for our various reasons. I did not want to start thinking about Hugo here. I took another pull at my glass, and it was empty. I would have to be careful not to get drunk.

When I went back in, the bar was three-quarters full. Again I had the sensation of being brushed by dozens of eyes. Archer vouchsafed me a nod and a grin before returning to his conversation with a public relations adviser from the NCB. Johnny Forsyth winked conspiratorially, then answered a summons from the other side of the room. Forsyth the freelance, I thought. Like all freelances, always on duty. I looked around for a friendly face; Sally wasn't there. Instead I saw the synthetic tan and flashing teeth of Hector Pollitt bearing down.

'Hello,' said Pollitt, with a large, insincere smile. 'Recovered from the other day?' I nodded. 'Bad luck,

76

that. How d'you rate the chances of getting one of your boats in the Captain's Cup now?'

I felt myself begin to bristle; then I thought, hold on a minute, he must have had a couple, to say a thing like that. Perhaps I could get him to talk.

'Have a nice evening with Protheroe?' I said.

Pollitt gazed at me with slightly bloodshot eyes. 'Didn't go back till late,' he said. 'Things to do, people to see, y'know.'

'On a story, were you?'

He laughed. 'You might say so.'

'Did I see you at the Shamrock?'

He wasn't as drunk as all that. 'I don't know,' he said. 'Did you? Seems unlikely, because I wasn't there.' He laughed again.

'Oh God, it's you,' said a woman's voice at my elbow. I looked down. It was Amy, in a high-necked dress that was black, for mourning presumably, which managed to emphasize the jut of her pointed, little breasts and the sharpness of her aggressive chin. Her mouth was an ugly red line, and her eyes were creased with spite. 'I'm surprised you've got the nerve to show your face.'

Hector laughed. I said, 'Hello, Amy,' as pleasantly as I could.

'Don't you hello me,' said Amy, in a high, carrying voice. 'I had the bloody police round asking nosey questions. I told them they should have been talking to you.' Hector was nervously smoothing his glossy, brown hair with a nicely-kept hand.

There was silence in the bar, now. A lot of rich, new Pulteney faces were looking worriedly in our direction or staring hard at the floor. A big hollow had opened where my stomach was meant to be. Then I smelt perfume, and Sally's voice said, 'For God's sake, shut up, Amy, you're making a fool of yourself.'

Amy's eyes narrowed to slits, and she whirled on Sally. 'And as for you, you scrubber,' she said. 'How you can stand there, next to your boyfriend, and – put me down!'

77

For I had picked her up and carried her out of the room.

Ed Beith was in the hall. He raised his eyebrows, grinned, and said, 'Is this wise, Charlie?'

Too angry to answer, I carried her through the hall and onto the quay. She hammered at me with her fists and screamed. Outside in the air, she stopped screaming, and I put her on her feet. A small crowd had followed us out, glasses in hand, to watch. Her make-up was smudged, her face twisted with rage.

My own heart was thudding unpleasantly. 'Tell me one thing,' I said. 'Was it you taking walks on the cliffs near Kinsale on Saturday night?'

For a moment her face smoothed out and she said, 'How on earth . . .?'

'And Hector,' I said, pressing home my advantage. 'Did you have him with you? A quick stroll on the beach, down to Crosshaven?'

Her eyes were black, and they flicked like windscreen wipers between me and Pollitt. The surprise in her face abated, and the tensions of rage and calculation returned. She laughed, a high, ugly laugh that bounced round the stone faces of the harbour, and said, 'Well, you can bloody well find out.'

'What about it, Hector?' I said.

He flashed his teeth, spread his hands and said, 'Like she says, old boy.'

'Let's go,' said Amy. 'I don't like the company.'

I turned back towards the clubhouse. As I entered the door, Frank Millstone stepped in front of me.

'Agutter,' he said. 'We don't like chaps who lay hands on ladies in this club. Maybe you'd better get off home and think about that.'

I looked up at the jovial face with the cold, satisfied eyes. Then I shrugged my shoulders and walked off along the quay, head down. The Yacht Club was everything that stank about the new Pulteney.

A voice at my elbow said, 'Take it easy, Charlie.'

I looked up. It was Johnny Forsyth, his leathery neck incongruously trapped in a white collar and a Pulteney Yacht Club tie. I said, 'I should keep away, if I were you. I'm not nice to know.'

'I just thought I'd tell you I know how it feels,' said Johnny. 'It's not much fun, being at their mercy, is it?'

'No,' I said, screwing up my eyes against the dazzle of the late sun in the harbour.

'But look at it like this. Some years you work, some you don't. Like us. This year, the wife's doing okay with the restaurant, I've got a bit of work, and if Frank can find a Captain's Club boat, I'll be doing the tactics. Oh Christ, sorry Charlie, I'm not trying to rub your face in it.'

'No,' I said. 'Thanks.'

'I just wanted you to know.'

'Thanks,' I said again. 'Look, you'd better get back to the party.' And I trudged off up Quay Street.

It has always been one of my difficulties that I am constitutionally unable to accept defeat. My main emotion was one of intense anger, and by the time I was brushing under the honeysuckle that overhung my front gate, I knew what I had to do to get into the Captain's Cup. I pulled the Famous Grouse out of the cupboard and tipped quite a lot of it into a glass. It was a scheme that required a certain amount of Dutch courage. Then I heard the squeal of tyres on the cobbles and the creak of the gate, and Sally and Ed Beith were coming down the path.

'That bitch,' said Sally. 'Are you all right, Charlie?'

'I feel a bloody idiot,' I said. 'I shouldn't have touched her.'

'You should have dropped her in the harbour,' said Ed.

'It was nice of you to . . . defend my honour,' said Sally, avoiding my eye. 'That scrubber.'

'Scrubber?'

'She used to lead Henry a dance. She even made a dirty great pass at Hugo once.' Sally was calm and matter-of-

79

fact, but I could see that she was very angry. 'She's really got an itch, that one.'

'Do you think she's scratching it with Hector Pollitt?'

Sally looked surprised. 'Hector? It's possible, I suppose.'

'Because they were off on Saturday night, in Ireland. And I found what could have been her footprints on the cliff top. So she was at least close at hand when sabotage was being covered up.'

'Sabotage?' said Ed. 'What's this?'

'Tell you later,' I said. 'And if she covered up that sabotage, what's to stop her covering up the sabotage of *Aesthete* to get rid of Henry?'

'Pretty unreliable method,' said Ed.

'It's you they're after,' said Sally. 'Why should Amy want to ruin you?'

'God knows,' I said. 'But she's doing a grand job.'

'It's not so good to be on the wrong side of Millstone,' said Sally. 'What are you going to do about him?'

'Sail the bastard under the water and forget about him.'

'But he hasn't got a boat,' said Sally. 'Nor have you.'

'I'm getting one,' I said. 'A revelation came to me on the way home tonight. And Millstone's expecting to find one. Johnny Forsyth told me as much, tonight. Know anything about it, Ed?'

Ed was staring at his whisky. 'He's looking for one, all right,' he said, without looking up. 'I don't know what's come over this town. I reckon he'll make me an offer for *Crystal* any day now.'

'Would you sell?'

'Oh, I don't know really,' said Ed, and fixed me with a steady eye above a big grin. It was the eye I remembered from teenage contests in Pulteney regattas. 'So what are your plans?'

'Oh, I don't know really,' I said, and looked him straight back between the eyes. We had been playing these games for twenty years and we both knew exactly what we were planning to do.

80

Ed finished his whisky and stood up. 'I must pop off and transact this and that,' he said. 'Sally?'

'Could you drop me home?'

She put her hand on mine. Her fingers were warm and dry. 'Take care, Charlie.' It was no good trying to hide it from myself. I liked it.

They left. It was only eight o'clock. I picked up the telephone and dialled Billy Hegarty in Ireland.

The lines were in their usual demented state, and when I got through I had had to chase him from his home, via two pubs, to Jury's Hotel in Cork. He sounded slightly drunk, and there were convivial noises off.

'Charlie,' he said. 'Cripes, aren't I after trying to get hold of you all day?'

'What's the problem?'

'Well, after you went I had the vet over to take a blood sample out of that dog. And you were right, the brute was full up with sleeping pills.'

I could feel my face stretching in a grin, and the horror of the cocktail party receded. 'You're a great man, Hegarty,' I said. 'Now, listen to this. I want you to tell the story to one man, and I can promise you that he's a boat owner who wants to win, and the only way he'll win is if he never tells a soul.' Billy was making doubtful noises at the far end. I cut him off. 'And, Billy,' I said. 'Would you ever find out if there was anything peculiar the day Protheroe had the rudder checked? Any strangers in the yard, sleeping dogs, you know?'

'Ye're a hard man,' said Billy. 'I'd say I'll have to.'

After he had rung off, I started to look for Breen.

He was not easy to find. First of all, I rang his office and there was no reply. Then I rang his home, and someone who might have been a butler said that Mr Breen was out, and had, as far as he knew, gone to a party, but it was hard to say where. The manservant then began to show signs of extreme discretion, and put the telephone down as I was in the middle of asking him to go and look in the boss's diary.

81

At this moment, I had an inspiration. About six months previously, when we had been making early drawings for Breen's boat, he had had occasion to give me the number of his car phone. So I ran out of the house and down to my office, and looked under the diary entries for last November. And there it was.

I was sweating as I waited for the call to go through. This was the last throw between Agutter and Queer Street. The ringing tone sounded twice, then someone picked up the receiver and said, 'Hello.' It was not Breen.

'Hello,' I said. 'Jack Danforth here. Would you mind coming half an hour late? I'm a bit tied up at nine.'

'What?' said the voice on the other end. 'Er . . . Mr Danforth . . . nine when?' The man sounded like a chauffeur.

'Tonight, of course,' I said, gaining confidence. 'Bloody hell, man. He can't have forgotten.'

'Forgotten?' said the chauffeur, sounding nervous.

'Well, he'll just have to fit it in,' I said. 'We're only in Nottingham for the night. Could he drop by?'

'Nottingham?' said the chauffeur. 'That's a very long way. He won't be able to do it. We're in Lymington, in Hampshire.'

'Know it well,' I said. 'Not at old Harry Foster's?'

'It's a dance,' said the chauffeur. 'At Mr Birkett's.'

'Oh, well,' I said. 'That's that, then.' I put the telephone down. It had been almost ludicrously easy. I only hoped that Breen would not find out, or his chauffeur would be out of a job.

After that, all I had to do was ring up my friend Harry Chance in Lymington. Harry knew everyone there was to know and specialised in big shots. He informed me that Septimus Birkett was giving a fund-raising dance for someone's America's Cup challenge, and that he lived at Reynolds' Stone Hall, three miles out of town.

All that remained was for me to stroll back to the house, climb into my dinner-jacket and take a couple of deep breaths for my nerves' sake. Then I was on the road for Lymington.

82

Chapter Fourteen

Two hours later, I parked the BMW under some trees on the verge of a wooded lane. I straightened my bow-tie in the driving mirror. My face was what I had to call haggard. I climbed out, walked up the road to the tall gate-pillars, and turned into the drive.

The drive was gravel, beautifully raked. It led between banks of rhododendrons to a house, large, white and latter-day Georgian, nestling under the eaves of the New Forest like a cuckoo chick in a wren's nest. The night air was cool on my face as I skirted a gravel sweep with perhaps fifty expensive cars parked on it. From the gardens on the other side of the house came the thud of a bass guitar and a muffled roar of voices. I walked round. There was a lawn, grey in the moonlight, surrounded by high black trees. Attached to the garden front of the house was a marquee, lit yellow from within. I walked down a turf walk between two flowerbeds, pulled back the flap and slipped inside.

The air inside was hot and the noise deafening. At the far end of the tent, a band was playing, but it was nearly drowned by the voices. The men looked smooth, and some of the women wore tiaras. There was a fair sprinkling of New Pulteney. It was what Hugo would have called the Royal Yacht crowd.

I stood for a moment with the sweat breaking in my palms. Now all I had to do was find Breen. The crowd stretched before me like a sea. I dived in.

If I had been a terrorist, I could have wiped out a good slice of the royal family. But I was only a yacht designer in search of an owner, and for five minutes I patrolled the groups of expensive men and women without any success. Then I saw a pair of square shoulders topped by a head of close-cut brown hair and a brown neck, sitting at a table with four young women, all of whom were laughing. You could feel the charm radiating from him like heat from an electric fire. Archer.

I went up and touched him on the shoulder. He looked round, flushed and smiling, his blue eyes sparkling in the light, and I remembered what Georgia had told me about Archer and the ladies. The smile stiffened a little when he recognized me.

'Archer,' I said. 'I must have a word.'

He stood up. 'Of course,' he said. We walked away into a corner. As we went, he said in a low voice, 'What are you doing here?'

'I've come to see Breen.'

'Breen?' Archer said the name as if he did not know what it meant. 'Look, Charlie, if old Septimus Birkett sees you, he'll have you tossed out. Millstone's here. A lot of people from that cocktail party. He's been spreading the word about you. Forgive me for saying so, but you were a bloody fool earlier on this evening.'

'Possibly,' I said. I was keyed up past the point of listening to anything except what I wanted to hear. 'Where's Breen?'

'He was in the house earlier,' said Archer. 'Having dinner. For Christ's sake, Charlie. You know I'll do anything for you in the normal way. But tonight . . . you're out of order, mate.'

'Everything I do, I do for Padmore and Bayliss,' I said, with a smile whose ugliness hurt my face. Archer raised his hands; on your own head be it, the gesture said. Then he turned away and walked greedily back to his table of lovelies, a pint-sized ball of sexual fire.

I moved quickly to the green-and-white striped tunnel

84

that led into the tent from the house. A crowd of men and women were coming down a passage lined with paintings of Dutch sea-battles. The men were smoking cigars. Breen was not among them. I walked on, looking into doorways. The first was a drawing-room. A very old man was talking to two middle-aged women by the fire. I said, 'So sorry to interrupt. Have you seen Alec?'

'Washing his hands,' said the old man.

'Oh,' I said, and went back into the passage.

At that moment, Breen came out of a door under the staircase, looking chubby and well-scrubbed. I saw his eyes flick towards me, move away, then flick back. I walked quickly up to him.

'We have to talk,' I said.

He put his cigar in his mouth, and sucked. 'I've got nothing to say,' he said. He advanced down the passage. 'Excuse me.'

I was standing by a door. Inside was a small room that might have been a library, with books on the walls, and armchairs and a desk. On the desk was a telephone.

As Breen passed me, I grabbed his wrist with both hands, and heaved him in. He looked solid, but he fell with surprising ease, and we both landed in a heap on the library floor, Breen uppermost. I got out from under him, and slammed the door. Breen had got as far as his knees, and was staring at me with a face frozen with shock and anger.

'I'm sorry to have to do this,' I said. 'But would you mind sitting down?'

He got up, brushed the dust from the knees of his dinner-jacket trousers, and retrieved his cigar from the Bokhara rug. Then he said, 'Let me out of here, Agutter.' His eyes were more than ever like gun barrels in his mild, podgy face. Nobody I have ever met, having been thrown on the floor by a surprise attack, could have turned round and dominated the room twenty seconds later. But Breen managed it.

'No,' I said. There was a key in the door. I turned it,

and dropped it in my pocket. 'Not until we have had a little talk.'

'Brute force does not speak to me,' said Breen.

'Be reasonable,' I said. 'You were about to walk straight through me. You've done worse, in your day. I just want you to make one telephone call. After you have made it, you can turn me over to the police, or do whatever you want.'

Breen pondered a moment. He took out another cigar, cut it and lit it. When it was burning to his satisfaction, he took a deep breath and shouted, 'Help!'

His voice was surprisingly loud. I had not imagined that he would shout. The sweat began to pour inside my shirt.

'Help!' shouted Breen, opening his mouth wide.

I pulled out my handkerchief and stuffed it between his gaping jaws. Tasselled cords hung by the curtains. I tied him to the chair with one, and put the other round his face to keep the gag in place. He struggled, but he was a desk man and his strength was in his will, not his body.

When he was tied up tight, I picked up the telephone and dialled Billy Hegarty, in Ireland. As the telephone rang, someone knocked on the door and said, 'Are you all right in there?' The knob rattled. 'It's locked,' the voice said.

'It shouldn't be,' said another. 'I'll get the spare key.'

Billy answered. I said, 'Billy, it's Charlie Agutter. I want you to explain exactly what's been going on round your yard, as far as you know. It'll go no further.' Breen's eyes stared at me, cold and distant.

I held the telephone to his ear while Billy said his piece. When his voice stopped, I said, 'Goodbye, and thanks.'

The voices were back at the door, now. I said, 'We're fine,' and slipped my key into the keyhole, half-turning it so they couldn't put theirs in. Then I returned to Breen.

'Billy Hegarty runs the yard at Crosshaven,' I said. 'Somebody's been drugging his guard dogs in order to get in and sabotage *Ae*'s rudder. Someone removed the original titanium bolts and replaced them with aluminium.

86

Then they reinstated the titanium bolts in time for the Lloyd's inspection, having first broken them with a mechanical hammer. Billy has told you enough to wreck his reputation as a secure yard and I can now be charged with assault. Consider this before you decide what you want to do when I take off the gag.'

A voice outside the door shouted, 'Security! Open up!'

I went to Breen, untied him from the chair, and took the gag out of his mouth. Then I poured him a glass of whisky and soda from the tray in the corner, and said, 'You'd better open the door before they break it down.'

Breen pulled his small, thick body out of his chair and walked slowly across the room. He ran a hand across his iron-grey hair, turned the key, and opened the door.

A big man in a dinner-jacket said, 'Why did you lock this door? We're security.'

'We're having an important meeting in here,' said Breen. The sweat was sticking my shirt to my chest, and my heart was banging. 'Could we have a little peace?'

And the balance of power shifted, as it always did, from the big men in dinner-jackets, back to Breen. They melted away.

Breen took a drink of his whisky and soda, and sat down behind the desk. Then he leaned forward and hissed, 'I have ruined men for less.' He held his position, face suffused with blood. Then he relaxed. 'Now, then, it strikes me that this story of yours is even odder than the way you have chosen to tell it. You'd better explain.'

My throat was so dry I could hardly speak. 'Nothing to explain,' I said, reaching with shaking hands to pour myself a drink. 'Some bastard's trying to wreck my business and keep me out of the Captain's Cup.'

'So your brother's death was not an accident.'

'It would appear not. But we won't know for sure till we pull up *Aesthete*.'

'So there could be murder involved.'

'Yes.'

'You must be angry.'

87

'I am.' But I was beginning to relax. For the first time ever, Breen was talking to me like a human being, not a machine paid to give results.

He leaned back in his chair, and smoke wreathed his head like clouds wreathing a small mountain. Finally he said, 'I used to build motor-bike sidecars. With my own hands.' He held them up. They were small and thick. 'I had a workshop in Coventry. I rented it from a bloke called Purdue. Well, I had a new suspension system, and I knew Purdue wanted it, and sure enough he found out I was in trouble at the bank and then he quadrupled the rent. Thought he'd bankrupt me as principal creditor. But I got angry and I got organized and I raised some money and bought out his lease and I booted him into Station Road.' He took the cigar out of his mouth and opened his eyes and looked straight at me. The whites showed all the way round. 'It was being angry made me win,' he said. 'I wouldn't have, else.' He paused. 'But you have to learn to control it. You controlled it tonight, I suppose.'

I said nothing. Dealing with clients has given me a sort of extra sense that tells me when we are getting to the heart of things. I knew, now, that this was the pivot of matters between me and Breen.

'It could be any of those people out there who are doing this to you,' said Breen, gesturing towards the distant hum of voices. 'Millstone included. Did you know he's going for the team?'

'Yes,' I said, 'but he hasn't got a boat.'

'He'll get one,' said Breen. 'He's in the process just now. Determined man, Frank Millstone.'

He sucked at his cigar for a moment. The dance band was thudding away in the garden. Finally he said, 'I won't finish the new boat. We've lost a week; it's too late. Besides,' – the eyes came up like gun barrels – 'I'm only ninety-eight per cent sure you're on the level.' My heart sank. 'Hold on,' he said.

He picked up the telephone and dialled a number. I went and mixed myself another drink while he spoke in a

88

low voice. After five minutes, he put the receiver down. 'Well, there you are,' he said. 'You can sail for me in the Captain's Cup. In *Sorcerer*.'

'*Sorcerer*?'

'I've just bought her,' he said. 'Well?'

Sorcerer was a fast boat I had designed the year before last, for an owner who had subsequently got himself killed in a helicopter crash. That was elderly by Captain's Cup standards, but she was a good hull. In fact, it was a good offer.

'New sails,' I said. 'And you take care of that unfinished hull at Neville Spearman's. I'll organize the crew.'

Breen's chubby face stretched into a grin like a ventriloquist's dummy. 'You have quick reactions, Charlie. Very well.' I got up. 'Wait a minute,' he said. 'Get angry enough to win. But don't get angry enough to . . . take liberties with me. You're on my time, now.'

He placed his fists softly on the desk and leaned forward a fraction. The smile disappeared, and once again I could feel the strength of his will and his gun-metal eyes boring into mine. 'And don't ever tie me up again.'

Then he got up and spread his arms, waving his cigar in his blunt, cheque-signer's hands. His face came alive and his voice sounded almost springy. 'Now, let's go through and meet some people.'

I followed him, slightly dazed. At least I had a boat to sail. At least I had designed her myself. But she was two years old . . . He forged a path down the passage and into the marquee. More people were dancing, now. This time, I was calm enough to take in some details. The band was playing on a dais. It was a full dance orchestra, with sequined music stands, playing under full-sized date palms.

Breen paused in front of them, and turned to me, and, for an insane moment, I thought he was going to ask me to dance. Instead, he said, 'Let's go!' and jumped up on the stage. The leader looked round and Breen said,

89

'Stop.' Then, without looking back, he stepped over to the microphone and waited. He was stocky and intensely energetic and his cigar jutted over the dancers like a gun barrel. The band stopped playing.

Breen said, into the microphone, 'May I have your attention for one minute? I'm sorry to stop the music, but I know you'll all want to hear that Charles Agutter is sailing *Sorcerer* for me in the Captain's Cup trials. Good luck, Charlie!'

He began to clap. Some of the other dancers followed his example, then others. I saw Millstone, not clapping, and Hector Pollitt, clapping with a cynical grin on his even brown face, and several Pulteney people. Not Archer, though. It was the second party that night where all eyes were on Agutter, and a lot of these people would have heard about the first one. The sweat of embarrassment broke out on my temples and I forced a smile. The clapping was ragged, itself slightly embarrassed. Breen put his arm round my shoulders, standing on tiptoe to do so. I waved, and we climbed down from the stage.

'Drink,' he said. I needed one badly. People came and talked. I answered as best I could, scarcely conscious of what was said. I kept thinking that to be thrown out of one party and to be the hero of another, all on the same night, must be some kind of record. As soon as I could, I detached myself from Breen's circle and went out onto the lawn and beyond the marquee.

The air was heavy with the scent of azaleas, and behind it the invigorating tang of pine trees. Above, the sky was clear.

'Hello, Charlie,' said a voice at my shoulder. 'Congratulations.' I turned. Light shone from the speaker's shirtfront and from his glistening white teeth.

'Thank you, Hector,' I said, with as much enthusiasm as I could muster.

I could smell whisky on his breath. 'Seen Amy?' He seemed very drunk.

'No,' I said. 'I was just going for a walk.'

90

'Ah,' said Hector. 'Yes, it's a nice night. I'll join you.'

This was by no means what I wanted. But I could not politely tell him to go away, so we strolled across the lawn under the stars.

'We haven't had a chat,' said Hector. 'Nasty scene on the quay, there. 'Motional lady, Amy.'

'It's understandable.'

'Understandable? Oh, I see. Henry and everything.' He paused. 'Charlie, what do you think happened to your rudders?'

Drunk or not, Pollitt was on duty. 'No idea,' I said. 'If I hadn't seen it with my own eyes, I'd have said they had been interfered with.'

Hector chuckled. 'Who'd do a thing like that?'

Abruptly, I said, 'What were you doing on Saturday night in Kinsale, Hector? You weren't at Protheroe's.'

'No, I was . . . seeing some people.' His voice had changed. It was defensive, now. 'Is it any of your business?'

'But were you with Amy?'

The whites of his eyes glared in the moonlight. 'What if I was?'

'You could be of help.'

He was quiet, then. We walked on across the lawn, under a yew arch and into a rose garden. The turf paths of the garden converged on a cone-topped summer-house with lattice windows. In the summer-house, a woman's voice said, 'Oh!'

It was not a startled sound. In fact, it was quite the reverse – as if the woman had got something she had been expecting for a long time, and was pleased about it. More sounds followed it. The maker of the sounds must have been quite unconscious that she was making them, probably because she was concentrating on whoever was in the summer-house with her. They developed a rhythm, and the rhythm accelerated until it was an incoherent moaning working up to a high animal pitch, and the woman cried out a name. Then the sounds stopped.

91

I stood and listened; not through prurient curiosity, but because I recognized the woman's voice. It was Amy's and the name she had cried out at the moment of climax had been, 'Archer.'

When I turned to go away, Hector was no longer at my side. Sound travelled well in the shelter; I heard the thud of running footsteps receding across the lawn, the slam of a car door, and the howl of tyres in the gravel. Then the scream of an engine disappearing down the long tunnel of rhododendrons.

Soon after that, I went home myself.

Chapter Fifteen

Next day, I felt almost human. I called in on Sally, and over breakfast told her about the party and Breen. She laughed, and her cheeks went small and round and pink, like a little girl's. As I left, Ed Beith's Subaru was turning in at the drive gates. Good old Ed, I thought. Solid as a rock. Not like those perpetual adolescents at the party.

I went down to the office and rang around for a crew. I loaded up Scotto and another couple of hands and drove over to Lymington, where the marina already had *Sorcerer* in the crane. I looked her over. She was in terrific shape, crisp and clean as the day she was built. She'd spent most of the previous year in a shed.

Scotto spat out his chewing gum. 'Not bad,' he said. We dropped the mast in, and by four o'clock we were nosing into the Solent under the eyes of the Isle of Wight ferry passengers.

The shipping forecast for Portland, Plymouth and Wight was force four to five, southerly. We made very good time down the coast. *Sorcerer* went well; she needed a new mainsail and a couple of genoas, but if we could get her worked up in the very short time available, she had a good chance for the Captain's Cup team. Actually, she was better than good; and I could see that Scotto thought so too.

At midnight, the flash of Portland Bill light was well astern, and Scotto had up a kite and a blast reacher. I had forgotten how to be tired as she hurdled the long black

93

seas under a high half moon. I had sailed this course dozens of times with Hugo, and now, tired as I was, I could almost feel him standing at my shoulder. He would perch on the weather deck and the red ends of his bloody awful Players would glow against the black hulk of him, and he would talk. He was a much better hand at talking than me, and what he really excelled at was in stripping people's polite actions down until the bare motives showed, like gears, slippery and dirty. I wondered what he would have made of *Aesthete* and *Ae*, and all these broken rudders. Myself, I didn't know where to begin. Last night had complicated matters still further.

What the hell was Amy up to? Assuming that she had been with Pollitt in Ireland, that she'd been having an affair with him, and that she'd been cheating with Archer in the summer-house, why should any of it be connected with the rudders?

By four a.m., we were off the Teeth, opening Pulteney Harbour light. Scotto was watching the suck of foam among the rocks. I was trying not to, because there was no Hugo smoking next to me, and the Teeth were the reason.

'Wind's dropping,' said Scotto.

We arrived off Pulteney in the last ghostly whisper of breeze. I put *Sorcerer* on a mooring in Lower Pulteney, just around Beggarman's Point from Pulteney proper, and went home. First I rang Neville Spearman to arrange the salvage barge. Then I had four hours sleep. When the alarm went off, I stumbled into the garden. The wind had dropped and the midday sun glittered off a sea smooth as satin. I went down to the quay and collected my diving gear. Then I went looking for Chiefy.

He was in the bar of the Mermaid, as usual. Ed Beith was with him. I ordered a pint and drank it; I was parched and tired. Then I said to Ed, 'I'm sailing *Sorcerer* for Breen.'

'Sally said,' said Ed, in what I thought was a lack-lustre manner. 'Glad to hear it.'

94

'Don't see why,' I said. 'It'll be my regrettable duty to sail the pants off you.'

He smiled. Again, it seemed a little forced. 'You may not get the chance,' he said. 'Millstone made his offer for *Crystal* today.'

'*Crystal*?'

'A big offer. For boat and crew.'

'Tell him to get stuffed,' I said.

Ed finished his whisky. 'My exact words to the bank manager only this morning.' He rose stiffly to his feet, ape-like in his foul boiler suit. Presumably he had worn it to see his bank manager. 'Well, see you around.' He walked out of the bar.

'Ed's not too happy,' said Chiefy.

'He'll never let Millstone have the boat, though.'

'Ed'd be well shot of her, if you ask me,' said Chiefy. 'Better off farming than sailing them things. Come on, then. Today's the day.'

We went round to Spearman's to pick up the salvage barge. I humped my mask, bottles and weight belt across to where Johnny Forsyth was watching a couple of Spearman's men buffing the hull of a forty-foot sloop he looked after for its absentee owners, ready for Regatta Week.

His eyes flicked to the diving gear. 'Hear you're sailing for old Breen,' he said. 'Nice work, if you can get it.'

'Thanks,' I said. 'Who told you?'

'Frank Millstone.'

'I hear Frank's getting close to a boat.'

Forsyth looked at me sharply, his narrow eyes gleaming above his lunar cheeks. 'Is he?' he said. 'Wish I was getting the broker's commission.'

'Aren't you?' I said.

He laughed, not very humorously. 'Some chance,' he said. 'Frank likes to do his own deals, or he uses the big boys up the coast.' He jerked his acid-stained thumb in the general direction of Lymington and the Hamble. 'It's

95

hard to scrape up a general purpose longshore living these days.'

'You do okay.' I was edgy. A lot of questions were due to be answered today. 'I've got to go.'

'I'm coming with you, for Lloyd's. And so's he.' He pointed to a small figure in a brown suit smoking a cigarette in the lee of the yard office. It was Inspector Nelligan.

The sea was flat as a pancake all the way out to the Teeth. Nobody said much. The engine clanked and spat out black diesel smoke, and Nelligan sat downwind of the smoke until I pointed out to him that he'd be more comfortable upwind.

'Ta,' he said, twitching his little moustache at the diesel. 'I'm not much of a sailor.' Besides his brown suit, he was wearing shiny leather shoes that the salt would ruin, and a nylon shirt.

'What are you trying to prove out here?'

He looked at me from under the ridge that bore his eyebrows. 'Oh, not prove. Just want to be on hand during the recovery of evidence.' He turned away to look at the low, blue line of the shore and, as he doubtless intended, I felt disconcerted. If there was evidence of sabotage, Nelligan would assume that I'd done it, to get rid of my brother. If there wasn't, Agutter's rudders were unreliable. Heads I win, tails you lose.

We came up to the Teeth on the last of the flood. The sea under the salvage barge's rusty bow was a shiny green. The only sign of the big humps of rock below was a couple of patches of weed and a line of scum running a quarter of a mile away along the edge of the tide, where three boatloads of holidaymakers were feathering for mackerel. Chiefy's hands moved over the worn paint of the wheel and caressed the throttle. The clank of the engine died to a chug, and the blunt nose crept in among the patches of weed. Forsyth nodded to the two wet-suited men sitting

96

alongside him in the cockpit. They got up and began struggling into diving gear.

I pulled my own gear out of the locker. Nelligan looked across sharply and shook his head.

'What?' I said.

'That's evidence down there,' said Nelligan. 'Not worth sending police divers after, of course. But we wouldn't want you too close to it, would we? I'm sure you'll understand.'

I caught Johnny Forsyth's eye. 'Little bastard,' said Johnny under his breath. I shrugged.

Chiefy said, 'Drop the 'ook, Charlie.'

As I went forward, my heart was thudding with rage. The anchor plunged into the green gloom, trailing a cloud of bubbles. The barge fell back ten yards and swung to. I stayed forward, hearing the splashes as the divers went down, the tiny cries of tourists hauling mackerel out of the tide a quarter of a mile away, consumed with my powerlessness. Then I leaned on the side, looking at the oily slop of the sea, and making resolutions; whoever had done this, interfered with my rudders and killed my brother and gone tale-bearing to Nelligan, was going to pay dearly.

Forsyth leaned on the rail next to me, tapping his wide, flat fingers on the rusty iron. Finally he said, 'This must be pretty horrible for you, Charlie.'

'It is not the greatest fun I have ever had,' I said.

For a moment, I was going to tell him all about Hegarty and the sabotage. Then I remembered my promises to Hegarty. Gossip is the staple diet of freelancers like Forsyth.

'Put it like this,' I said. 'I'm getting a new set of engineers' reports before I build another rudder like that.'

'Bloody bad luck,' said Forsyth. 'Bloody bad luck.' And we stood and watched our reflections wobbling in the water.

The divers' bubbles moved aimlessly round for ten

97

minutes. Then they converged and combined. A moment later, a black rubber head came up alongside.

'Got her,' said the diver. 'She's on her port side. Stove in. You sure you want her?'

'Take down the airbags,' said Chiefy. They took them, with the slings and the compressor hose. Then we put the crane cable overboard.

The first thing to come up was a twisted tube of aluminium, trailing steel wires. Nobody who did not already know what it was would have been able to identify it as a mast. After the mast was a netful of junk: a spinnaker pole twisted like a corkscrew, three winches still embedded in fragments of white composite deck and a tubular aluminium bunk with pieces of the space frames still attached. It was revolting, like the exhumation of an old corpse.

'Strewth,' said Forsyth. 'She must be in bits.'

I did not answer. Instead I watched the bubbles, feeling sick and numb at the same time. The pile of dripping wreckage in the barge's well grew higher.

When I looked up, Nelligan was watching me, his eyes impersonal above his cigarette. The diver-to-ship telephone squawked.

Forsyth said, 'Inflate.' Then he waved a hand at the compressor and said, 'After you, Charlie.' I hit the switch and the sea began to boil.

You raise a wreck by threading slings under the hull and attaching a big rubber bag to each end of each sling. Then you put a couple more bags inside the hull and pump in air. Because of the need to inflate the bags evenly, it is a slow business. The bubbles rose for what seemed like an eternity. The divers came up twice to change tanks. They did not say much, and nobody asked questions. Around us, the tide ebbed hard and great forests of weed waved below the glass-green surface. Chiefy ate a vast tea of ham sandwiches, and offered me some. I refused; my stomach was too tight for eating. The mackerel boats had long since gone home, and a thin

98

evening breeze began to steal across the sea.

At six forty-three, Forsyth's telephone squawked and he said, 'Up she comes. Stand by.'

And up she came.

The floats came first, huge black bubbles like the heads of nightmare octopuses. They rose in a nest, and in the middle of the nest was *Aesthete*. Not that it looked like *Aesthete*. *Aesthete* had been a knife-edged silver thoroughbred: this thing was a dull bone colour, scoured by waveborne particles of sand to look like the derelict skull of an old sea monster.

The divers came aboard and crawled out of their suits. I said to one of them, 'Is the rudder still there?'

He turned towards me a face with white, exhausted circles under his eyes. 'Yeah,' he said. 'Why?'

'We'll all take a look at the rudder tomorrow,' said Nelligan. His shoulders were hunched in his thin brown jacket; he must have been freezing.

'Why not now?' I said.

'Tomorrow'll do,' said Nelligan. 'It's all arranged. We'll leave it in a locked yard and make our inspection first thing.'

'What will you lose by checking now?'

'I don't know anything about boats, Mr Agutter. I think the inspection should take place in the presence of . . . er . . . qualified parties.'

'How about Mr Barnes? Or Mr Forsyth?'

He looked down, felt in his pockets, and extracted a cigarette. Without looking up, he said, 'Perhaps you know each other a bit well, Mr Agutter. They tell me you're a tight little lot, down here in Pulteney.'

'What exactly do you mean by that?'

He looked up at me with his soft brown eyes. 'What I mean is that we'll look at that boat tomorrow, with a few experts from Plymouth. And when we find nothing wrong with it, we can put it all to bed and I won't have to come out in boats and freeze to death. I hate boats,' said Inspector Nelligan. 'It'll be left in a locked compound

99

overnight, at Spearman's yard. And if they find nothing wrong with her tomorrow you're off the hook.'

Heads I win, tails you lose.

I went to the mast and looked at it, keeping my hands carefully behind my back for Nelligan's benefit. The aluminium was unimaginably battered, but the masthead fittings were still there, the jib halyard with a little scrap of white sailcloth still attached to the shackle. I looked at it, asking it for some sort of clue. I bent to examine it more closely.

The clue was there.

I walked aft to Chiefy, and said, 'Come and look at this.' He gave the helm to one of the divers and we clambered into the well, Forsyth following. I pointed to the corner of cloth. 'What's that?' I said.

'Looks like a corner of a jib.' Chiefy stooped to look at the little black number on the cloth. 'Number five.'

'The number five genoa. Heavy weather. About the size of a pocket handkerchief. Do you think a sailor with Hugo's experience would have taken a knockdown under storm jib?'

'Not likely,' said Chiefy. 'Not in just force eight.'

'So the rudder broke,' said Forsyth.

'Or it was sabotaged,' I said.

'Strewth,' said Chiefy.

They dropped me off at the quay. I went up the iron ladder and watched the rusty barge chug away into the dusk. The black airbags at its stern pushed a fat wave in front of them, and I listened to the tiny roar of its break against the outside of the quay as Helberrow Point came between me and the barge.

Spearman's was located on the flat between Pulteney and Little Pulteney. They built a good few one-tonners, which are radical boats that incorporate some new and original ideas; so if you build them you do not necessarily want every Tom, Dick and Harry strolling round your lot.

100

Hence the twelve-foot wire fence round the yard.

The barge disappeared into the gathering dusk. The quay was empty. I pulled in the painter of *Squid*, *Nautilus*' tender, moored with a little fleet of dinghies in the scummy water at the foot of the steps.

Squid was not one of your plywoods or inflatables. She was a sturdy ten-foot carvel rowing-boat and she was heavy enough to be well cursed by those unlucky enough to get the job of dragging her aboard *Nautilus*. On a night like tonight, she was exactly what I needed.

I went down the steps, climbed in, and pulled out to *Nautilus*. She was lying with her nose pointing to the west, in an eddy of the flood tide. I went up under her port side, and tied up to a stanchion out of sight of the shore. Above the harbour, Pulteney rose tier on tier, strings of yellow lights hanging across the face of the cliffs and wobbling in the ripples of the harbour.

I went forward and packed some tools, a flashlight and a camera into a canvas bag. Then I went through to the main cabin, ate a quick corned beef sandwich and washed it down with a slug of Famous Grouse. Finally, I pulled on a heavy oiled jersey and a dark cap with a shiny peak and the badge of the Agutter Line. Then I turned on all the cabin lights and returned on deck.

The sky had deepened from blue to black, and stars swam among the clouds. There was no moon. A hundred yards away the quay was empty. Lights showed in a French yacht a little to seaward, but there was nobody on deck. Very cautiously, I slipped into *Squid*, laid an oar in the notch of the transom and let go the painter. I gave two figure-of-eight twists to the oar, and the dinghy moved seaward. Anyone watching from the shore would be dazzled by *Nautilus*' lights. Ripples made tiny clocking noises against the planking as I came beyond the shelter of the quay, and the lights of the town wheeled, a mountain of fireflies, as the tide caught the dinghy and began carrying her eastwards.

Once past the end of the quay, I knew I would be

invisible against the band of darkness where the sea met the southern horizon. Setting the oars into the rowlocks, I began to row. The tide helped; five minutes later, Helberrow Point had passed to starboard, and I pulled hard with the left to bring her inshore, towards the flat stretch of sediments that the tide has deposited in the eddy behind Helberrow. As I turned, I felt the wind on my cheek. Above, the cirrus was already thickening into a layer of altostratus. Today's calm had been temporary.

It took another ten minutes to pull out of the tide and across to the shore of the flats. The sandy beach shone in the dying starlight, and I strained my eyes to look for the Bastion. The Bastion was a vast slab of concrete left over from the war, and a little past it was the mouth of the lagoon – or rather one of its mouths. The main mouth, artificially deepened, served Spearman's yard. The one by the Bastion served nobody but people like me and Hugo, when we had been young. It was a way of getting into the lagoon without anyone seeing you, which was useful if you wanted surreptitiously to fish for sea trout awaiting entry into the river Poult, which enters the sea here. It is also useful for anyone wishing to approach Spearman's unseen.

The tide swept me briskly through the Bastion channel. A bump on the shallow bottom, and I was into the lagoon. If anyone was watching, this was where they would see me. A puff of wind whistled across the lagoon; I was under the shore now, and it rattled the marram grass at the water's edge with a sound like light, dry bones. I felt acutely alone in the great sweep of beach and sky. I was taking a terrible risk; if Nelligan got to hear about this, he would assume I was a murderer, out to cover my tracks.

I rowed up the shore of the lagoon for perhaps five minutes, keeping low in the boat. Soon, the high wire fence of the yard cut the dark grey sky. I pulled perhaps another sixty strokes; then I found what I was looking for.

People like Nelligan, with shore-based notions of security, seldom appreciate that their standards do not

102

apply by the sea. Wind and waves blow down posts and rust barbed wire. In this particular case, the sand had simply eroded away from the base of a pole, leaving a two-foot gap under the bottom of the wire. I carried *Squid*'s anchor up the beach and dug it well in. Then I shouldered the toolbag and crawled under the wire.

I knew Spearman's like the back of my hand. It consisted of three long corrugated iron sheds set parallel in a large compound of landfill, on which wisps of sand blew to and fro among haphazardly-placed yachts chocked with poles and wedges. The dock was at the far side, facing onto the main channel of the Poult. That was where they kept the crane. That was where they would have hoisted *Aesthete* out of the water.

I crept forward, keeping under the side of one of the long sheds. The wind was getting up now, clattering the halyards against the metal masts. The hulls on their chocks loomed like a field of great beasts sleeping on their feet. A yellow square of light shone from the side of a shed; Harry Howe, the night-watchman. Harry would be watching telly, leaving his light to deter intruders. A car swept down the road inland and stopped in a lay-by favoured by young lovers, and I noticed one of its headlights was out.

I came to the end of the shed, and paused to listen. The only sounds were the slap and ting of the halyards and the distant bubbling yodel of a curlew.

I moved cautiously from the side of the shed to the lee of a chocked yacht, and paused again. Nothing, except that I could suddenly hear my breath roar in my nostrils, and my heartbeat – not particularly quick, but certainly louder than usual – in my chest. Small sounds suddenly became significant; the tiny crunch of grit under my feet as I moved down towards the crane, the slop of water against the pilings of the quay.

They had left *Aesthete* in the slings of the crane. I smelt her almost before I saw her, salt and weed, the smell of something that has been underwater for a long time. In

103

the darkness, she had a terrible, lopsided look. As I drew nearer. I could tell even in the blackness the extent of the damage. Her port side was stove clear in for half its length. Underneath, her fin keel was battered and twisted. My eyes travelled aft. The rudder was intact.

I put up my hand and touched it. It was still wet. I increased the pressure. The fin moved. I gave the stock mountings a quick flash of the torch. They were covered in weed. I clawed the weed aside. The torch's beam glittered on stainless steel. The darkness returned, thick and black, when I turned it off and groped in my toolbag for screwdrivers and socket wrenches.

I had not known if I could do the job in the pitch dark, but it was easier than I had feared. The detailed drawings of the rudder came up in my mind as if on a screen, and my fingers navigated surely by touch alone. And because of her broken keel the yacht lay low in the slings, so the work was at a convenient bench level. I put the bolts in my pocket and pulled at the fin. It came away easily. Holding my breath, I pointed the flashlight at the cams and clicked the switch. Then I released my breath in a long, slow sigh.

In place of the titanium bolts specified were two empty holes. Lining the holes were a few crumbs of minced aluminium – all that remained of the aluminium bolts substituted by whoever it was who had meant *Aesthete*'s steering to fail. Whoever it was who had murdered Hugo and Henry.

For a few moments, I stood completely absorbed in those little grey flecks of metal, the night-noises of the boatyard entirely shut out. Then I bent down and pulled from the bag the brass chronometer I had brought from *Nautilus*. It was a pretty chronometer, built as a navigational instrument, not a clock. I stuck it on the rudder with a lump of putty, took my camera out of its case, and then draped myself, rudder and camera in folds of the black polythene I had with me and focused as best I could inside my miniature lightproof tent. As I lined up, I

104

thought: right, Nelligan, let's see if I'm still a murder suspect after I've recorded my own sabotage.

My finger tightened on the shutter, and the flash exploded in a sudden glare of white light. Then something twitched violently at the polythene and smashed into the back of my head and the light seemed to rush back into my eyes and mix with a sudden enormous pain at the nape of my neck. It turned from white to red and roared. My hands no longer existed, nor did my legs, which was why my face was grinding into the sand. There were two ideas in my mind. One was that someone had hit me from behind, very hard. The other was that I had been an idiot to leave violence out of my calculations. I could taste oily grit. The last thing I remembered was another big pain, cut off suddenly by black night, no stars.

Chapter Sixteen

Someone was flicking water into my face. At first, I thought I was at home in bed and that my father had broken out of his wing and was down getting prankish. I said, 'Get away,' and tried to bat at him with my hand. But my hand seemed oddly heavy, and I could not move it. Also, I was being thrown about and it was playing hell with my co-ordination. In fact, I could not see. It occurred to me that this was because my eyes were shut, so I opened them. This did not help, as there was as much blackness beyond my eyelids as inside them. But it did open the gates for other sensations.

For one thing, I realised that my head contained a terrible, jagged ache, as if it was full of cubes of hot stone. For another, I felt sick. And I was, hideously and agonizingly sick, onto whatever I was lying on, while the stone cubes rattled against the tender lining of my skull. With the nausea came cold. Shuddering violently, I relapsed into coma.

The next time was just as horrible, though it was an improvement in a way. I could move, as I discovered when I managed to put my hand to my forehead. My forehead was wet, as was my hand. In fact, I was lying in six inches of water, which was sloshing violently to and fro, impelled by the heaving of the surface on which I was lying. It was still very dark, but now I could see pale patches overhead.

Muzzily, I came to the conclusion that I was in a small

boat. My fingers explored the planking. I knew those planks; I had repaired them myself – *Squid*. How had I got aboard *Squid*? There were no memories. And where was she now? It was a hard struggle to get upright, and not worth it, because on the way back the nausea returned. But this time, the idea of lying down again in the mess was unacceptable, so I achieved a sort of halfway house against the thwart, propped my chin on the edge and tried to persuade the agony in my head to behave like a brain.

There was a wind. I could feel it, and the sea was feeling it, too, because the waves were big. The sprinkling I had felt earlier was spray. In the darkness, the waves were already evil black hills, up whose sides the tender lurched, sometimes broadside-on, sometimes end-on. Now I was propped against the seat, the centre of gravity was higher. I pondered this fact, as *Squid* slithered down the side of a dark wave and up the side of the next. I saw the white water of the crest hang over the gunwale and flung myself towards it to stop her rolling. The sudden movement made me sick again. When I had finished, I groped around on the bottom boards for the oars. If I could keep her head to sea, I would be fine.

There were no oars.

I tried again, groping in the water. It must be the brain that was at fault. *Squid*'s oars lived where all oars should live, under the thwarts unless they were actually in the rowlocks. I searched twice more in the black water. The oars were not there.

I was already shivering, but now I started to shiver in earnest. It dawned on me that these were not inshore seas. Somehow, *Squid*, with me in her, had arrived a long way out in the English Channel in what felt like the run-up to a gale. I was as defenceless as a kitten in a shoebox. I braced myself against the sides, rigid with panic. Another wave sloshed in, half-filling the boat with water that made me gasp as it came up to my waist. But as the water came in, the panic left me. There were things you

107

could do in this situation. The first requirement was to get her head to sea.

Groping forward of the bow thwart, I discovered the painter. I blew a short breath of relief. The painter was thirty feet long. It needed to be, to moor the tender among the gaggle at the quay steps. Then I took off my jersey, ignoring the icy cold of the wind on my wet T-shirt. 'Sea anchor,' I said to myself. I stripped off the T-shirt and pulled the jersey back over my head. 'Wool next the skin,' I muttered. 'Always wear wool next the skin. Wool warm when wet. Wet when warm. Warm when wet.' Babbling foolishly, I tied the T-shirt's arms in a knot, hitched its hem to the end of the painter, and paid it out overboard.

There was a slight – very slight – easing of the dinghy's motion. But she was sluggish still; the water in her made her slow to recover from rolling. So I took off my left shoe and began to bail.

The wind was freshening, to perhaps force six, and there was a lot of water flying about in that black hissing. I bailed a hundred strokes with my left hand, then a hundred with my right, and then changed back again. I changed hands dozens of times. I could feel the sweat running down my back. A hot metal band lay round my forehead and I could hear someone talking. The person was me, I was pretty sure, but I had no time to listen to myself. Instead, I sat on the thwart facing forward and glared into the darkness at the wind that howled over the wavecrests and split itself on the bridge of my nose before it tumbled away into the night astern.

There were two complete certainties in my mind. The first was that I had to keep bailing, and the other was that I was going to die. After a while, my arms knotted with cramp and I felt a raging thirst. From then on, death seemed preferable to bailing. But I kept bailing anyway, and entered a curious zone.

In this zone, people appeared to me. There were my father and mother first of all, asking me (I was five

108

years old) why I had gone out without oars in an offshore wind. When I told them I did not know, they smiled and wandered off into the darkness. After them came Hugo. Hugo's lips were moving, but no words came out. So he merely shook his head and looked depressed, and left. This upset me, and I wept. Then, very close to my face, there appeared the bronzed visage of Richard Mitchell, my Olympic coach. Richard told me to pull my finger out, and counted the strokes of the bailing shoe at the rate of one a second. After he had done his bit, I was visited by a committee of my clients, requesting a sail-powered ocean liner with an air-powered rudder. I began lecturing them. Sally was there, smiling encouragingly. So were Amy Charlton and Frank Millstone and Archer and Ed Beith and Hector Pollitt and Johnny Forsyth. They all listened for a while, then tiptoed round behind me, keeping step, like Ali Baba's Forty Thieves in a pantomime. Each of them was carrying an enormous titanium bolt. I did not look round because I knew they were going to hit me on the head. I screamed at them not to, and the darkness whirled down again.

I do not know how long it was before I got up again. This time, I was better. Now I knew I had severe concussion. I knew from the alternating dry heat and shivers that I was running a fever. But as I strained my eyes over the stern of the boat, I began to feel a tiny shred of hope. For on what might have been the eastern horizon, a narrow band of paler darkness ran. It must be the dawn. Grinning at that stripe of daylight, I continued to bail. After a while, I could no longer see the daylight and my mind was wandering again. The bailing must have become slower, I suppose. Vaguely, I remember slipping down into water that came all the way up to my neck and laying my face in it gratefully.

This time, I thought I really had gone to Heaven. There was a roaring in my ears, and a sensation of floating, then

109

rising and flying. I tried to open my eyes, but shut them against the brightness. After that, a powerful smell of fish. That was odd; I had never imagined fish in Heaven, somehow, though there must be some in the Glassy Sea. After that, a deep and healing rest, on a surface that yielded and was warm and dry.

When I opened my eyes, I was in a small cabin with a cream-painted ceiling with pipes running across it. I sat up. My head spun. There was a bowl beside the bunk to be sick into. I used it. After a while, I could sit up. My clothes were on the end of the bunk, rough-dried. I pulled them on and stumbled out onto the bridge of a ship. Through the glass, I could see a low, green coast across five miles of dark blue sea. A man with a heavy black moustache turned his head towards me.

'Salut,' he said. 'Ça va?'

'Ça va,' I said, through a mouth that seemed to lack its usual connection with my brain.

He asked me who I was and where I was from, and I told him in a halting French made even more dreadful than usual by the motor grinding between my ears. I was on the Breton trawler *Drenec*, he told me. They had found me awash in a dinghy at 0700 hours. I would have sunk pretty soon. I was in luck.

I agreed that I was in luck, and he told me that we would be ashore in an hour, and that I could just walk onto the ferry and I'd be in Plymouth before I knew what. I asked him what port was this, and he told me Roscoff, which is in Brittany. *Drenec* seemed to be a fairly ancient boat, and the time on her chronometer was 1850 hours. I asked him where he had picked me up, and he told me about fifty kilometres southwest of the Isle of Wight.

I went back to the hot little cabin and searched through my pockets. They were empty. 'Of course,' I said aloud. But I was disappointed. Camera and chronometer and crumbs of aluminium were in the mugger's pocket or at the bottom of the deep blue sea, and would never be seen

110

again. I sat down on the bunk, wincing at the jar of pain at the base of my skull.

When I felt a little better, I went to the bridge and got myself patched through to the telephone system via VHF. I sat down and watched the shearwaters cutting the white wavetops, and the sharp blue horizon waving from side to side, and listened to the hisses and clicks in the receiver. Eventually I heard the voice I wanted: Neville Spearman's.

'Who's there?' he said.

'Charlie Agutter.' The long waves of the static rolled between us. 'You inspected the yacht's rudder. What did you find?'

'You should have bloody well turned up to the inspection,' said Spearman. The hostility in his voice was audible even through the electronic soup.

'I couldn't,' I said. 'Previous engagement.'

'We found two broken titanium bolts,' said Spearman. 'And before I build any more boats for you, I will want structural engineers' reports and guarantees in blood. The amount of dirt that's flying round here, some of it's going to stick to my yard.'

'I'm sorry.'

'Me too,' said Spearman, and the line went dead.

I shuffled back to the cabin. It was no more than I had expected. I should have felt gloom. What I actually felt was a twinge of pleasure that the sabotage had conformed to pattern. And stronger than that, an urge to lie down and go to sleep for a long time, which I duly did.

I slept off some more of my headache on the night ferry and Sally was at Plymouth to meet me. As I walked down the echoing baggage hall, she was by a pillar at the far end, looking more than ever like an Egyptian temple sculpture. She smiled, but there were black smudges under her happy green eyes. I kissed her on the cheek.

'I'm glad you're back,' she said matter-of-factly, as we climbed into the car. 'You look bloody awful.'

111

I squinted into the rear-view mirror. The face that squinted back was the usual one, spiky hair, sunken eyes, bat ears and all. But this version looked as if it had been starved for two weeks, then whitewashed and smeared with green paint under the eyes. The eyes themselves had an unhealthy, glassy look.

'Undead,' I said.

'Yes.' She was driving, threading crisply through the morning traffic along the Hoe. 'What happened?'

I was getting good at answering this question now.

I told her. Her white face jerked towards me and the Peugeot swerved violently across the nose of a builder's van.

'But you could have been killed,' she said.

'That was the idea,' I said. 'I'd just discovered that somebody did sabotage *Aesthete*.'

I had meant to put it more gently, but my neck hurt and the engine was still buzzing between my ears, and besides, Sally was not the kind of person who appreciated having important things put gently. This time, the Peugeot remained steady in its tracks.

'How?' she said, in a small, cold voice.

I told her.

'The same way as *Ae*,' she said. 'But why?'

'Do you think Amy would sabotage a boat to kill her husband and give Pollitt a clear field?'

'Do what?' She laughed. 'Amy couldn't change a lightbulb.'

'Well, what about Pollitt, to give himself a clear field with Amy?'

'Not exactly up his alley, is it? That means it would have been him who hit you on the head.' She paused. 'And it couldn't have been him, because he was off somewhere boozing. Apparently he got himself breath-alysed the night before last, down on the coast road.'

'Really?' I said, not too interested.

'Three times over the limit. I reckon it's Amy's fault. She doesn't half muck him about. They stopped him for

112

having a headlight out and he fell out onto the road.' She turned onto the A303, driving a Morris 1000 into the kerb of a roundabout. 'What's wrong with you?'

I was gazing through the windscreen. But I was not seeing the streams of traffic heading down the dual carriageway. Instead, I was back there at Spearman's in the dark, watching a car pull into the lovers' lay-by. A car with only one headlight. Perhaps Pollitt did know something after all.

She tried to take me to see Dr Allison. But the headache was down to a dull thud now, and the cotton wool wrapping my thoughts was losing its grip. So I asked her to drop me at the office, and she looked across at me and must have seen some convincing reason for not objecting, because she did as she was asked.

I rang the *Yachtsman*. Pollitt wasn't there; they said he was supposed to be in Pulteney, so I asked Chiefy if he'd seen him. Chiefy, who had a special talent for knowing exactly what went on, said Frank Millstone had lent him an office in one of his buildings down by the harbour. Then he asked me what had been happening, and I told him I'd fallen into my tender from the quay steps and come round in mid-Channel. He did not tell me how lucky I was to be alive, because he knew I knew. When Chiefy rang off, I went to see Pollitt.

It was a small room above a yacht-chandlery. As I walked in, Pollitt was typing.

He looked round, rolled his piece out of the platen and placed it smoothly face-down on the desk. Then he smiled broadly and said, 'Well, well, Charlie!' He came round the desk, hand outstretched. 'You look as if you've been in the wars!'

So did he. His tan looked greenish and I could smell the drink on him when he was ten feet away. His hand was cold and wettish.

'I have,' I said. 'Bloody stupid thing happened.'

113

'Really?' said Pollitt. 'Do tell.'

'I fell down the quay steps when I was untying my tender,' I said. 'Late at night. Offshore breeze. Woke up in the middle of the Channel.'

'The middle of the Channel?' His amazement sounded genuine enough. But then it was a pretty amazing story.

I explained to him my subsequent tribulations, searching his face for hints the while. I didn't find any.

'You were lucky,' he said, when I had finished. Was there a double meaning there?

'I was. Heard you had a spot of bother the other night.'

'Ah,' he said. 'Yes. The officers got me.'

'Bit of a shocker,' I said.

'Well, you know how it is. I went out to dinner at the Lobster Pot, and there they were on the way back.'

'Was Amy in the car?'

'No. I'd dropped her – ' He stopped himself. 'How did you know I'd been having dinner with Amy?'

'I guessed.'

'Bloody nymphomaniac,' said Pollitt. He sat down at his desk and pulled out a half-bottle of whisky and drank from it. When he looked up, his face had turned weaselly. 'None of your bloody business, though, Agutter. What do you want, anyway?'

'Social visit,' I said.

'How's your deal with Archer?' said Pollitt.

'Fine.'

'That's not what I heard.'

'You didn't hear anything from Archer.'

'Sources close to Archer.'

'Like Amy?'

He clamped his hands on the desk and came at me. But he was unfit and half-drunk, so I picked him up and put him back in his chair.

'You're not yourself, Hector,' I said. 'You finish your nice story and then get some kip.'

He subsided. 'She doesn't love Archer,' he said. 'She was drunk at the dance the other night. That's all. And as

114

for you, you just watch it. It's the Captain's Cup soon and the selectors read my column.'

'Easy, Hector,' I said. And I left him there, in the sleazy little room in his wooden chair, with his typescript of cheap secrets flat on the desk in front of him.

I went back to my office and dialled Sally. 'Come on,' I said. 'We're off for lunch.'

'Where?' she said.

'The Lobster Pot. Try out your friend Pat Forsyth's cooking. See you there in twenty minutes.'

I got there first. In earlier days, it had been called the Angel, but in the wake of the Millstone invasion the brewery had strung fishnets across the ceilings and nailed dried starfish to the walls, and Pat Forsyth had got the bistro franchise in what had previously been the skittle-alley. The food was medium to bad, but there was nothing they could do to the tomato juice, so I ordered one.

Johnny Forsyth came out of the kitchen with a sandwich in his hand. 'Charlie,' he said. 'Just pinching a snack off the wife. Heard you had an accident.'

'Amazing, the way news travels in this town.'

He looked slightly wounded. 'Just taking an interest,' he said.

'Sorry,' I said. 'Sore head. Have a drink.'

He grinned at me. 'Nope,' he said. 'I'm painting a picture for Millstone this afternoon. Got to keep a clear head. Hey, there's Sally.' He watched Sally's graceful walk as she came across the room. I felt his eyes on us as we talked, quietly, and ordered potted shrimps from the bar. After a while he said, loudly, 'See you, then,' and left.

Sally and I sat down at a table. There were a couple of other lunchers, but the place was by no means full. It very seldom was.

'I wonder how they make a profit here,' I said.

'I'm not sure they do,' said Sally. 'They always seem to be just about bankrupt.'

115

'Listen,' I said. 'Go and have a word with Pat. Ask her if Amy and Pollitt were here all evening the night before last.'

Sally looked at me, hard. 'Is that why we're out to lunch?'

'Please,' I said.

Sally got up. 'If you insist,' she said, and dived into the kitchen area.

She returned twenty minutes later, with our order of potted shrimps. 'Pat says that they were here all evening,' she said.

'Pity.'

'Except that Pollitt had to go out and telephone some people. He was gone about three-quarters of an hour. After about nine-ish. Amy sat up at the bar and talked to Pat. Then Pollitt came back and they started eating again.'

'Did she notice anything strange about him?'

'He was drunk. He was quarrelling with Amy.'

'Nothing strange about that.'

'I suppose not,' said Sally. 'Bloody hell.' She paused. 'I used to think Pulteney was the most beautiful place in the world. Do you remember the fun we had, Hugo and you and me and Ed Beith? And now it's all gone miserable and ugly, and there are things going on that nobody understands.' Her long green eyes were glassy with tears. 'And even the potted shrimps here are disgusting.' She pushed her plate away, and took a long, juddering breath. 'Charlie, I've got to go.'

'I'll take you home.'

'No,' she said. 'Don't. I'll be fine.'

She got up and left.

I paid the bill. Pat Forsyth smiled at me; an artificial smile. She was an unhappy woman, who liked to give the impression of being the patient victim of malevolent fate, but actually merely seemed to complain a lot about very minor afflictions.

My head hurt. I was tired and fed up. So I took it slowly

116

back up the hill to the house where the aspirins lived.

Evidence or not, I didn't believe Pollitt had left dinner, driven a mile to the marina, whacked me on the head, loaded me into the boat and cast me adrift. He didn't have the strength. And he didn't have the guts.

It was a fine afternoon. The sky was blue, with a light southwesterly breeze herding clouds like sheep. George Evans the postman, late as usual, was ducking under the honeysuckle over my garden gate.

He said it was a nice day, but privately I was studying his red face and light blue eyes and wondering, was it you who smashed me one at Spearman's?

'Not looking too good,' said George.

'Overwork,' I lied, and watched him go down the road, whistling. I didn't believe in Pollitt as saboteur and mugger. That left the field wide open; anyone in Pulteney might have Agutter on his mind. It was a nasty, naked feeling.

I went in and called Scotto, telling him to have *Sorcerer* ready for an outing on the afternoon tide. What I really wanted to do was go to bed for a couple of days. But the start-gun waits for no man, and we had six months' practice on *Sorcerer* to cram into three weeks. I could always grab forty winks on a bunk.

Also, I admitted to myself, nobody was banging anyone on the head on *Sorcerer*.

I had ten minutes to spare before I had to leave, so I shaved quickly and then went to see my father. The nurse was reading the *Daily Post* in the kitchen. She put on her large, lipstick smile above her starched apron.

'He's very well today,' she said. 'The doctor gave him some new pills, and he's had ever so many visitors.'

He was under a tartan rug in the armchair by the window. *Lloyd's List* trembled in his bony fingers. He recognized me and laid his newspaper aside. He said, 'You've been very quiet for a couple of days. Where've you been?'

'France,' I said.

117

'Oh,' he said. 'My bloody memory. Archer told me.'

'Archer?'

'Everyone in Pulteney knows.' He laughed. 'Clumsy oaf. Falling down the quay steps into yer own tender. Hee!' His liver-spotted hand spanked mirthfully at the arm of his chair. Then he looked at me sideways, as he did on the rare occasions he wanted to make a confession. 'Nice to see yer, though. Sounded nasty.'

'It was a bit.' If Hector Pollitt was useful for anything, it was as a spreader of rumours.

'Charlie,' he said. 'Are you in money trouble?'

I was taken aback. We rarely discussed money. 'Why do you ask?' I said.

His fingers plucked nervously at his rug. 'Frank Millstone came round,' he said. 'He said you were going broke. That you'd have to sell up. You know he wants to turn this house into a hotel or something. He said he'd make me an offer for my half, a decent offer, so I could be comfortable for the rest of my life.' He was grabbing handfuls of the rug, now. 'Are you going broke, Charlie?'

I said, 'No. There's nothing to worry about.' Inwardly, I was furious.

He grabbed my hand and shook it. 'Be careful,' he said, and in the watery eyes, I read affection and perhaps fear. 'Now tell me the gossip.'

We chatted for five minutes, then I went out and used the telephone in the hall to call Millstone.

'Frank,' I said. 'Charlie Agutter. What do you mean by sneaking round here and trying to frighten my father into selling you the house?'

Millstone said coldly, 'He's over twenty-one.'

'And what do you mean by telling him I'm going broke?'

'What I said,' said Millstone. 'You're in big trouble, Charlie.'

'You may not have heard,' I said. 'I'm sailing one of my boats for Sir Alec Breen, in the Captain's Cup trials.'

118

Millstone chuckled his ripe, jolly chuckle. 'Well, then, you'd better make sure you win,' he said.

I rang off.

Nurse Bollom was watching me, her mouth a thin red line. She had an idea that there was something unhealthy about the house. She would have preferred a bungalow, with me far away.

As I opened the garage doors, I indulged in a little paranoiac fantasy. Why had Frank Millstone chosen yesterday to make another offer to my father? Was it because he knew about my financial state? Or did he have reason to be sure that the obstructive Charlie Agutter was out of his way, for good?

I climbed into the car and my hand went to the ignition key. I drew it back. Climbing out, I looked carefully under the bonnet, then under the car itself, seeking unfamiliar bulges. There was only the usual mixture of rust and oil. As I drove between the banks of yellow gorse flowers to New Pulteney, the feeling of vulnerability returned.

Of course, I thought, as I parked the car in the New Pulteney Marina car park, I could always tell Nelligan. Assuming he believed me, he could launch a full-scale murder investigation.

On either side of the gently bouncing jetty, the racing-boats lay low and sharp. The sight of the boats and the nip of the wind reminded me why I was here: to race. No, I thought. No Nelligan. Just you and me, you murdering bastard, whoever you are.

Sorcerer carried a crew of ten men. Offshore racing is a small world, so I already knew the four who had come with the boat. There was Dike the foredeck man, wearing an obscene T-shirt to which his head seemed connected without benefit of neck. Halyards Joe was reputed to originate near Burnham-on-Crouch, but it was hard to confirm this since few had ever heard him speak. George,

119

known as Walter because he was a winchman, had enormous arms that hung to bare brown knees. These three crouched on the deck next to Scotto and a bearded Henry the Eighth lookalike called Al, who specialised in mastwork. Their appearance made it easy to understand why mastmen, winch-grinders and other classes of essential and highly-skilled deckhands are classed under the general heading of gorillas.

The more intellectual section of the crew included Morrie, a sail-trimmer who had come with the boat and was an authority on the tuning of her mast. Further, there was Doug Mitchell, tactician and navigator, who had sailed himself round the world twice without getting lost; Nick Thwaite, special trimmer, who had been sent down by Capote's the sailmakers to make sure we got the best of any new sails we might chance to order from them; Crispin Hughes-Affrick, winner of the Flying Dutchman Championships the previous year, mainsheet and spare helmsman; and me, helmsman and managing director of the yacht *Sorcerer*, a wholly-owned subsidiary of Breen Holdings.

We exchanged courteous greetings, as befitted gentlemen amateurs. Then we had a serious discussion, as befitted amateurs who were all being heavily subsidised by the boat's owner. Scotto, as full-time boatnigger, was the only one who drew a salary. The rest of them had to put up with free air tickets, lavish living expenses and fast cars on loan. Or, in my case, a potential boost to a very bad reputation.

The Captain's Cup trials are a series of races that begin in early summer. From the contenders, the selectors pick out the three boats that will sail in the English team. Most of the opposition had been working since before Christmas, so by that standard we were a late-come and disunited crew. On our side was the fact that *Sorcerer* was nicely tuned, and that the gorillas knew each other. It was only a matter of fine tuning, brisk routines and luck. Quite a lot of luck.

120

That day, I started with a violent headache and a fuzzy mind. But the breeze was crisp, and though the routines were a little slack the potential was there. After three hours, my head was clear and *Sorcerer* was once again an extension of my mind, as she had been when she was on the drawing-board.

There were a couple of things that needed changing: she was wearing a straight keel when she needed an ellipse, and I would have liked to put a cam rudder on her, but for the moment it seemed scarcely politic. So I called my office on the VHF and Ernie the draughtsman pulled *Sorcerer*'s original plans out of the chest and began drawing a keel.

We reached home with the big spinnaker, red and gold with the *Sorcerer*'s caduceus, ballooning huge against the horizon. Seeing that cloud of sail against the sky, hearing the sharp fizz of the wake, there was a moment when I felt a pang of pleasure in being alive. Then I remembered that someone among the folds of the green cliffs on the port bow wanted to kill me, and the pleasure faded.

As we motored in, I called a crew meeting.

'Out again first thing tomorrow,' I said. 'Then we'll lift her out and they'll put a new keel on at Spearman's. That'll take two days. Back in the water on Tuesday. Scotto, a word.'

After we had tied up and the crew were drifting off towards their Red Stripes, I said to Scotto, 'Big favour. Stay with the boat, could you?'

'What did you think I'd be doing?' said Scotto.

'I mean really stay with her. They're taking her into a shed, and they're locking her up. Even so, I want you not to let her out of your sight. Sleep aboard. Okay?'

Scotto stared at me. 'Bloody hell,' he said. Then he shrugged. 'You're the boss. What's happening?'

'Enemy action,' I said. 'Lock her up and nip over to Spearman's with me.'

Neville Spearman was in his office, at the drawing-

121

board with Johnny Forsyth. There was a set of plans in front of them. I saw the name *Crystal* at the top.

'What are you doing to that thing?' I said. 'Ed Beith rebuilding her again?'

Forsyth grinned at me, showing widely-separated teeth. He looked particularly pleased with himself. 'Ed?' he said. 'No. We were just . . . looking into her a bit. You might meet her on the water.'

'She's falling apart, I heard,' I said. 'Hull delaminating.'

'Not any more,' said Forsyth. 'I've fixed her.' There was real conviction in his voice. 'You want to watch out for her, Charlie.'

'Anyway,' I said. 'A word, Neville?'

Spearman went round to his desk and sat down in front of an array of photographs of boats: fishing-boats and customs launches as well as yachts, all built by Spearman's. The skin around his eyes was dark from overwork. He did not look particularly pleased to see us.

'This is private, I'm afraid, Johnny,' I said.

Forsyth stuck his big hands into his pockets and shouldered his way out of the door.

'What's so private?' said Spearman.

'Oh, you know how things get around,' I said. Spearman nodded, without much conviction. I could tell that my stock with him had not been improved by my acquisition of *Sorcerer*.

'Your office rang,' he said. 'Keel's on its way from Wolverhampton in the morning.'

We discussed the keel for a quarter of an hour. It was not an enormous job, but Neville was wary. When I told him that Scotto would be sleeping aboard, and that I wanted *Sorcerer* in a locked shed, he looked even more tired.

At the end, I said, 'I'm upset about *Aesthete*'s rudder. I'm sorry if it's put you in difficulties.'

'So am I,' said Neville. 'And I don't like it.'

'They were titanium bolts.'

'But they broke. Frankly, Charlie, it looks like you

ballsed up the calculations.' He drew papers towards him. The subject was closed.

'Bring her in tomorrow,' he said. 'We'll lift her straight out and get to work.' He returned to the papers on his desk and we left, dismissed. Three weeks ago he would have been all over me.

As we left the yard, Scotto said, 'I'm minding the boat. Spearman's looking at you like a leper. What's going on?'

He stared at me with his faded blue eyes, hands in the pockets of his jeans, six and a half feet high and three feet wide. I thought for a moment. What the victims of attempted murder need are bodyguards. Well, why not?

'Let's get a drink,' I said.

We drove to the Mermaid. Scotto ordered lager, and I had a pint of Bass. Then I told him the truth about what had happened the night before last.

'Ugh,' said Scotto, when I had finished. 'What did they do that for?'

'Sporting manoeuvre,' I said. 'When I was in Montreal for the Olympics, some enterprising person put a coat of fresh varnish on my boat very early one morning, so when we dropped her on the gravel before we put her in, we would get a lot of stones and whatnot stuck to the bottom and we would go a bit slower as a result. We were lucky, because we spotted it and wiped it off. You can't always be that lucky. And we are playing for big money, so people are just naturally going to be rougher. Now then, I'm going to Ireland for a couple of days and when I come back I'll need a bit of minding. Meanwhile, you're in charge of *Sorcerer*.'

Scotto sucked at his lager. 'Yeah. Shall I get my gun?'

'Gun?' I said.

'I was one of the armed guards on *Australia II* at Newport, 1983. I've got it in me bus.'

'Just get a bit of iron bar and keep your eyes open.'

Scotto's enormous face took on a disappointed air. Then he cheered up. 'Right,' he said. 'Let's get to it, shall we?'

123

The following morning it was apparent that he had slept on board. We had a good outing practising sail changes. When we came in, we had a crew meeting and Scotto took her round to the yard for her new keel. I went home, packed a bag, drove to Plymouth and caught the Brymon Airways flight for Cork.

Chapter Seventeen

After we landed, I picked up a hire car and drove to the Shamrock Hotel in Kinsale. Next morning, I got up early and took my headache down to breakfast. The dining-room was cold and empty, full of the bluish-grey light of the sea. I sat and crumbled the soda bread in the basket, and wondered where to start. Then the holiday break-fasters started to trickle in, fathers heavy-eyed with last night's stout, and the drifts of cigarette smoke drove me out into the telephone box.

I had to start with Hegarty. I was nervous about Hegarty. I had to hope that his regard for the truth was greater than his regard for his own reputation. If this was the case, he would be unique in the world of offshore racing.

I need not have worried.

'Hell, yes,' he said, when I asked if I could come down and do some interviewing. 'I'll set you up a desk and you can ask who you like what you like, and we'll tell 'em you're going to give us some work, and you're checking us out. You could send us some, come to that.'

'Next job that suits,' I said, and meant it.

The desk he had promised me was in a small green office. The first man I talked to was Sheehy, the yard foreman. He was small, with twitching hands and shuffling boots; he gave the impression of acute nervousness until you noticed the steady eyes under his sandy brows. Sheehy kept track of all boat movements through the yard.

'*Ae*,' he said. 'We had her out of the water. I looked at her keel bolts and the rudder assembly my own self, and they was fine. That would have been Thursday evening, before the weekend when the rudder came off her.' He blew smoke at his square, twitching hands.

'Where did she stand the night?'

'Beyond in the yard, on her props,' said Sheehy. 'We put her in the water the next day.'

'What time did you check the rudder?'

'It would have been five in the evening. Tight as a drum, it was.' He shook his head, his eyes never leaving mine. 'Bloody odd, them bolts going. You'd hold a steam train with one of them.'

After he had gone, the whole yard trooped through and I asked them to corroborate Sheehy's story, which they did, and then to add anything of their own. Nobody added anything important. After all, most of them were carpenters or painters or riggers, and they saw hundreds of boats every year.

I was shown over the lofts by the Construction Foreman, a blond Dutchman. Then I saw the paint sheds with White, an old man wrinkled like a walnut and coughing from years of solvent vapours. Last came the rigging sheds, for which my guide was one Dennis, with black hair growing low on his forehead and one finger distorted by what must have been an accident with some kind of power tool. It was a lovely yard, and perfectly secure. But I was not here to admire the view.

My last interview was with Garrett, the watchman, a tiny brown man in a filthy brown raincoat and enormous boots.

'What time do you come on?' I said.

'Six o'clock in the evening,' said Garrett. 'But you understand I'm busy part of the time.'

'How's that?'

'The Archaeological Association,' said Garrett. 'We meets in the Marine, nightly.' He looked at me, hard. 'And we drinks Lucozade, in case you was wonderin'.'

126

'I was,' I said. 'How d'you make sure nobody gets into the yard?'

'I turns the dog loose,' said Garrett.

'He's a fierce dog?'

'He would have the leg off you and still call to the house for his breakfast,' said Garrett, matter-of-factly.

'And do you remember him behaving differently, ever?'

'There was only the Saturday night, when that boat of yours come in with the bust rudder.'

'Nothing before that?'

'Nothing. He's a very lively dog altogether.'

'Oh.' It was beginning to look as if my Irish trip had been a waste of time. I decided on one last try. 'But before the boat came in with the bust rudder, was he not behaving strangely then?'

'I could not say,' said Garrett.

'I see,' I said. 'Well – '

'And the reason I could not say was because I did not then have the pleasure of the dog's acquaintance.' Garrett drew himself up to his full four feet eleven inches. 'The reason being that I was then in possession of the previous dog, Brian. Two days before your troubles with the rudder, Brian was found stiff. Poison was suspected. But then he was a bloody man-eater, so I wasn't surprised.'

I stared at him. He was eyeing me with triumph, as if I were the captain of a rival Archaeology Association that he had just worsted in debate.

'He was poisoned on what night?'

Garrett calculated on his fingers. 'It would have been the Thursday.'

'And you noticed nothing strange in the yard.'

'I did not.'

'Very well,' I said. 'Thanks for your help.'

'Not a bit. Are ye done?'

'I am.'

He turned and marched from the room. So Thursday night was dog-poisoning night in Crosshaven. From my

127

notes, I made a table of the movements of everyone in the yard. Now I would have to go round their houses, twenty-three of them, and check out the husbands' stories with their wives. Any discrepancies might be significant – assuming the saboteur was employed by the yard. It was a big assumption.

As it happened, it didn't work out like that.

At six o'clock, Billy Hegarty put his head round the plywood door and asked me how I was getting on. I told him. He shrugged, and asked me to dinner in Kinsale that evening. I refused, on the grounds that I had to work. I could see that he didn't think I'd get anywhere. At six-thirty, I drove off to the Marine Bar and ate smoked salmon sandwiches and drank a pint of Murphy's, the best stout in Ireland. Then I walked back into the car park, got into the car, and looked at the first address on my list. It was in Crosshaven village, so I started the engine and pulled out onto the road. Something was digging into my back, so I shifted position. The lump did not go away. It dug in harder.

A voice from the back seat said, 'Keep drivin' and do as you're told and ye might not get hurt.'

My heart gave one leap and seemed to stop. The world became very still. The voice said, 'Turn left, after the post-box.'

I turned left, into a narrow lane that wound up a steep hill, overhung with oak trees. I shifted my eyes to the rear view mirror. The back seat was empty; he must be down on the floor.

'Keep yer eyes ahead of yiz,' said the voice. It had a nervous, strangled quality. The accent was Northern Irish, but there was something not quite right about it.

'Who are you?' I said, keeping my voice steady with an effort.

'Ask no questions and ye'll hear no lies. Turn right at the end of the brick wall.'

The curtain of oaks had parted a fraction, to reveal the mouth of a cart-track. The track wound through thickets

128

of brambles. There was a distant flash of blue sea, a huge mound of ponticum, covered in mauve flowers. My mouth was dry.

'Turn left,' said the voice. We turned away from the sea. Ahead were rhododendrons, and above them pillars and window sockets entwined with brambles – the ruins of a big house. 'Don't do nothing stupid, and let me see yer hands.'

I got out. The wind sighed in the trees. The air was soft, with that Irish smell of bracken and recent rain.

'Turn around,' said the voice. I turned towards the house, but not before I had seen him getting out of the car. A chill came on the air. It was the figure of the bogeyman who follows the coffins in West Belfast. Black balaclava, black woollen gloves; and in the hands the gun. Not an Armalite, though. A sawn-off shotgun, pump action.

I said, 'Is this political?'

'Shut yer mathe,' he said. Again, there was something wrong with the accent. Carefully, the man lit a cigarette. He put it through the mouth-hole of the balaclava. It looked ridiculous. And the fear went, for a moment, and I began to think clearly. People in England are under the impression that the Provisional IRA spends its leisure time robbing and intimidating in the South. But I had been to Ireland enough times to realise that the Provos had better, or anyway different, things to do than intimidate private citizens for no good reason.

Some smoke had caught in the wool of the balaclava. The man coughed. I smiled.

'What are ye laughing at?' he said.

What I was smiling at was the fact that the accent was a fake, a County Cork approximation of Belfast. The man threw away the cigarette and gestured with the gun. The fear returned. The gun looked real enough; and as long as the gun was real, it didn't really matter much who stood behind it.

'What do you want?' I said.

129

'Less of you,' said the man. 'Some of the lads doesn't want you stickin' in your nose where it don't belong.'

'What lads?' I asked.

'You don't want to find out,' he said. His black-gloved hands shifted nervously on the stock of the gun. I watched him closely. There was something odd about one of the fingers. 'This is your first and last warning.'

'I see.'

'Now,' he said. He pulled a metal tool from his pocket and tossed it on the ground at my feet. 'Take out the valves from the wheels of the car.' Picking it up, I crouched and unscrewed the valve pistons. The tyres subsided with a hiss. 'Don't you be bothering us again.' He aimed the muzzle of the shotgun at my feet. I watched it, halfway between fear and amusement, thinking: this amateur IRA-man doesn't know what he's doing. He hadn't even asked for his pliers back.

The bang of the shotgun made me jump nearly out of my skin. He fired again, kicking up soil between us. I threw myself behind the car. Pigeons clattered away from their roosts, and a cock pheasant crowed in alarm.

'Stay away, you Brit bastard,' he said. I crouched behind the car, shaking. Pathetic he might be, but his gun had been loaded. 'You have been warned.'

He backed away from me towards a rhododendron bush, the gun still trained. Then he dived into the bush. I watched him from behind the car. My fingers closed on a large stone. He came out of the bush wheeling a moped. He levelled the gun, leaning the moped against his hip.

'Stay where you are,' he said. 'Don't try nothing.' He sounded a little desperate and the Northern accent was slipping badly. He was perhaps twenty-five feet away. I said nothing, waiting. The birds began to sing again. This man was the key. I couldn't let him go.

He began wheeling the moped away sideways, pointing the gun at me one-handed. I hoped it was as awkward as it looked. When he was twenty yards off he straddled the moped, slung the gun, and started pedalling frantically. I began running after him, clutching the stone like a rugby ball. His black and khaki figure was outlined against the bushes. I smelt raw petrol from the moped's exhaust. I was six feet behind him when the engine caught and whirred. Raising the stone in both hands, I flung it at his back.

It hit him between the shoulder blades. His head jerked round in surprise just as the front wheel of the moped lurched into a deep rut in the road, and he went flying over the handlebars. I kept running. The last two paces I covered in mid-air. I saw the whites of his eyes swivel in the holes of the balaclava. Then I landed with both feet on his stomach. The air went out of him with a whoosh and the gun flew into a bramble-bush. I pulled it out and pointed it at him. The moped engine coughed and stopped.

He lay folded like a clasp-knife, retching, as peace returned to the woods. Pigeons cooed in the canopy of leaves, and flecks of dappled sunlight shifted over his gaping mouth. One of his gloves had been torn off in the crash. The strangely twisted finger was now revealed. Half the nail was gone, as if in an accident with a power tool of some kind. It belonged to Lenny Dennis, who had shown me round the rigging loft at Hegarty's yard that afternoon.

After a while, he rolled onto his back and struggled into a sitting position.

'Take off your hood, Mr Dennis,' I said.

He pulled it off. He was red and puffy, and his eyes shifted left and right like the eyes of a dog in a crate.

'How long have you been a member of a paramilitary organization?' I said.

He swore at me.

'Shall we pop down to the Gardai and tell them what's going on?' I said. 'I'd say you'd be safer with them than with the Provos. The Provos can get a bit nasty with freelancers.'

He did some more swearing.

131

'Or you could just tell me why you put on this little play, and I'll decide what to do about you after.'

This time he did not swear, but stared at me with eyes that were sullen and angry.

'Are you going to answer?' I said. 'Or are we going to walk down the hill and talk to Billy Hegarty?'

'Hegarty?' he said. His forehead was suddenly white and sweaty.

'And then the Gardai. Think about it.'

He thought about it. Finally, he said, 'And if I tell you?'

'Not a word, if you do what you're told.'

His eyes searched my face for guarantees. I don't know if he found what he was looking for, but he began talking. 'A fella telephoned and said would I poison that bloody dog,' he said.

'Who was he?'

'I never heard him before. Some English fella.'

'What made him think you'd consider poisoning dogs?'

'He said he knew I needed the money. He said he'd seen me credit rating.'

'Your credit rating? How did he get hold of that?'

'God knows. I had a bad year on the horses, and the wife ran berserk with the Access card,' he said, pathetically. 'Yer man said he'd give me two hundred quid, cash. Anyways, I hated the bloody dog.'

'And the other dog?'

'I run out of poison so I give it some of the wife's sleeping pills.'

'How did the fella with the English voice pay you?'

'In notes. In the post.'

'You're sure you didn't see him? Why should I believe you?'

'For Chrissakes,' he said. 'I have the envelope here.' He pulled a crumpled paper out of his pocket. I looked at his face. It was stupid and desperate.

'Okay,' I said. 'Now what about all this Provo stuff?'

'You was askin' questions,' he said. 'I wanted to give yez a scare.'

132

'Your own private idea,' I said. 'No suggestions on the telephone.'

'No.' His arms hung limp by his sides and he was staring at his feet. He looked like a man who would back three-legged horses and have a wife who went mad with the Access card.

'Anything else you can tell me?'

He shook his head.

'Because if there's anything you've left out, I'll come for you.'

He shook his head again. I smoothed the envelope over the barrel of the gun and glanced down at it. It was typed with Dennis's address, and postmarked Bundoyle, County Longford.

'You can explain to the hire mob about the car,' I said. 'I'll have the moped. And if your Englishman telephones again, tell him you'll call back, and get his number, and then you bloody well ring me.' I jacked the cartridges out of the gun and flung it far into the rhododendrons. 'And you'd better pray to God that I find what I'm looking for.'

He stared at me for a moment. He was sniffing. His eyes were red and tears were running down his face. "Tis me brother's gun,' he whimpered, and blundered like an animal into the rhododendrons after it.

I got onto the moped and drove away.

Chapter Eighteen

I rode the moped as far as Cork and left it on St Patrick's Quay, where a Mr Flynn was pleased to rent me an accident-damaged Opel Kadett. It was completely dark as I threaded the grim northern suburbs of Cork, and the Opel was barely controllable. But my mood was as bright as the undipped headlights of the oncoming cars. I had another lead. True, it was a slender one. But the envelope had been typed on a word processor and the person who had arranged the dog poisonings had access to credit ratings.

Bundoyle was marked on the map as a town of between one and two thousand inhabitants, which meant that very few industrial establishments within its boundaries would be big enough to own a word processor, or to have access to credit ratings.

Bundoyle, as it turned out, was a few miles northeast of Longford. On the map, it looked like a four-hour drive, but the Kadett and the roads between them made it more like six. I pulled off the road at about two a.m. and caught three hours' fitful sleep in a lay-by.

Eight o'clock saw me driving across a flat green bog in a grey drizzle that limited my field of vision to two hundred yards. A concrete grotto with a concrete Madonna loomed out of the murk, then a double line of grey cement houses, one with a plastic Guinness sign. I was dirty and ravenous. The pub looked nasty and shut tight. But I got stiffly out of the car and hammered on the door.

After a couple of minutes, a fat woman answered, wearing a man's check dressing-gown. Ten minutes later, I was seated in the lounge bar with a large pot of mahogany-coloured tea, eating a toasted sandwich which contrived to contain not only cheese and ham but also mashed potato.

The fat woman came back, tightly corseted now, to clear away the dishes. I showed her the envelope. She said it was nice, but had no idea where it had come from.

'We'll ask Thomas,' she said, drawing herself a small glass of stout from the pumps. I was about to ask who Thomas was and when he would be arriving when brakes screeched outside and a head in a peaked cap stuck itself round the door.

'Ye have the phone bill, God help ye,' said the postman.

'Come in, Thomas!' cried the fat lady. 'We have an English gentleman with a mystery.'

I showed him the envelope. He put his head on one side, with a proprietorial air. ''Tis one of them word processors, right enough. I'd say it was from Curran's.'

'Curran Electric,' said the landlady. 'They sells fridges,' she added.

'On the road, a couple of miles out,' said the postman.

'Who runs it?'

'Fella name of White.'

'What about Mr Curran?'

'Sure there does be no Mr Curran. I'd say it's only a name.'

'Good,' I said. 'I think I'll pop out and pay them a visit.'

'Yer man's not there,' said the postman, with authority. ''Tis his daughter's half-term in England.'

'Ah,' I said, slightly taken aback by the breadth of his knowledge. 'Well, I'll go anyway.'

'Fine,' said the postman.

Curran's was a white concrete-and-metal shoebox in the grey drizzle on the outskirts of town. I parked between the only other two cars in the car park and

135

pushed open the swing door marked RECEPTION. There was a small area with a bench, some magazines and a painting of a lorry among mountains. The receptionist looked up and smiled. She was operating a word processor. I walked over to the desk.

'Is Mr White in?' I said, allowing my eyes to stray over the letters on her desk. They were all in the same typeface as the envelope.

'Mr White's in England,' said the receptionist. She was pretty, with dark hair, a roman nose and the restless eye of a thoroughbred mare. 'What was it in connection with?'

'Oh, business,' I said, vaguely. 'Credit control.'

'Mr White looks after that,' she said.

'Ah. Could you ever tell me where he's gone in England?'

'By all means.' Her fingers battered at the keyboard. The printer screamed, and a sheet of paper wound itself out of the slot. 'There you are, so,' she said.

'Thank you,' I said, and took my leave.

The address was in London. But what sent my heart slamming against my ribs, as I sat in the driver's seat of the Opel, was the list of directors at the bottom of the page. The list that began F. Millstone (*Managing*).

I got home in a state of greasy exhaustion. The only sign of life was a faint smell of dettol drifting through from my father's wing. There was a note on my table in his ancient, spidery handwriting:

Millstone rang up. He says that he is going to keep on trying to buy the house until one of us sells it to him. He is a terrible nuisance, could you have a word with him, he is making me very tired.

My father was not the only one who was tired. After I had swallowed a cup of coffee, I rang the London number on the Curran Electric paper. The voice that answered was Irish.

136

'Mr White?' I said.

'Speaking.'

'I've just come from Curran Electric,' I said. 'My name's Charles Agutter. Tell me something, are you interested in sailing?'

'Sailing?' said White. 'No. We're an electrical goods company. What do you want?'

'Are any of your staff English?' I asked.

'No. We're all – excuse me, who are you? Why are you asking me all this?'

'Because someone with access to credit ratings has been bribing people to poison dogs and sending the money in Curran Electric envelopes and this person speaks with an English accent. What have you got to say, Mr White?'

'Is this some class of a joke?' White's voice was full of genuine exasperation and puzzlement. 'Who are you and what do you want?'

'This is a murder investigation,' I said.

'Murder?' he said.

'Tell me now,' I said, injecting my voice full of menace. 'Do you remember any unusual transactions in your department this last week?'

'I do not,' he said sharply. 'We are after having our Board visit, and everything has been most regular and proper.'

'I see.' I paused. 'And was Mr Millstone there?'

'He was,' said White.

'I'll send him your regards,' I said. 'Thank you for your assistance.' And I put the telephone down.

I spent the rest of the morning trying to concentrate on the numberless petty chores of getting *Sorcerer* ready, and at half-past twelve I went down to see Scotto and inspect her new keel. Scotto had been doing odd jobs all weekend. There had been no trouble of any description. Having conferred, we went and had some lunch in the Mermaid.

'Find anything?' said Scotto.

'Yes.' I told him about Curran Electric.

137

'What does that mean?' he said.

'I don't know,' I said. 'Dennis's telephone calls could have come from England and the money could have been despatched by one of the directors at the meeting, namely Frank Millstone.'

Scotto placed two crab sandwiches in his mouth at the same time, and frowned. 'But why would he fix the rudder? He was on the bloody boat.'

'He wouldn't have expected any problems; maybe a sort of dignified rudder failure, but not a crisis. When we were poncing about by the lighthouse there, he said something very interesting. He told me he never thought I'd bring her in that close.'

Scotto pondered once again. 'So you reckon he did it?'

'Not himself,' I said.

'So you reckon he got Pollitt to do it?' He posted in two more sandwiches and washed them down with lager. 'Why?'

'No idea,' I said. Actually, I was begining to have various ideas, but none of them was yet strong enough to stand the light of day. 'Shall we pop along to Millstone's?'

'Let's go.'

I rang him first.

Georgina answered. She was his secretary. I had known her for twenty-five years. 'He's in a meeting, Charlie,' she said. 'But he wants to see you anyway. He has a call in to you.'

'He does?'

'Could you manage ten past two?'

'Yes.'

Millstone's house sat on the south side of a hill overlooking Pulteney. It was made of concrete, steel and large expanses of plate glass and it crouched in a six-acre garden surrounded by a high wall. The gates were locked. I spoke into an entry-phone, and we drove between beautifully-mown lawns and onto a tarmac sweep. I had

138

been to the house several times before, on business – I was not part of Frank's social circle. Each time, I had been made vaguely uncomfortable by the blank, eyeless look of the thing.

The man who opened the door was as big as Scotto, and looked hard. We went into an anteroom. Georgina Pearn asked if we wanted coffee.

At precisely 2.10 Frank Millstone came to his office door. His hair was wet, and he was wearing a towelling robe and a large, tough smile. He ignored Scotto, and said, 'Come in, Charlie.'

I said to Scotto, 'I won't be long,' and went in.

Frank lowered his huge frame into a chair behind a big desk with four telephones and a Reuters screen.

'We'd better forgive and forget about the Yacht Club party,' he said.

I ignored him. I'd already worked out the approach.

'My father tells me you've been pestering him about our house.'

'I expressed my intention of pursuing it,' said Frank.

'Is that why you were going to ring me?'

'Correct,' said Frank.

'Well, it's not for sale. As he told you and I have told you.'

'Charlie.' He purred the word like a big cat, and his eyes practically chirruped in their nest of wrinkles. 'Look here, we don't need bad blood between us. I'm sorry your rudders aren't working out. I'm sorry your contract with Archer isn't going too well. And I'm sorry if anything gives you the idea that I'm not on your side. But I asked you here because I want to help you.'

'I didn't know I needed help.'

He pulled a sheet of paper towards him. 'You've got a big overdraft, Charlie. And a couple of nasty-looking loans to pay, your father to support. And you've got no income.'

'Clever of you to find this out,' I said. 'How do you do it?'

139

He laughed, and flattened the timber of his desk with his big, hard hands. 'We call it credit control,' he said.

'Do you really?' I said, mildly.

'So all you've got is Alec Breen taking up your time for the summer with that old boat of his.'

'She's a good boat.'

He rolled on, still smiling. 'So I'm making you a proposition. I want your house for a nice hotel, very select. I'll make a deal with you now. You can have two hundred thousand quid for it, and your dad can stay on for as long as he wants. Okay?'

It was a tempting offer. Two hundred thousand pounds would have solved a lot of problems. The trouble was, most of my problems seemed likely to have been created by Millstone, and I have never enjoyed being black-mailed.

'Not for sale,' I said. 'In fact, it is even less for sale than it was before, because I don't deal with people who try to frighten my father out of his wits.'

Millstone's eyes were earnest. 'Listen,' he said. 'When I came to Pulteney it was a dirty little hole. You could smell the fish miles away. I've changed all that. It's been my life's work. Other men collect paintings. I've tried to turn Pulteney into a place people can enjoy.'

'Very noble,' I said. 'Pity you didn't ask the people who live here, first.'

'Be practical,' said Millstone.

'I think that's up to me.'

'I'm worried that you're going to go broke,' said Millstone earnestly. 'Then I'll get your house anyway. Couldn't we keep it amicable?'

I was tired and I was edgy. The hypocrisy of the man disgusted me. Anger bubbled up, and I stopped being sensible.

'Do you call arranging for my boats to be sabotaged amicable?' I said.

The smile clicked off. He frowned. His eyes lost their twinkle and became flat and hard, like pebbles. 'Your

140

boats weren't sabotaged,' he said. 'The rudders bust because they were badly designed.'

'Not because someone with his eye on my house decided that I needed ruining?'

Millstone rose and leaned forward over his desk. 'I think you're under a lot of strain, Charlie. Because if you weren't, you certainly wouldn't be suggesting what I think you're suggesting.'

I could feel the hammers of anger beating in my temples. I got up and walked towards the door.

Millstone said, 'I want your house, Charlie. But, if I hear any more accusations of sabotage, I'll sue you for your last – ' I slammed the door on him.

Georgina showed me and Scotto along the concrete-walled corridor to the front door of the house.

'I hear you've got a boat for the Cup trials,' she said. 'Congratulations.'

I thanked her. Then it occurred to me that a little digging might be in order. 'And Frank's buying Ed Beith's, I hear.'

Georgina looked around, and put a finger to her lips. 'Not so loud,' she said. 'It's confidential; they're still arguing.'

Well, I couldn't help it if she assumed that the person I had heard it from was Millstone himself.

'Nice pool,' said Scotto as we went through the hall.

I looked into a plate glass conservatory. Inside were tropical palms and a pool with blue water and white marble dolphins. Beside the pool, reading a book and wearing a minute bikini that showed off her creamy redhead's skin and foxy little breasts, was Amy Charlton.

'Lunchtime swim with Frank, is it, Amy?' I said. 'You do get around these days.'

She looked up. 'Oh, piss off, Agutter.'

As we walked towards the car, a blue Mercedes drew up, and Jack Archer got out. He looked neat and dapper as ever, carrying a pigskin briefcase.

'Ah,' he said. 'Hello, Charlie.' His square, brown face

141

was smiling, but I thought he looked a little worried. 'I was going to ring you. Sorry to hear about the results of the *Aesthete* inspection the other day. I . . . that is, unless something happens to make me decide to the contrary, I may have to start thinking about putting out some of those design jobs elsewhere. I'm sure you understand. Unless, of course, things go very well for *Sorcerer*.'

'Are you sailing?' I said, to cover up the fact that my heart was beating too hard. It was no more than I had expected, but now that it had happened it was very unpleasant.

'With Frank,' he said. 'If he gets a boat.'

'I'm sure he'll do his best,' I said, not altogether succeeding in keeping the irony out of my voice.

As we went down the drive, Scotto said, 'What was that all about?'

'Millstone wants my house,' I said. 'Archer wants me to stop designing boats for him. The bank manager wants my skin. And the only way out is to get into the Captain's Cup team, and win. Is it possible?'

''Course it is,' said Scotto. I wished I shared his confidence.

As we drove, I thought about Amy. I was now good and sure that Amy was mixed up in it somewhere. She had been two-timing Henry with Pollitt, and two-timing Pollitt with Archer. Was she also two-timing Archer with Millstone? And where, if anywhere, did bashing Charlie Agutter fit into her complicated love-life? As we drove back down to the village, I decided that I should go and see Sally. She knew Amy well. Perhaps she'd have some ideas. And then I'd visit Ed Beith. Georgina had mentioned his discussions with Frank. It would be interesting to find out their content.

But first, there was work to do.

With Scotto and a couple of yard hands, I spent the afternoon and early evening re-rigging *Sorcerer*. As it was getting dark I called Sally, but there was no answer. So I thought I might as well go and see Ed first.

142

I drove out of Pulteney fast. It was dark, and the sky over the whalebacked hills was pricked with stars. Ahead, the lights of a town reddened the sky. I frowned. There should be no town. I forked left where the signpost said Lydiats Manor Only – Private Road. The glow intensified from dirty red to glaring orange. I put my foot on the accelerator and the BMW tyres screamed as I breasted the rise and dived into the deep lane that led down into the valley.

The valley was burning. That was what it looked like at first; but once the eyes had accustomed themselves to the glare, it became apparent that it was not the whole valley. Ed's house stood at the far end of the lake of flame, untouched, its windows yellow with electric light. I drove through the gate, past the burning turkey huts, and came to a halt in the gravel sweep in front of the house. A man ran past with a bucket in each hand, the sweat on his face blazing red in the glare. The heat was fierce. A gust of smoke whirled down the house's front and I choked. It stank of feathers. Then the meaning of that sank in, and I stood quite still for a moment. Above the roaring of the flames, I heard a voice yelling my name, and in the red glow I saw two figures standing at the end of the stone barn. Behind them, a fire-engine was sending a wholly inadequate jet of water into the nearest part of the fire. I went across. It was Ed Beith. He was standing, with his hands in the pockets of his boiler suit, shaking his head. The person next to him was Sally.

Ed said, 'Oh, Charlie. How are you?' as if we were at a cocktail party. Sally looked at me, then back at the flames. The red light painted her face with black hollows. I wondered what she was doing here.

'Buckets,' I said.

Ed raised his black eyebrows, as if surprised. 'Buckets?' he said. 'Ah, buckets.'

The word set him going. He ran for the stables, and we ran after him and got a dozen buckets. By now, there were several farm-hands there and neighbours who had

143

seen the glow and come down the hill. So we got a bucket chain going from the cowshed tap and as the flames rose and danced and sparks whirled high above the red ruins of Ed's turkeys, we splashed our buckets at the edges.

But the huts had been made of wood and we might as well have tried to bail out the sea with a teacup. Four more fire-engines arrived, and a fireman asked us politely to stand back. The bucket chain faltered and stopped.

Ed thanked its links, and said, 'Not much we can do here. Let's go in and have a drink.'

We went into the kitchen. It was much tidier than usual. Ed pulled a bottle of champagne out of the fridge, divided it between three tumblers and gave Sally and me one each.

'Let's drink to 'em,' he said. 'One hundred thousand Christmas dinners, all bloody burnt.' He drank deeply. Sally was eyeing him.

'Listen,' I said. 'Can't we stop it spreading?'

'It's spread,' said Ed. He had already been drinking, by the sound of him. 'Those little gurks were sitting in dry wood-houses on wood-shavings. They're the only thing that'll burn. House is quite safe.' He slapped the kitchen wall. 'Stone. Proper job, Lydiats.'

'I'm sorry,' I said.

Ed shrugged. He sat down with a thump on a wooden chair. 'No insurance. Thank God they weren't any older. Poor little gurks.'

'No insurance?' I said.

'Ah, well. Hundred thousand quid down the drain. So what?' But the thought seemed to depress him. Sally was standing close to him, drawn and silent. The ticking of the clock was loud in the foreground of the roar and crackle outside. Ed sat and stared bleakly at a silver salt-cellar on the kitchen table.

Then he reached out a large hand, picked up the telephone and dialled.

'Frank Millstone, please,' he said. 'Frank, hello. D'you

144

still want to buy the yacht *Crystal*?' I started forward.

'Ed!' I shouted. 'Wait a minute – '

Sally grabbed my hand. 'Sit down and shut up,' she said fiercely. 'This is nothing to do with you.'

A tinny voice muttered on the other end. 'Very well,' Ed was saying. 'You've got her. Sails and all. Send me your contract.'

He put down the telephone. His face was grey and hard, and he picked up his tumbler of champagne and drained it. 'Well,' he said. 'Who needs insurance when you've got a boat to sell?'

The kitchen door opened, and a man with a smoke-streaked face said, 'Wind's changing. Fire's heading for the barns.'

'I'm there,' said Ed, and rushed out of the room.

I ran after him, out into the yard. The flames were leaning downwind, clawing hungrily at the range of old stone and clapboard buildings on the side of the hill, where Ed kept his machinery.

'Get a hose!' shouted Ed. 'Any hose! Damp down the weather-boarding!'

The smoke was choking, and the heat tightened the skin on my face. I ran for a tap, screwed up the hose, and started soaking the elm boards. A tractor started up inside. Ed roared out, parked it upwind, and ran back to collect another.

Steam drifted from the weather-boarding. It was very hot. When I looked round, Sally was standing next to me, with a scarf wrapped round her face against the smoke.

I said to her, 'What's Amy up to?' I had to shout, above the roar of the flames.

'What's what?'

'Amy. Up to. She's all mixed up with this.'

Sally said, 'No. She can't be.'

'She's been screwing Pollitt. And Archer. And she was at Millstone's today, looking like a fixture.' A wall collapsed with a roar into the lake of fire.

'A what?'

145

'Fixture. Concubine.'

'I told you,' she shouted. 'She's got an itch. It doesn't mean anything.'

'People are getting killed,' I said. 'Things are happening, all around her.'

'Shut up!' screamed Sally. I stared at her in amazement. The hose's jet strayed onto the ground. She was saying something, but I couldn't hear. Deep in the burning sheds, something went whoomph. A mat of flame licked across the ground at us. I charged at her and shoved her out of range, into the darkness. Two firemen appeared with a big hose. We lay in the shadow where we had fallen. I could feel her body shaking.

'Are you hurt?' I said.

'No.' Her voice was unsteady. 'But I've had enough.'

'It's all right,' I said soothingly.

'No it bloody well isn't.' She sounded panicky. 'There you are playing bloody boats, taking yourselves so bloody seriously. And you say it's only a game. But it's not a game anymore, Charlie. It's got on top of you. And it's killed my lovely Hugo, and Henry, and someone's trying to kill you now. And Ed's poor turkeys. I suppose someone did that to make him sell his boat, is that it?' She laughed; the sound was unpleasantly shrill. 'You're not looking for a saboteur, you're looking for a madman. But don't kid yourself that this madman's any different from you. He's just another brat playing a game that's got out of hand. Well, I'm not a child any more.'

'Wait,' I said.

'No,' she said. 'The only sane one's Ed. He's selling his boat and getting out. He does it for fun, and when it stops being fun, that's it. Why don't you leave it to the police?'

'Sally,' I said, and tried to take her arm. 'You're not making sense.'

'Leave me alone!' she cried. 'I've had enough! You're all mad!'

There was a cracking roar from the turkey sheds, and the night sky was filled with a blizzard of sparks. Ed

146

Beith's voice shouted, 'Come on, Charlie!' He was silhouetted against the flames, struggling with the hitch of a water trailer. I ran down to help him. Halfway, I looked back for Sally.

She was gone.

I ran on into the red glare and the disgusting stink of feathers. I have never felt lonelier in my life.

The night went in the slop of water and the taste of soot. We kept the fire off the barns. By dawn, it was under control and I drove home to bed for a couple of hours. When I woke, I tried to ring Sally. Nobody answered the telephone. I made some coffee and put in extra sugar. Perhaps I was trying to console myself for the fact that the closeness we had felt in Kinsale was gone.

By eight-thirty, I was shuddering in *Sorcerer*'s trench as we moved down-channel for the day's practice.

Chapter Nineteen

Slowly, I woke up. The boat was going well with the new keel, and the crew seemed none the worse for a three-day lay-off. We spent a cold, wet day slamming through a short sea to the south of the Teeth. *Sorcerer* had a lighter feel; she was sailing more than ever like a giant dinghy, which was what I wanted of her. It wasn't until we were sliding downhill, homeward bound, that the no-talking rule was relaxed and I got a chance to talk to Scotto.

Crispin, the relief helmsman, had the wheel, and Scotto and I were sitting with our legs under the windward lifelines, gazing down the coast of England towards the murky grey clouds in the general direction of the Isle of Wight.

'Did you hear Millstone's got *Crystal*?' he said.

Scuttlebutt moved at amazing speed. 'I heard.'

'Not a bad sled, that *Crystal*.'

'We can beat her.'

Scotto slapped *Sorcerer*'s hull with his vast hand. ''Course we can,' he said.

And there we were again, playing the children's game.

I got up from the rail. 'Right,' I said. 'Final exercise.'

The windburned faces the crew turned to me were not at all enthusiastic: it had been a long, hard day.

'Channel buoy to harbour light,' I said. 'We'll try the tri-radial.'

The Channel buoy marked the outer extremity of the Pulteney channel. It was a red cage with a bell, a relic of

148

the days when my father's big ships had used the harbour. Now it served as a handy mark for yachts wishing to cut a dash on the way in. Furthermore, it was precisely one sea mile from the light at the end of the quay, so it gave competitors watching from the Yacht Club a rough measure of the way the opposition's boats were travelling.

The buoy came up to starboard. As the huge red-and-gold sail collapsed, its smaller brother blossomed, and *Sorcerer*'s bow came up until the readout by the mainsheet track read 100 degrees off the wind. Nobody spoke as the cockpit tilted and the water began to fly. *Sorcerer* leaned steeply over and the water slithered under her and up from her retroussé transom in the fan of thin spray that meant high speed. The rigging groaned and she heeled a degree or so more; there was a slight shudder and she was up.

The speed of racing-yachts was once limited by their waterline length. A yacht used to send up a bow wave at its nose and a quarter wave at its tail and sailed along in the trough between the two, unable to cross its own bow wave. The theoretical maximum for *Sorcerer*'s forty-three feet of waterline was less than nine knots. But obviously nobody had told *Sorcerer* this, because she skimmed across the water like a flat pebble, with no bow wave and a V of spray at her tail while the log needle went round to fourteen knots.

'Strewth,' said Scotto.

It took us dead on five minutes to make the harbour light.

'Sails off,' I said.

'Hardly worth putting 'em up,' said one of the trimmers, and everyone laughed. It was partly a release of tension, and partly that this was the first time *Sorcerer* had ever got up and gone off the clock like that. Suddenly we weren't just a good crew in an old boat, but a good crew in a boat that could do it.

I raised my glasses and trained them on the balcony of the Pulteney Yacht Club. Despite the overcast sky and

149

the cool wind, there were several people out there. I moved my glasses slightly and found myself looking at another pair, trained on me from above the well-filled blazer of Frank Millstone. I waved. Millstone lowered them quickly and turned to the group at his elbow. I identified Hector Pollitt, Jack Archer and Johnny Forsyth. Johnny said something, presumably about *Sorcerer*'s turn of speed, and they laughed and shook their heads. But Millstone did not laugh. Instead he drained his drink and walked quickly in at the French windows. Inside the windows, I saw the figure of a woman, white-faced against the dark interior of the bar. Amy.

As we motored up-channel towards the marina, I called the crew together.

'We've got over two weeks till the first of the trials,' I said. 'We'll be out every day. Now she's shown what she'll do with the new keel, I want her moving like that all the time. But the boat's only half of it. The rest of you stay off the beer and no picking fights with grizzly bears. Watch yourselves and we'll win.'

There was some grinning, and some serious nodding. The word for crews at this level of racing was dedicated. The free air tickets and the living expenses were only icing. The cake was winning. Winning was the only thing they didn't make jokes about, and the will to win was what made them different from other people. Inhuman, some would say. Or mad.

I stayed to talk to Scotto after the rest of them had cleared up and filtered away.

'Watch out,' I said.

'What's happened?'

I took a deep breath. 'I think someone set fire to Ed's turkey shed to . . . persuade him to sell his boat.'

'You mean Millstone did.'

I shrugged. 'Would he do a thing like that?'

Scotto said, 'I dunno.'

'He'd be a fool to.'

'Who else would?'

150

There were alternatives. Hector Pollitt, for one. Amy, for another. Anyone who didn't care what they did to get Millstone a boat.

'Get the law in,' said Scotto.

'Not yet,' I said. 'The papers'd get it. Hegarty'd lose most of his customers. And if it got to court, Millstone'd get a million quid's worth of barrister and the case'd be flung out for lack of evidence.'

'Strikes me there's loads of evidence,' said Scotto.

'Courts want things proved beyond reasonable doubt. What we've got is coincidences.'

Scotto shook his massive head.

'So what we want to do is beat him in the trials.'

'You're going to wait that long?'

I tried to smile at him, but I could feel my face ugly and stretched. 'I have an idea. If we win the first race of the trials, I can get going on it.'

'We can but try,' said Scotto. 'You got a definite plan?'

'Tell you later,' I said. The idea was so horrible that I could scarcely even bring myself to think about it.

'Am I still sleeping on board?' he said.

''Fraid so.'

'It's a bloody salt swamp down there.'

'You'll survive.'

He nodded. 'How about if I got Georgia down?'

'Why not? But there's not much room for two in one of those bunks.'

'We'll manage.' Scotto paused. 'She says she's got Red Indian blood. Her ancestors did it in canoes, standing up.'

I laughed and jumped onto the jetty. Outside the car park, I turned automatically in the direction of Sally's house. Then I remembered last night, did a three-point turn in the gateway, and drove back towards Pulteney. Children's games, ending in tears.

But not hers this time. Or mine. Millstone's.

151

Chapter Twenty

When I got home, I poured myself a large Famous Grouse, looked at the answering machine and decided not to listen to the messages until I had got the salt off. So I took my glass upstairs and stood under the shower for ten minutes, hot as I could stand it, trying not to listen to the shouting from next door. My father seemed to be having a bad day. My throat was sore from the smoke of Ed's turkey chicks. I was looking forward to a bit of telephoning, dinner and ten hours' kip. I stepped out of the shower and pulled on a pair of O.M. Watts trousers and an *Aesthete* crew shirt, for old times' sake. Then I went down to the living-room, feeling pink, clean and a bit woozy from the hot shower and the whisky.

There were a dozen or so messages, mostly from newspapers. The only important ones were from Breen and Sally. The one from Sally was important because it wasn't there. Breen's secretary wanted me to ring him, and had left a number. I called the number. A woman told me that I was expected to dinner. She then gave me an address between Marlborough and Newbury and put the telephone down. I sat down and held my head in my hands for a couple of minutes. Then I changed into a blazer and my RORC tie, and trudged wearily through to the garage.

Two hours later, I was winding through the manicured lanes of North Hampshire, reflecting that it was only a matter of time before the inhabitants of the area erected a

152

fence around it and posted security guards to spare them the necessity of contact with the outside world. Breen's home was long, low and half-timbered, with an immaculate garden and a lake beside which was sited the helicopter pad.

Breen was waiting in a large, beamed room full of chintz furniture. He was dressed in a khaki safari suit, drinking what looked like Coca-Cola and chewing the inevitable cigar. He looked uneasy in the sea of chintz; at last, I thought, a room he could not dominate. He introduced me to a tall, pale woman in a pair of expensively modified silk pyjamas.

'My wife, Camilla,' he said. 'Charlie Agutter, who's sailing *Sorcerer* in the Captain's Cup trials.'

She had once been beautiful. Now she looked tired of doing nothing. 'The Captain's Cup trials?' she said. 'What are they?'

'A series of races between boats who want to get into the Cup team,' I said. 'Half a dozen inshore races and three long offshore races.'

'I'm afraid I know absolutely nothing about boats,' she said.

Dinner was steak and a bottle of very good burgundy, of which Breen drank none. Lady Breen asked me questions in whose answers she was obviously not interested. I wondered why I had been asked. It was as if by doing Breen violence in Lymington, I had cracked his shell, and he felt I should be admitted to some sort of intimacy. But he was obviously a man not used to intimacy, so the dinner had an aching formality that none of my previous encounters with him had shown. Afterwards, Lady Breen said she had a headache and asked to be excused.

After she had gone, Breen lit another cigar, gestured at the long oak table with its Paul de Lamerie silver, and said, 'Shall we adjourn?'

He led the way down a passage to a heavy oak door, which he unlocked. The room behind it was filing-cabinet

153

green and dove-grey, with a big oak desk on which sat a computer terminal and a telephone. It might have been any office in any high-rise block in London. In it, Breen regained the poise that the chintz had upset.

'Right,' he said. 'Nice dinner. Let's talk.'

I told him about the success of the new keel. He seemed gratified. 'Anything else?' I told him that a new mainsail would be useful. 'More bloody Kevlar, I suppose,' he said. 'Costs twice as much as Dacron and lasts half as long.'

I began to explain.

'I know. They don't stretch, and you might get an extra twenty-fifth of a knot. There again, you might not. Whoever said this game was like tearing up tenners under a cold shower had it right, except he should have said fifties.' The eyes above the cigar had a little glint of excitement in them. I was surprised. He was positively talkative, for him. 'If you need a mainsail, get it. But you'd better win with it.' He leaned back in his black leather swivel chair, blowing a thin stream of smoke. 'Now, tell me about the opposition.'

I ran down the list of entrants to the Captain's Cup trials, discussing their boats and their crews. As we went on, I began once again to see the qualities that had set Breen apart from the crowd. He had no scruples at all about being boring, and even fewer about being bored. When he got at a subject he picked it up and worried it, and would not leave it alone until he had modified it into a form he could digest.

It took us three hours to discuss the first eleven competitors, and never once were we allowed to stray from the point. When we had finished with the eleventh, he cut the end off a fresh cigar.

'That leaves *Sorcerer* and Millstone,' he said. 'Tell me, Charlie, why have you been saving Millstone till last?'

'No reason,' I said. Well, it was true; there were no conscious reasons.

'I'm going to ask you an insulting question,' said Breen. 'Are you frightened of Frank Millstone?'

154

I was; insulted, I mean. I said, 'No.'

'Badly put. Does he worry you?'

It sounded better that way. 'Yes,' I said. 'He worries me. But not for long.'

'How's that?'

'Because I am going to beat the hell out of him, and then I am going to turn him over to the law.'

'Charlie,' said Breen, 'I like you. Also, I like your priorities. But one of the reasons I asked you over here was to remind you that the first of the trials is very soon and that you are my employee. There are thirteen boats in the race, Charlie, not two. Your job is to come in first.'

'Yes.'

'I like to offer carrots, Charlie. If you win this race, you can design me a 150-foot schooner and name your fee. Also, I will influence Archer to give you your contract back. If you lose it, you don't get the schooner, or any help with the contract, but you keep your legs. But if you start mucking about with Millstone off the water and by so doing prejudice my chance, you can wave your legs goodbye, because I will have sawn off your arse. Understood?' The eyes above the cigar now held no trace of amusement. They seemed to fill the room. 'Now then, it's midnight. You're going to need your kip. Get out of here.'

I got out, as instructed. I was exhausted, but I had no trouble staying awake.

Whoever was sabotaging boats and burning turkeys had so far done it to his own timetable. This time, he was going to do it to my timetable and I was going to be ready for him.

Unfortunately, the method used had to be one that would prejudice Breen's chance for the Cup.

Next morning, I went to Portsmouth to put the first part of my plan into operation. As I was leaving Pulteney, I saw a green Cortina in a lay-by, with its bonnet open and

155

a man bending over the engine. The legs were long and lanky. I slowed down, and stopped. It was Johnny Forsyth. His hands were covered in oil and his acne-scarred face sullen.

'Bloody distributor,' he said. 'Shorting out.'

'Where are you heading?' I said.

'Hamble,' he said.

'Hop in.'

When we were in the car he said, 'Saw you coming off the harbour buoy last night. Going nicely.'

'Yes. Are you sailing the day after tomorrow?'

'On *Crystal*. I was working on her hull for Ed Beith. I'm staying with her for Millstone.'

'What have you been up to?'

'A few bits and pieces.' Johnny's face was watching the road, his eyes narrow, his cheek flat and grainy, not giving anything away. 'Bit of work on the rig. Cheering up the hull.'

'How's it going?'

'She'll be very nice.' His narrow eyes moved across at me. 'Very fast. A bit of serious competition for you.' He laughed, with that lipless stretch of the face. 'I'm doing tactics, too.'

We left it at that. I dropped him at the Hamble, went on to a security consultant to pick up some brochures and price lists, and collected him on the way back. I dropped him at the marina. He climbed out of the car and said, 'Thanks,' but I was looking past him. Archer's blue Mercedes was parked two cars down. Archer was in it. So was Amy. They were kissing, long and very, very hard.

Forsyth followed my eyes. His face reddened and his eyes narrowed. He said, 'Bitch!'

'What?' I said, taken aback.

He turned back to me with a smile that was visibly false. 'Nothing,' he said. 'Must dash.'

I returned to Pulteney quay and the Zodiac which was waiting to take me out to where *Sorcerer* was playing jibing. Chiefy was driving, but we did not talk. I was

156

watching *Sorcerer*'s big orange spinnaker against the blue-green sea, and thinking. Breen wanted me to win the race, and that was the limit of his interest. For me, winning was only the first step to finding out who was trying to wreck my career. And if I had to fly across Breen's bows in the process, it was just too bad.

Just too bad for whom? For me, more than likely.

The next two weeks went well. By dint of tinkering and fine tuning, we got the boat up and onto her running legs again; and each time, it seemed to come easier. The routine took over: up before dawn, running with the crew, sail till dusk or after, then work on equipment modifications far into the night. After ten days, we started some night practice. It was solid, concentrated effort.

On the seventeenth evening, I left Scotto and Georgia to sleep aboard and drove home in a trance of exhaustion. I crawled back to my house, showered, boiled an egg and sat down to eat it. The next thing I knew it was pitch dark and the telephone was ringing, and I was still in the armchair.

'What?' I said into the receiver, gluey-mouthed.

There was the noise of someone forcing money into a callbox.

'Charlie? It's Georgia.'

'Georgia?' I said, and looked at my watch. Two a.m.

'You'd better get down here,' said Georgia.

'Where are you?' I could remember my own name now. And hers. She sounded out of breath, as if she had been running.

'Marina callbox. I was on *Sorcerer* with Scotto. He's hurt. You'd better come.'

I went. Fog lay over the road in grey wisps and the grit of the marine car park was damp with it. Navigating by the tap of halyard against mast, I blundered across to the jetties. Lights shone yellow from a cabin hatch. The fog seemed to be inside my head as well as outside it.

157

'Who's there?' A small, shapeless figure loomed out of the darkness, crouching.

'Me.'

The figure relaxed and said, in Georgia's voice, 'Charlie, thank God you're here.' As we entered the lamplit circle of fog, I saw that she was wearing three jerseys and carrying a baseball bat.

'Where's Scotto?'

She switched on a flashlight and we climbed aboard *Sorcerer*. The deck rocked a little. Scotto's voice came hoarsely up from the hatch.

'Georgia?' he called, and ended on a grunt of pain. Until I felt the relief wash over me, I did not realise I had been expecting the worst.

He was lying on his back on the cabin floor. It was not a comfortable place to lie – a bit like an oversized fibreglass coffin, stark white under the unshielded bulbs, clammy with the condensation that ran down the walls. He had a sleeping bag over him, and his tan was yellow, not brown.

'What's wrong with you?'

Scotto grinned, a weak approximation to his normal rat-trap. 'Fell on my back,' he said.

'Let's have a look,' I said. 'Move your toes.'

'Nothing's bust,' said Scotto. 'Look.' He did a straight leg-lift that turned his face from yellow to grey and brought beads of sweat popping out on his forehead. 'She made me lie down, that's all.'

'Turn over,' I said.

'I'm okay,' said Scotto, and turned with difficulty onto his face. A broad red weal ran across the huge brown pads of muscle on either side of his spine. I prodded the weal. Scotto said, 'Hey!'

'What happened?' I said.

'Someone pushed me down the hatch.'

'Oh,' I said, as if it happened every day. 'You'd better get down to Casualty for an X-ray.'

Scotto said, 'I heard someone moving about on deck. I went up to the hatch nice and quiet, but the boat must

158

have moved about a bit. First thing I knew, I got a knee in the chest and down I went.' Scotto paused. 'S'pose I screwed up,' he said. 'But Georgia went out with the baseball bat.'

'Somebody was running down the jetty,' said Georgia. 'They were running pretty fast, considering.'

'Considering what?'

'I got a swing in,' said Scotto. 'That's why I went down the hatch, because I was hitting the guy with the hand I was meant to be holding on with. I got him smack in the mouth.'

'How d'you know, if you couldn't see him?'

'Because I've got his toothmarks in my knuckles.'

'Great,' I said. 'Now all we've got to do is find someone with your knucklemarks in his teeth.'

'I thought of that,' said Scotto.

'The guy went off in a car,' said Georgia. 'I heard the engine.'

I sighed. I was very tired. 'Georgia, I'm going to stay with *Sorcerer*. Can you get him down to the hospital? Take my car.'

Georgia sighed back, and sat down. The light threw golden reflections on her warm brown skin. 'He's not going to be much good to me here. C'mon, Scotto.'

Between us, we managed to get him on his feet and drag him to the car. Then I trudged back down to the jetty and aboard *Sorcerer*. I went below, pulled Scotto's sleeping bag over my clothes, and lay down on the bottom bunk. For a moment, I lay listening to the slap of the ripples echoing in the hollow hull. Then I went to sleep.

I was beginning a very nice dream, in which Sally and I were in a biplane flying over a range of mountains. The engine of the biplane had a knock. The knock got louder and louder. 'We'll have to go down,' I yelled in the rush of the wind. A landing strip opened below a crack in the clouds, a postage stamp of concrete among grey rocks. But the aeroplane would not go down. The knocking was hideously loud now. I opened my eyes. It was still dark and someone was banging on the hull.

159

'Arright,' I croaked. I felt like death. 'Wharrisit?'

'It's me, Georgia!'

'What time is it?'

'About three, I dunno. Listen, come quick.'

I lurched out of bed and crawled up the companionway. Georgia dazzled me with a flashlight. 'Come to the hospital.'

'Something wrong?'

'Scotto's gone berserk.'

'Cool him down, then.'

'No. He wants you.'

'Oh.' I started for the jetty. 'Hey. No. I've got to stay with the boat.'

'I will.'

'You bloody won't.'

'I will. I've got Scotto's gun.'

I fought an urge to sit down on the jetty and weep. 'Get back to Scotto.'

'I'm staying,' said Georgia. 'I might scream.'

My arms were pig-lead and I still felt weepy. I said, 'Don't shoot anybody,' and trudged off up the jetty.

The BMW was hot, and smelt of burning clutch-plates. I took it back towards Pulteney, hypnotised by the white lines in the yellow headlamps. I sang, trying to stay awake. Even so, I bounced off the hedge and dented the driver's door. But at least that woke me up. Ten minutes later, I was turning into the car park of Pulteney Cottage Hospital.

The long, white building was dark and quiet. The only sign of life was the cold light burning above the casualty department door. The Cottage Hospital was staffed by a single night nurse. In an emergency, she called a duty doctor, who zigzagged sleepily up from the village. I climbed out of the car and went in.

Tonight – this morning, rather – the duty doctor was a smallish, timid man with large eyebrows, who did not approve of Pulteney's irregularities. But he didn't look at all sleepy. He was standing to attention, with his fists

160

clenched at his sides, saying, 'Nurse! I said call the police!'

'No reply from the station,' said the nurse, who was called Hilda Hicks, a round, philosophical Pulteney native.

'Can I help?' I said.

'Ah,' said the doctor, rounding on me. 'Who are you – Mr Agutter, ah, yes. Nurse, dial 999.' But Hilda, not wishing to miss anything, stayed where she was.

I said, 'What's the trouble?'

'An Australian with spinal contusions has gone berserk in the sluice room,' said the doctor, his eyebrows working. 'He weighs about twenty stone, and he has the biggest dorsals I have ever seen.'

'New Zealander,' I said. 'Is he concussed?'

'Not noticeably,' said the doctor, wincing.

'But we don't know about the other chap,' said Hilda. 'Evening, Charlie.'

'Evening, Hilda. What other chap?' I said.

'The chap he was chasing. He's got him locked in the sluice now,' said Hilda.

'Ah. Perhaps I'd better go and have a look. Don't let's call the police just yet.' A dreadful burst of New Zealand shouting came from above.

'That's him,' said the doctor.

'I recognise the voice,' I said, and started up the stairs. 'Scotto!'

'Charlie!' said Scotto's voice from behind a locked door. 'About bloody time.' The door opened. Scotto had no shirt on. His mighty torso was half-covered with an elastic strapping, which finished in a twisted end, as if he had torn himself away halfway through the operation. His face was greyish-yellow.

'What the hell are you playing at?' I said.

He pointed at the inside door of the sluice-room. 'The bastard's in there.'

'What bastard?'

'I was getting bandaged up when this bastard came in wanting two of his teeth put back, and I was trying to ask

161

him a few questions when he made a run for it.'

'Is he the one you hit?'

'I dunno. But he didn't seem too pleased to see me. Did you, you sneaky little bastid?'

'Easy,' I said. Doctor Harris and the nurse were in the room now. I addressed myself to the closed door. 'This is Charlie Agutter,' I said. 'If you come out, we'll just ask you a couple of questions and you can go. If not, I'll call the law and it'll be GBH. Well?'

A high, panicky voice behind the door said, 'Piss off, Agutter!' It was a voice I recognized.

'We're coming in.'

There was a silence, then the sound of a window opening.

'Look out!' said Scotto. Leaping to his feet, he slammed his shoulder into the door. It burst inwards and he went down after it, groaning in agony. I stepped over him and stuck my head out of the window.

A narrow ledge ran across the plain brick of the Victorian building. Hector Pollitt had made about ten feet, and was hanging on to a drainpipe thirty feet above the tarmac.

'For heaven's sake come back, Hector,' I said quietly.

He jerked his head round to look at me. The blood on his chin was black in the reflected light from below. 'Get away from me!' he said, in a high, panicky voice.

'Take it easy,' I said. 'Come back. Nobody's going to hurt you.'

'Oh, yeah,' he said, sarcastically.

'Scotto won't touch you. I won't touch you. Just come back.'

'Ask him what he was doing on *Sorcerer*,' yelled Scotto from behind me.

'Come on,' I said gently. 'Take a couple of steps. We know you haven't done anything. You'll be fine. And you can have the whole story for your magazine.'

I could see the whites of his eyes, big as moons. And I could smell the drink on him.

162

'You're a nice chap, Hector,' I lied. 'But you've got some nasty friends. That's all over now.' I climbed out onto the window sill, and held out my hand. I could see his knees shaking. He stretched out a hand towards me. 'It wasn't you who clobbered me at the marina, was it?' I said quietly. 'Who was using your car?' Then I cursed myself.

Because Pollitt froze and I saw his eyes flash as they swivelled in the moon. He pulled his hand away and gripped the drainpipe to swing himself onto the continuation of the ledge. As his weight reached its furthest outward point, I heard myself shout, 'No!' For the upper section of the drainpipe was bending under the weight. Slowly, horribly slowly, it keeled outwards. I saw Pollitt's bloody mouth, silver and black in the pale, cold light as, still clinging, he lay backwards in space and fell.

At last he yelled. The yell was cut short by a horrible crash. I clung to the window, shaking. In the yellow square of light below was the shadow of my own head, and something else. It was human, but its limbs were sprawled like a starfish's, and no living human head had ever been at that angle to a body. And the eyes looked up at me, wide, wide open, seeing nothing at all. Hector Pollitt of the *Yachtsman* had written his last story.

Chapter Twenty-One

We stood jammed in that window for a long moment, the doctor, Hilda and I. Then the doctor's professional reflexes starting working and he dashed down the stairs, closely pursued by Hilda. Scotto was on his hands and knees now. He was still groaning.

'Things are going to start happening,' I said. 'I'll be back.'

'Where the hell are you going?' he said.

'Never mind.' I ran out to the car park, turned on the headlights of the BMW, and made the tyres screech as I reversed away.

I was aware that someone behind me was yelling, but I paid no attention. I was entirely awake, now.

The road howled under the car's bonnet, but I was hardly there. I was in the marina again, the night after we had pulled *Aesthete* from the Teeth, creeping among the chocked boats in the dark, watching a car parking in the lay-by. A car with one of its lights out: Pollitt's car, in which he had later been breathalysed. But had Pollitt been driving it? When I asked him five minutes ago, it had frightened him. Frightened him to death.

But I couldn't see Pollitt as a saboteur and a killer. Had somebody else been driving that night? Someone of whom Pollitt was frightened enough to go swinging on drainpipes high above tarmac car parks?

The tyres screamed on the bends, the headlights muddied with grey fog. I saw the marina entrance at the

164

last moment and went through it broadside. *Sorcerer*'s lights were still on. I jumped onto her deck and Georgia rose from the cockpit.

'Don't!' I roared. 'It's me!' Her hands went down.

'Charlie?' she said. 'What is it?'

I took the .38 revolver out of her hand and flung it as far as I could into the fog-shrouded water. 'Police'll be here any minute,' I said. 'Clean it all up. Don't tell anyone anything.' Then I ran back to the car and drove back to the hospital, fast.

My watch said I had been away twenty minutes. As I approached, I could see the flashing blue glare in the fog. The car park seemed full of police cars. I climbed out and went to the Emergency door.

The constable inside it said, 'Can I help you, sir?'

'I saw what happened.'

'What did happen, sir?'

I told him. He said, 'If you would care to step this way?' in a voice full of old-world Devonshire charm. We went through into an office with tatty black PVC furniture illuminated by a fluorescent tube. Scotto was there, the colour of a corpse under the greenish light. So was the doctor. So was Detective Inspector Nelligan.

'Well, well, well,' said Detective Inspector Nelligan. He paused to extract a John Player Special and light it. 'Mr Charles Agutter. I was just saying I wondered where you had gone. Where had you gone?'

'Back to the boat,' I said. 'I wanted to tell the person on board what had happened, and that I might be . . . delayed getting back.'

'Considerate, and true,' said Nelligan. He turned and murmured to a uniformed policeman, who left the room. 'Now, are you in a position to tell me what is taking place? I believe you know Mr Hector Pollitt. Knew, I should say.'

'Hasn't Mr Scott already told you?'

'I haven't told anybody anything,' said Scotto.

'Yes,' said Nelligan, blowing smoke. 'Dead unco-operative. I wonder why.'

165

'Perfectly straightforward,' I said. 'Mr Hector Pollitt had been writing things about me I didn't like. I'd told Mr Scott as much. So when Mr Scott chanced to bump into Mr Pollitt, Mr Scott, er . . . espoused my cause.'

'Let's not be flippant,' said Nelligan. 'There's a dead man here, and Scott was chasing him when he died.'

'Correction,' I said. 'Scott was on the other side of a window when Pollitt fell to his death from a ledge from which I was attempting to rescue him. Dr Harris and the nurse will tell you so.'

Nelligan said, 'Mr Scott was still chasing him. And I'd like to know how he came by those bruises.'

'He fell down a hatchway on the boat. Is that illegal, nowadays?'

Nelligan lit a new cigarette from the stub of the old one, and said, 'Perhaps Mr Agutter and I should have a private chat. If you would excuse us?'

After the room had emptied, he poked fussily at a speck of ash on the sleeve of his jacket and said, 'Of course, you're right, Mr Agutter. We could nick your friend for breach of the peace, assault maybe. But is it worth it?' He paused, interrogating a cloud of smoke. 'Of course it isn't. Not so much because of wasting magistrate's time, because I don't much care about that. But here we are with a dead body that's written some nasty things about you. And the dead body has two front teeth missing, and there are toothmarks in your mate's hand, and the doctor says they match. And you go belting out into the night as soon as the balloon goes up.'

I said, 'Was it Pollitt that told you I was having an affair with my brother's wife?'

'The first time I met you, you mean? Yes, it was.' He paused again, looking at his lacquered shoes. 'I have a terrible prejudice, Mr Agutter. It is a prejudice against people who take the law into their own hands. If someone is getting across you, why not tell me, and we can apply the sanctions of the law?'

I laughed at his mild, sallow face. 'What we're in here is

166

offshore racing,' I said. 'The law of offshore racing is, if you can get away with it, do it.'

'Ah,' said Nelligan, vaguely. 'Very glorious. Are you telling me that three men have suffered fatal accidents so someone can win a boat race?'

'No,' I said.

The vagueness left his face and the brow-ridge came down and it was hard and pugnacious under the lights. 'You've got a lot of enemies in this town, Agutter. Powerful ones. Personally, I don't like any of you rich gits in your smart boats. But it's my job to keep the Queen's peace, and that's what I am going to do. So you can settle your quarrels by the law, and I mean of England, not the jungle. Understand?'

It was five in the morning, and I was beginning to judder with exhaustion. This new, hard Nelligan was real enough, but I did not believe in him. He was between me and whoever had sabotaged my rudders and killed my brother; and he was between *Sorcerer* and the Cup. I was going to fix them both, in my own way.

'Can I go now?' I said.

'Oh,' said Nelligan, vague again. 'By all means, yes.'

'And Mr Scott.'

Nelligan spread his hands.

I took Scotto back to *Sorcerer*. It was grey dawn and the last police car was leaving. Georgia's face still wore traces of outrage.

'Body search,' she said. 'Every sail out of its bag. The lot.'

'What did they find?'

'Nothing. What did you expect?'

'Oh, dope. Corpses. Just as well that gun's in the drink.'

'How's Scotto?' she said.

'Stiffening up,' I said. 'Can you stay with the boat? Scotto can have a bath at my place. I'll drop him off, and

167

you can nip over when someone arrives to relieve you.'

'And then you might explain.'

I laughed.

I took Scotto back to my house, showered and shaved. I groaned at the mirror. My face was about the same colour as the shaving-foam, and the bags under my eyes looked like lumps of slate. For someone who needed his eight hours a night, I was staying awake an awful lot.

Scotto was slumped in the corner of the drawing-room. He stank of embrocation. 'You want to go sailing?' I said. 'Coffee first.'

He shrugged, and winced with pain.

'Pollitt,' I said, as I brought in the jug. 'Do you think he was coming aboard *Sorcerer* to bend something?'

'Why else?' he said.

'Did you have the lights on?'

'Yeah.'

'So what if he wanted to talk?'

'I've got nothing to say to him.'

'What if he thought it was me?'

Scotto drank his coffee in silence, then said, 'Yeah.'

'Maybe he wanted to tell me something?'

Scotto nodded his vast head slowly. 'So maybe I shouldn't have slapped him.'

'Too late now,' I said. 'Anyway, he might have been trying to bend something, at that. Let's go boating.' But privately, I thought: Pollitt had reason to be fed up with Amy. What if he had found out something about one of Amy's lovers, and got drunk enough to tell me what he knew?

As we drove back to the marina, I could not get rid of the picture of his terror-frozen face, black and white under the moon.

By eleven-thirty, the Official Measurer had finished his pre-race inspection and *Sorcerer* was out and propped. The crew were back. Scotto started on her bottom with the pressure hose, making sure no particle of muck remained. The rest of us milled around, scrubbing, oiling

168

and making sure that she wasn't carrying an ounce more weight than she had to. Some of it was useful, and some of it was superstition. But then, in my experience, races are won by ninety per cent sailing, nine per cent luck and one per cent superstition. This may not sound like much, but in an offshore race lasting a hundred hours, a one per cent margin means a commanding lead.

At two o'clock, we had the final crew meeting. I issued last instructions and told everybody to be on the dock at eight. Then I went home.

First, I went to see my father. He was watching sails through his telescope, banging the arm of his wheelchair with his fist and swearing continuously.

I said, 'Hello.' He wheeled round. 'Race day tomorrow,' I said. 'Trials begin.'

'What races?' he said.

'Captain's Cup trials. Olympic Triangles tomorrow and Tuesday in Pulteney Bay. Then the Duke's Bowl, offshore, a week on Tuesday.'

'Yes,' he said. 'Saw you with the glass. Got that boat going well, boy. You'll smash those idiots out there.' He gestured at the window with a clawlike arm.

'Yes.'

'You look shagged,' he said. 'Get yer head down. Good luck.' He fumbled in the pocket of his dreadful tartan dressing-gown.

The nurse said, 'Here, let me.'

He said, 'Damn your eyes, woman, I'll do it myself.' She stepped back, drawing her breath in sharply, and he found what he was looking for. 'Here,' he said. 'Take this. First sovereign I ever earned. Put it on yer watch-chain.'

'Thanks,' I said.

'And beat that Millstone feller.'

'Has he been pestering you?'

'Mr Millstone called round,' said the nurse. 'He was ever so nice to us, wasn't he? Captain Agutter – '

'Get out, blast you!' roared my father, with astonishing vigour.

169

She said, 'Well!' and scuffled off.

My father pulled a bottle of whisky from under a draped table. 'Bloody Millstone trying to buy the house again. Said it was the last chance.' I wondered what he meant by that. 'Nerve of the swine. Sent him packing. Decent whisky, this. Chiefy brought it,' he said. 'Don't bother about glasses.'

His liver-spotted hands trembled as he raised it to his lips. He took a shaky gulp and passed it to me. 'Here's to Agutters in Pulteney,' he said.

'Agutters in Pulteney,' I said.

'Now you get along.'

I patted him on the shoulder. It was like patting a skeleton. 'Goodbye,' I said.

Downstairs, I rove a bootlace through the sovereign and hung it round my neck, feeling a bit of an idiot but strangely moved. Then I called Breen's office. It took some time to get through; he was probably in his helicopter.

'Ready to go,' I said.

'Splendid.' There was a strange, whining hum behind his voice.

'Shall we expect you on board?'

'Not on the Olympic Triangles. But I'll come on the offshore race. The Duke's Bowl.'

'Bring your seasick pills.'

He laughed. 'I was talking to Peregrine Apsley today,' he said. 'He's on the selection committee. He thinks we're in with a good chance. Mind you, he's about the only one who does.'

Peregrine Apsley was an ex-Submariner, tough as old boots and a hideous snob.

'Oh well, we'll try to bring 'em round,' I said.

'By the way, I'd like a report on that business last night. Dead bodies. Don't like it. Telex me, would you, by tomorrow at the latest?'

Exhaustion and whisky combined to make me resent this. I said, 'Haven't got time. If you want a private

170

detective, hire one. Meanwhile, get stuffed.'

Then I put the telephone down and stared at the receiver. Dear, dear, I remember thinking, getting tense before the race, Agutter. This was not the way to speak to an owner. Then I thought, well, compared to the stroke I intended to pull on his boat, slamming the phone down wasn't all that serious.

I poured myself another Famous Grouse and sat staring at the telephone. Outside, the wind huffed petals off the last tulips in the garden and the afternoon life of Pulteney hummed along in its usual calm style. I felt out of it, in a backwater. I should be doing something. There was one thing I wanted to do, more than anything else. But I didn't dare.

'Yellow rat,' I said to myself, aloud. Then I lifted the telephone and dialled Sally's number.

The telephone rang and rang, until it began to sound hollow, as if I could hear it in the emptiness of her house. And as it rang, I felt lonelier, less and less equipped to go on the cold sea and out-think the meanest and sharpest sailors in England. There was only one place to go, when you felt like that: bed.

So I went.

Next morning, I got up very early, walked the quiet streets down to the quay and put in an hour's hard work on *Nautilus*' moorings, preparing a little surprise for later in the day. When I got home for breakfast, the kitchen clock said 7.15.

171

Chapter Twenty-Two

The battle flags of the moored Trials boats were fluttering straight out as I walked down the jetty an hour later, greeting acquaintances and mentally checking the competition rocking under the feverish activity of its crews. There was enough wind to start the halyards singing, but not to make them scream; force five westerlies, the early shipping forecast had said. I could still taste the triple-strength coffee, thick and black, with the race day breakfast of three eggs, ham and fried potatoes, two slices of toast with honey and an orange to follow. I did not want to eat it; the nerves had shrunk my stomach. But if I didn't, there was always the possibility of the low-sugar shakes out there on the course. There were too many imponderables in racing, without the shakes. No sense in risking any that could be avoided.

I was getting some looks, this morning. The rise and fall and current shaky resurgence of Charlie Agutter was a topic of great interest in the fleet and among the spectators, Press, and other hangers-on who had been filtering into Pulteney during the past couple of days. It was not surprising. From the point of view of those who knew no better, Charlie Agutter had several weeks ago killed his brother. And now he was going out in an oldish boat to risk everything on winning a boat race. Had I been a journalist, I would probably have thought it quite a good story. As Charlie Agutter, it made me more than somewhat nervous.

172

Sorcerer was looking businesslike with her red-and-gold caduceus battle flag billowing from the forestay. I was the last aboard; I had timed it that way, because the crew was a good unit and I wanted them to feel at home together before I went aboard. Scotto was there, his bandages invisible under his bulky wet-gear. I said, 'How are you?' and he looked at me as if I was mad. If Scotto was not admitting any disabilities, he would not be acting disabled. It was as simple as that. 'Okay,' I said. 'Any problems?'

There were no problems. *Sorcerer* was in as good shape as she would ever be.

'Cast off,' I said. 'Flags, Scotto.'

Scotto went for the locker, plied the halyard, and the two flags went up the backstays – the Royal Ocean Racing Club Class 1 pennant, and below, the C flag flown by all Captain's Cup boats. They snapped and fluttered in the stiff breeze as we motored down the creek, past the ends of the jetties.

The creek widened. I said, 'Number two genoa.'

Ahead, the sea was grey, with the occasional white horse. The wind blew flat and hard along the coast. Nobody on the boat spoke, except me.

'Up main,' I said.

The grinders applied their colossal arms and shoulders to the Lewmar halyard winches, and the ochre-and-white Kevlar sail ran briskly up the mast.

'Up genoa.'

The trimmers squinted at the tell-tales, playing the sheets. *Sorcerer* leaned smoothly away from the wind and accelerated for the open grey horizon. Her crew arranged themselves in position; right aft, me at the wheel, and Doug the tactician with his clipboard. In the cockpit, Nick the trimmer, a mastman, a halyardsman and Crispin, the spare helmsman, on the mainsheet. Then there were the gorillas; Scotto in the cockpit and Dike, the foredeck hand. We all sat to weather, on the uphill side of the boat, and sucked glucose tablets. The crew gazed out at the

173

grey sea and the far-off white triangles of sails by the tiny black shapes of the committee boats. It was cold and raw and peaceful. But I could feel the boat alive under the wheel. Doug the tactician flicked buttons on the digital readout by his seat, and peered through his binoculars at the distant white sails, and scribbled in waterproof pencil on his clipboard. The peace was purely temporary. This was the moment of drawing breath, before sailing became war.

We put in a couple of practice tacks, feeling our way through wind and water. At first we were overstrung; Nick the trimmer oversheeted the genoa, and I swore harder than was necessary. But after ten minutes or so, we began to quieten down as everyone found their groove of concentration. I was telling people to do things; adjust the backstays, ease sheets, shift their weight. But if you had asked me afterwards, I wouldn't have known what I was saying. I was part of the equipment.

'Coming up to five-minute gun,' said Doug. 'We'll take the right-hand end.'

The first leg of an Olympic triangle heads into the wind, which makes the pre-start manoeuvres complicated. The basic idea is to cross the line bang on the start-gun, travelling at maximum speed. In theory, it is a good idea to start at one end or the other, since the eyesight of the starters on the committee boat has been known to be unreliable. If you start at the right-hand end, close-hauled on the starboard tack, with the wind blowing over the starboard side of the boat, you have the right of way over other boats. If you start at the left-hand end of the line, away from the committee boat, you tend to have clearer water.

In practice, it is not as easy as that.

We sailed up to within fifty yards of the minesweeper that was doing duty as committee boat, picking our way through the dipping masts and gleaming hulls crowding the start area.

'Five minutes,' said Doug. As he spoke, one of the

174

minesweeper's turrets boomed a puff of white smoke and the crowd of yachts bore away. I could see Archer, his close-cropped brown hair fluttering in the breeze at *Crystal*'s helm. He saw me, too; he gave no sign of recognition.

Race rules begin at the five-minute gun. Pre-start manoeuvres are so complicated that they are governed by special right-of-way rules which are stretched to breaking-point at every start. Offensive sailing can leave the opposition miles away from the line at the start-gun, or push them over it before the gun, which is just as bad. So as Doug muttered a string of suggestions in my ear, I steered my way through the tangle of jockeying hulls, reaching away for position from which to make the run-in, watching the digital stopwatch readout, which was count-ing down in ten-second jumps.

At three minutes and ten seconds, Doug said, 'Watch him.' I heard the clatter of waves on hull. Just behind my left shoulder, a silver bow was slicing the water. 'Can't tack across him,' said Doug. 'We'd hit.'

'Trying to force us off the line,' I muttered. 'Let's do him. Ready about!' I shouted.

A warning hail came down the wind from astern. I ignored it, pulling the wheel down until the luff of the mainsail shivered. The silver bow came on, shouting.

'Go!' I called. 'Go' was one of our codewords. It meant jibe; turn with the wind passing under the stern of the boat, not her head. The boom swung over. Two minutes, the readout said. We sagged away to starboard. After perhaps thirty seconds, I brought *Sorcerer*'s nose hard on the wind. The start-line on the committee boat's side was bang on the nose; there was clear water between us and it, and it was our right of way. Ahead and to port, the boat which had tried to ease us out had thought better of it, and was going down for the start. But she was going to be early, and too far down the line.

'No protest flag,' said Doug. 'Yet.'

'She didn't have to alter course. We're in the clear.'

'Correct. You were lucky, though. Go for it.'

The start boat came closer. She was long and grey and high. The wind would do funny things round her hull and upperworks; I didn't want to get too close.

'Look out,' said Doug.

I had seen. Down to port, a gaggle of five boats was approaching, close-hauled on the port tack. They were led by a green-and-orange hull that I recognised as *Crystal*. They were on a collision course.

'They'll tack,' I said. 'Hail.'

'Starboard,' yelled Scotto. Archer was perhaps a hundred and twenty feet away. He glanced over his right shoulder, then returned his eyes forward. The boats astern of him were tacking.

'Bastard,' said Doug. 'We'll cut him in half.'

As I looked down *Sorcerer*'s deck, I could see green-and-orange hull and ochre Kevlar where there should have been clear water. It was my right of way; Archer knew it. I could hear myself yelling, but I did not alter course. I could see the place where we would hit, felt *Sorcerer* falter as he took the wind momentarily from her sails as he crossed her.

I think it was that little falter that saved him. His transom went past *Sorcerer*'s nose with perhaps two inches to spare. The faces of his crew were round-eyed, except Johnny Forsyth. Johnny was grinning his hard, evil, racing grin.

'Bastards,' said Doug.

The green-and-orange hull turned in the water ten feet from the minesweeper's side. Boom and genoa came over. They were level with us and to windward, and we were getting dirty wind from them.

'Wait for it,' I said.

And it happened as it had to. The back-draughts from the minesweeper's sides bulged his genoa and main back the wrong way, and for a split second *Crystal* wallowed.

'Zero,' said Doug.

Above our heads the start-gun boomed, and we were away, ahead and upwind of the fleet on the starboard

176

tack, with Archer's nose a couple of feet aft of our stern. When I glanced back I could see his foredeck man at the hatch, his crew out on the weather deck and above them, the flicker of back-draughts in his luffs as they in their turn caught the dirty wind deflected by *Sorcerer*'s main. Behind him and to leeward, the rest of the fleet jostled, a chaos of sails and hulls.

'He'll have to tack,' said Doug.

'Never mind him,' I said. 'Let's get to the mark.'

The windward mark lay a couple of miles southwest of Beggarman's Head, at the western end of Pulteney Bay. It was slack water, so tide was not a factor until the beginning of the ebb. By that time, we should be round the mark. I could see the buoy, a big orange inflatable against the dark cliffs of the headland. Doug and I knew what we were going to do. I looked to port. The remaining eleven yachts were tightly bunched, masts bristling from the pack. The best of them was ten seconds behind us; two of the last boats had protest flags fluttering on their backstays. *Crystal* was a quarter of a mile away, on the port tack. As I watched, she tacked again onto starboard. We were well clear of her.

'Tack now,' said Doug.

We tacked, and tacked again. Now we were on the starboard tack, to starboard of the rhumb line, the direct line between the committee boat and the buoy. *Crystal* lay a hundred yards to leeward. We were still clear of her. The rest of the fleet seemed in no hurry to follow.

'And again,' said Doug.

I waited, just to make sure. It was a short tack, this one, and it had to be in the right place. To leeward, there was activity on Archer's foredeck. He was setting his number one genoa. In my humble opinion, Archer was too far to leeward; he had miscalculated. I kept my eye on the wind-speed and direction readout. When I saw what I was looking for I said, 'Ready about. Helm's a-lee.'

I saw Archer look up and across. It was a struggle not to wave at him, because what we had done was sail into a wind-bend, where the westerly was bent southwards by the face of Beggarman's Head, so that instead of making the mark with another tack, we had enough of a lift to make it on this one. The nice thing about wind-bends is that they operate in a small area; this one had not yet affected anyone else in the fleet. Then I saw Archer's bow come up; he had got it too, but his wind was lighter than mine because he was too far over, in the shadow of the distant headland.

We stayed in that narrow corridor of sou'westerly breeze for perhaps five minutes. During those five minutes, the rest of the fleet fell back. Only Archer managed to stay in touch, and he was a good twenty seconds behind now.

We came round the first mark clean as a whistle, and the tri-radial popped up like a balloon. We settled down for the first reaching leg. There wasn't quite enough wind for *Sorcerer* to get out of the water and start tobogganing, but she dragged her old bones through the swell well enough, and I was able to relax a bit – but not too much; the first windward leg is always hard work, and there's a temptation to slacken off on the reach.

I had just checked astern. The fleet was round the mark, with Archer well out in front, but too far away to interfere with us. My eyes ran up to the hard curve of the mainsail with the huge swell of spinnaker beyond it, then caught on something. At first I didn't know what it was; it was merely a hangnail of the mind, something out of place. So I ran my eye back over it. And as so often happens, it chose the moment to do what it was going to do.

What I had seen was high at the masthead; a thread, fluttering where the starboard backstay joined the mast-head casting. I had time to say, 'Look out,' and then there was a bang and the boat lurched heavily. The tri-radial collapsed and the boom whacked across. I had to force myself not to shut my eyes, because if you were to choose the best way of losing your mast overboard, that would probably be it.

178

We lay head to wind, sail flapping. What had happened was that the starboard backstay had broken. The backstay is there to support the mast from astern, and to put the right degree of bend into it. Scotto stood on the transom, staring at the line trailing in the water.

'Move,' I said; he had been there all of two seconds.

'Get some headsail on her,' he said.

I yelled for the genoa, praying that he knew what he was doing, because if he didn't the mast was going to be a useful corkscrew. The fleet was on us now. The genoa went up and filled. When I dared look at the backstay, instead of double cables converging on the masthead blocks from the slope of the transom, there was only one. But at its base, the single cable forked, with a tackle leading to each of the chainplates of the original double backstay.

'Tri-radial!' I yelled, and pushed the wheel.

179

Chapter Twenty-Three

She came round like a dinghy, and there was a stiffening of the faces in the cockpit as the strain came on the jury backstay. The wind hit the tri-radial and we waited for the bang. But the bang didn't come. At that point we all stopped worrying about it, because we had a race on our hands.

We were now well down to leeward of the rhumb line. Amazingly, the whole process had only taken about twenty seconds. The bulk of the fleet was still astern, but our lead was gone. Also, we had managed to drift a long way to leeward. We still had a commanding position, though: as the wind struck into the sails again I pointed up, and we roared across the nose of the fleet on the port tack, pummelling the genoa into the rail and bearing off when the sightlines I had scribed on the deck told me we could make the mark on *Sorcerer*'s best point of sailing. There was one boat to windward: *Crystal*. She was screwed down tight and going for the mark like the hammers of hell. I couldn't crank *Sorcerer* that hard, not with one backstay gone.

But I did it anyway.

That reaching leg was more or less a drag race. I stayed as close to *Crystal* as I dared, trying to keep in close contact so I'd be ahead and inside at the mark, and Archer would have to give me room to jibe. But unless *Sorcerer* would get up and run, *Crystal* had the legs of her. *Sorcerer* showed no signs of getting up; *Crystal* edged closer.

180

At the jibe mark, boats turn with the wind passing across their sterns. A sailful of wind crashing from one side of the boat to the other is not, generally, cruel and unusual punishment. But it is a good idea to have your backstays in working order. I knew I was going to have to take it easy. Scotto was mind-reading.

'They've spotted us,' he said.

I glanced across, hearing the wind's roar in my right ear. A couple of hundred feet of grey water, then *Crystal*'s deck; and under her boom, the black circles of a pair of binoculars.

'They're coming up to cover,' said Doug. 'Two minutes to the mark.'

'We won't be able to stay ahead that long.'

'Can you luff 'em, then?'

Crystal answered that one. Her hail floated across the water. 'Mast abeam!'

'She's right, sod it,' said Doug. *Crystal* had now established an overlap, and we could no longer knock her off course by sailing across her bows on a course closer to the wind than hers. 'Let's make the buoy.'

'Look at her go,' I said. A dark shadow of wind was moving across the water at her. Archer took his gust nicely and it brought his stem past my sightlines and forward of the mast.

'Stay inside him,' Doug said.

I tried, hoping to get within that magic two lengths of the buoy where Archer would have to give me room to manoeuvre. But he was too far ahead. His jibe was beautifully smooth, and the spray from his quarter splashed over our bow. As we came up to the mark, he was already round. But the rest of the fleet was well behind. All was not lost.

'Cover him,' said Doug. 'Go on.'

The wind shadow of a boat on a broad reach on the port tack extends about a hundred feet onto her starboard bow. We luffed, sailing to the left of the rhumb line, trying to blanket *Crystal*. I saw Forsyth's face under the

181

boom. It was hard and preoccupied. *Crystal*'s wake crooked faintly to the left.

'Follow on,' said Doug.

We could afford a little boat-for-boat, because the rest of the fleet was between five and twenty seconds astern. I pulled the wheel and the trimmers took up the slack. A shadow was travelling out of the eye of the wind, darkening the grey waves.

'Look out,' I said. 'We'll do for him.'

As the shadow arrived, I pulled the wheel very gently. And for the first time that day, *Sorcerer* shuddered, came up and began to go. Spray fizzed astern and she made ground on *Crystal* fast – so fast that Archer failed to see what was happening until it was too late and his sails were shuddering in our dirty wind. He bore away for the mark, and we bore away with him, alongside.

The crews sat on the uphill rail, with their feet out. Doug and I crouched on the leeward side of the trench, looking across the twenty foot gap that separated us from *Crystal*. *Crystal* began edging ahead, but as soon as she got into our mucky wind she fell back again, until she was level. I could feel a tight grin trying to stretch my face, but kept it off; I didn't want to provoke the opposition, unless there was a special reason for doing so. Just now, we wanted things as calm as possible, because if Archer blew his cool and did an illegal luff we'd either have a collision, in which case we'd probably both be disqualified, or we'd have to take evasive action and protest. I wanted a clean win, boat-for-boat, not squabbles in the committee-room later. So I concentrated on the sails and the wind and the distant orange tube of the mark, and ignored the lines of eyes at *Crystal*'s weather rail.

Archer's head was only just visible, because of the heel of his boat. The wind was screaming in her rigging; we'd have to shorten sail if it went on freshening. Then I realized that there was another noise. Someone was shouting. It wasn't Archer; but Archer was looking pained, and beside him was Johnny Forsyth, his face

182

congested with blood and his lips moving. I couldn't hear what he was saying; but I saw his eyes glance across at *Sorcerer* and was surprised by the fury in them. Then Archer shook his head again, and Forsyth's hands went up and his head disappeared out of sight behind the boat's side.

Doug's face was stiff as a poker, but his voice was unsteady with suppressed glee. 'It looks like the tactician don't agree with the helmsman,' he said.

I nodded, not really interested. I had to stay on top till the mark; that was all. 'How close?' I said.

'Sorry,' said Doug, and began counting down. *Crystal* edged ahead again, and dropped back.

'Five lengths,' said Doug.

Crystal started up again, was backwinded and dropped back. She was perhaps five feet away now, creaking and drumming, the wakes quarrelling in the canyon between the shining hulls.

'Two,' said Doug. 'Water at the mark!'

I pulled the wheel across, and the tri-radial came down as the sheets came in, and the jury backstay tackle groaned as Scotto put his mighty shoulders into the winch, and the needles of the close-hauled dial came to rest at their marks.

'Excellent,' said Doug, and I glanced quickly over my shoulder.

Archer had had to bear quickly away at the buoy. He was on port tack, to leeward, but he had lost his overlap.

'Blew him away,' said Doug.

'Watch for the protest flag.' I settled down, squinting between the luff of the mainsail and the close-hauled indicator.

'Still nothing,' said Doug after two minutes. 'Fleet's round.'

'He's left it too late,' I said. 'We're clear.'

It is one thing being in front: it is another staying there. The difference was not so much on the windward leg as afterwards, on the run home. On the second beat to

183

windward we kept position between the wind and the fleet, covering Archer closely. We slipped round the windward mark, and the running 'chute popped out above the foredeck.

'Coming up to cover,' said Doug. 'Watch him.'

It was calm and still on the deck, with that peculiar stillness that always comes when you are running before the wind. The wind is blowing as hard as ever, but you are travelling at the same speed. It can be very deceptive, which is why things happen so fast and so catastrophically on the run.

What was happening on this run was that *Crystal*, a very fast boat downwind, was catching us again. Slowly, it was true, but catching us, Doug punched the readout, and narrowed his eyes. I waited for the computer between his ears to yield results.

'We'll do it,' he said. 'Unless the bastard covers us.'

'Then we'll have to stop him.'

We were both running with the wind on the quarter, rather than dead astern. You go faster that way, even though you travel in a series of jibing zigzags rather than a straight line. The trick is to keep the zigzags shallow, while at the same time preventing the opposition from stealing your wind.

Crystal was a hundred and twenty feet astern. As I watched, the clouds blew off the sun, and a ribbon at her forestay bloomed into a huge pigeon's breast of a running kite, gold and blue with a great cartoon diamond at its centre. She looked hugely beautiful, a tower of sail topping the blade of her green-and-orange bow with the bow-wave glittering below. She dipped like a Victorian dancer.

'On starboard,' said Doug, unnecessarily. I had been watching for half a second; few winning helmsmen spend much time admiring the opposition. 'Better jibe now.'

I said, 'Go!' and pulled the wheel a fraction. The boom smacked over. Up on the foredeck, they clipped on the spinnaker boom and the big sail swung smoothly across.

'Them astern,' said Doug. 'Covering now.'

184

'Go,' I said.

The boom went over again, and the spinnaker. Each time the mainsheet man had to retrim, the foredeck hands had to dip the spinnaker pole, and the grinders had to tail and trim the yards of slender spinnaker guys and sheets. A jibe swings an awful lot of wind through an awful lot of sail.

'They've gone again,' said Doug.

'Go,' I said.

We went. So did *Crystal*. We zigzagged down the final leg like two warplanes dogfighting. The sweat shone on the gorillas' faces. A sort of rhythm began to establish itself. That was what I had been waiting for.

'Go! Go!' I shouted, at the tenth jibe.

The pounding of feet sounded on the foredeck as the sweating hands went to the spinnaker pole. The mainsail boom crashed over. The spinnaker had moved round four feet when Doug said, 'Them astern's gone to cover.'

'Yes!' I yelled it much louder than was necessary to answer Doug. The spinnaker went back and so did the main boom. For the first time since rounding the mark, *Crystal* and *Sorcerer* were sailing on different tacks.

'That,' said Doug with reverence, 'is what is known as a dummy jibe.'

Down the wind there floated a hard, angry roaring as Johnny Forsyth came to the same conclusion. *Crystal* dipped and jibed, but it was no good. She was right out of touch now; she didn't have a hope.

We got the winner's gun twenty seconds ahead.

'Nice,' said Doug. And the whole boat was talking now, not roaring, but quietly satisfied. There were a lot of races to go; there was no point in getting over-excited. Still, it had been a good one.

'Class,' said Scotto, handing me a mug of Bovril. 'Showed the bastards.'

I sipped the Bovril, realising that I was shivering. The hot drink formed a lump of heat in the belly that made the spray seem even colder than it really was.

185

'Want me to take her in?' he said.

I shook my head. 'I'm fine.' This was a break with Scotto's personal tradition, and he looked surprised. 'How's the back?' I said.

'Great,' he said.

'Nice work with the backstay.'

He nodded, watching the rest of the fleet coming over the line. 'Fixed by tomorrow,' he said.

Little do you know, Scotto, I thought. I turned away and looked at the bleak, grey tunnel between clouds and sea, out of which the wind howled with the wail of a hungry ghost, and I spoke to Hugo, very quietly, and told him what I planned to do that evening. We were on the way back, but *Sorcerer* would not be racing tomorrow.

Chapter Twenty-Four

It is traditional, when returning from races, to pass by the end of Pulteney Quay. The tradition dates from the days when competitors at Pulteney Regatta kept their boats on moorings in the harbour. Spectators would gather on the quay in the hope of cheering heroes and gloating as the inexperienced missed their moorings. Of course, most of the racing-boats now lived at the marina, and the tougher international boats tended to ignore such courtesies. But I made a point of observing them. For one thing, I liked the old Pulteney a good deal better than the new. For another, the sail-past served today's purposes nicely.

The crowd on the quay head was thick. As the figures grew above pinhead size, I searched with Doug's binoculars. I felt a moment of extreme pleasure. Sally was there and beside her, in his wheelchair, my father, banging the armrest, with behind him Nurse Bollom, her wide face chapped and sullen.

'Some committee,' said Scotto, grinning.

I nodded, the pleasure fading at the thought of what I had to do. But it couldn't be helped.

I took *Sorcerer* right in close. The crew were all back in the trench now, and she was powering along on a beam reach under genoa and main, no spinnaker. The boats in the harbour grew bigger, and then we were among them. Sighting down the deck, I could see *Nautilus'* bottle-green hull and gold stripe to the left of my forestay. I gritted my teeth. The crowd on the quay were waving and cheering. I

187

passed the wheel between my fingers. The wake slapped against the sides of the moored boats. Sorry, folks, I thought, and twitched the wheel.

Sorcerer's bow came across, heading now for a sliver of open water beyond the head of the quay. It was then that I felt it: a steady wrenching of the wheel, plucking it out of my hand, blurring the spokes till they came to rest with a hideous clonk.

'What the hell?' said Scotto.

I pulled at the wheel. It was jammed hard over. Scotto joined me, and Doug and one of the grinders on the twin wheel at the far side of the cockpit. Sailcloth was rattling and booming overhead.

'Hooked a bloody mooring line,' I said. 'Get her straight.'

Above, the mast was bending nastily against the grey clouds. The wheel began to turn. I was shouting orders. Suddenly there was a lurch, and she was free.

'Fouled a hawser,' said Scotto.

He was right, of course. I had laid the hawser myself, at an angle to *Nautilus*' regular mooring, early that morning. It had been good helmsmanship to get the keel over the top of it and only hang up the rudder, while making sure the rudder would hit it so its leading edge wouldn't slide over the top.

'She all right?' said Scotto.

We were passing under the quay head. The crowd was cheering and waving again, except my father, who was shaking his head, and his nurse, who looked fed up. Sally was smiling. But it seemed to me that her smile was not so much for me as for the boat, because it had won.

'No,' I said to Scotto.

I gave him the wheel, and let him feel the vibration that meant a twisted rudder stock.

'We'll have to take her out,' he said. 'No bloody race tomorrow. If I find the bastard who hooked us up, I'll kill him.'

It was the only way I could get *Sorcerer* out of the

188

water. And I had to have *Sorcerer* out of the water to prove a theory about who was causing all this sudden death around Pulteney. But it did not make me feel very noble.

Round at the marina, we called the crane straight over and pulled her out. Scotto and I went and stood underneath and were dripped on by the hull. Doug, aloft, waggled the wheel. The stock was bent, all right; it was maybe five degrees out of true. We'd never bend it back. It needed a new one, and a new one would take at least twenty-four hours – as I had intended.

So I gave the orders to the yard men. I left Scotto to supervise the removal of the rudder, and went to ring Breen.

'Good,' he said, when he answered. 'You won.'

'Did you hear what happened next?'

'What?' His voice had gone cold.

I told him. I could almost hear him ticking away at the far end: cost, time, disadvantages.

'You miss one race,' he said at the end. 'Inshore. Not a major disaster. You'll have her ready for the Duke's Bowl?'

'Yes.'

'Good enough. Now tell me about the competition.'

I resailed the race for his benefit. At the end, he said, 'Good.' He sounded pleased. 'Keep her out of the water for as long as you need. The Bowl is in what, a week?'

'Eight days,' I said.

'Do what you have to do. I'll ask around behind the scenes. See how the . . . selectors view it. Bye.'

I uncoiled from the telephone box, smiling nervously at the fat woman who was waiting to use it, and went back to the crane. The rudder was already off; the crew was standing in the cold shed, reluctant to go home.

'Let's go to the Mermaid,' I said. 'Scotto, I'll give you a lift.'

'What about the boat?' said Scotto.

189

'Leave her,' I said. We got into the BMW. 'She's okay while they're working on her.'

He shrugged. Then he looked across at me, looked away again and said, 'How come you hit that thing this evening?'

'What thing?'

'The thing you hit. Charlie, did you do it on purpose?'

'Well . . . yes, actually.'

'So would you just explain why?'

'Because I want her out of the water. Somebody's sabotaged two of my boats so far this season. They were both contenders. So I reckon someone's going to sabotage this one, and I want to make it easy for them. So we'll have the boat out of the water for a week, and advertise the fact, and they can have their chance.'

'Are you crazy?' said Scotto.

'Like a fox,' I said.

We were in front of the Mermaid now. 'I'll drop you off here. Back in twenty minutes.'

When I got back to the marina, a small, red-haired man was waiting by the office. At his feet were two metal boxes, of the kind photographers use to carry their equipment. We shook hands, and went in to Neville Spearman's office.

Neville's manner was perceptibly warmer, though by no means effusive. That was what winning did for you. Agutter might, in his view, be on the way back, though there was still some distance to go. If we could win the trials and then the Cup, he would be so pleased he would hardly be able to stay off his knees – not because of his innate sportsmanship, but because a Captain's Cup winning Agutter would be very good for Agutter's local yard in terms of work and publicity and prices.

'This is Mr Brewis,' I said. 'He's a security consultant.'

Spearman said, 'Pleased to meet you,' but his grey-rimmed eyes were watchful and suspicious.

190

'We'd like to rig up a few bits on *Sorcerer*,' he said. 'If you wouldn't mind.'

'A few bits? We've got security of our own,' said Spearman.

'Which didn't stop you getting a yardful of policemen the other night.'

'I think you're being a bit . . . over-cautious,' said Spearman. 'I mean, what would happen if all my clients got the screaming abdabs?'

Mr Brewis coughed. 'That's unlikely,' he said. 'Mr Agutter has requested a couple of magic-eye devices, with radio link to a monitoring centre. Fitting and operation will be conducted with maximum discretion.'

'He means that we're not going to tell anyone,' I said. 'I'll bring *Nautilus* round, and we'll do some work on her deck and we'll keep the monitoring equipment below. Can you give me a berth the far side, where we won't be too obvious?'

'Hang on,' said Spearman. I could see that Charlie Agutter was not far enough on the road back to be worth much extra trouble, yet. 'I don't know about this – '

'I'm afraid it's necessary,' I said. 'And I have to ask you not to talk to anyone. Not anyone at all.'

There was a silence, while Spearman thought through the pros and cons of cooperating with Agutter. 'Of course, if you want it like that,' he said at last, sniffily. 'But I don't know what things are coming to.'

'That's Pulteney for you, nowadays. Bloody awful, isn't it?'

Spearman shook his head. Behind the dark eye-sockets, he would be thinking that Pulteney nowadays meant he built big, expensive yachts – not fishing-boats with owners who pared his prices to the bone.

'All right, Mr Brewis,' I said. 'I'll join you in a moment.' He rose and went outside with his boxes. Alone with Spearman, I said, 'I'll be brutally frank, Neville. Besides you and me and Brewis, only Scotto knows about this, and Scotto doesn't talk much. So if anybody else

191

comes to know, it won't be hard to work out who told them.'

He looked at me for a long, silent minute. Then he said, 'Why shouldn't I toss you off the yard?'

I let him work it out for himself. Then, in case he was coming to unhelpful conclusions, I told him about Breen's offer to commission a 150-foot schooner if we won the Cup. 'And you would probably like to build it, if you've got time.'

It was like offering fillet steak to a shark, if he had time. 'There's a big difference between winning the first Trial race and winning the Cup,' he said.

'If you don't cooperate, I've got no chance.'

He sighed, and said, 'All right. But the first sniff of a problem and we call in the police.'

'All right,' I said. 'How long for the rudder stock?'

'Not before the weekend,' he said.

'Fair enough. I also want a modification. I don't like that double backstay. Let's have a single one, please. My office will give you specifications.'

And I left to join Mr Brewis.

Chapter Twenty-Five

It was no hardship living on *Nautilus* for a few days. She was a pretty spacious old machine, and I established myself in her after-cabin, with drawing-board, and did some running with *Sorcerer*'s crew. Scotto spent the days with his head in *Sorcerer*'s electronics, and the nights in the fore-cabin. The alarm signals lived in the saloon.

After two nights, I was beginning to wonder if anything was actually going to happen. It was entirely possible that *Nautilus*' presence in the marina would prevent anything in the way of enemy action.

On the eighth evening, I had wandered up to the call-box to try to ring Sally. As usual, nowadays, there was no reply. I wanted to go after her, but I could not leave the marina. I walked moodily through the dusk, casting a jaundiced eye over the corrugated iron sheds and the rusty iron fence. It was a dull, chilly evening and the marina looked like a prisoner-of-war camp. I felt like a prisoner, too.

Nautilus' cabin lights were on. I walked down the hatch and found Scotto at the mahogany table in the saloon, playing cribbage with Georgia.

Georgia said hello, and we talked. I asked after Sally. Georgia said she was out at Ed Beith's, clearing up the mess. I felt a twinge of something very like jealousy, and poured some drinks, giving myself a larger-than-usual Famous Grouse to dull the ache. They asked me if I wanted to play poker. I refused, and sat on a berth half-reading a book. The whisky infiltrated my bloodstream, and the saloon gave off a mellow glow. I sat and meditated on the foul discomfort of racing-boats compared to *Nautilus*' solid mahogany and cushions. I moved only to throw another shovelful of coal on the stove that glowed in the corner, and sat back again, to watch the fingers of red spread through the black lumps. The sounds of the cribbage-players behind me were lulling, and my eyelids were heavy.

I sneezed. The next breath bore the smell of petrol.

'What's that smell?' I said.

'Petrol,' said Scotto.

I was still watching the stove. Something peculiar was happening. The air around it was shimmering, as if tremendously hot. The smell of petrol was suffocating. The cabin turned red, and a great whoomph blew me backwards and onto the card table. I could smell burnt hair, and the skin of my face was tight. The cabin was a sheet of flame. Georgia screamed. I could see a hulking mass of flames reeling across the cabin sole, and I thought: that's Scotto. I yanked the extinguisher off the wall and smashed in the plunger and great white loops of foam began to spurt out and at him, and his flames went out. The extinguisher ran out.

I shouted, 'Fore-cabin!' and grabbed Scotto's wrist and dragged him through the door. The flames were everywhere again, but not on Scotto.

I grabbed another extinguisher, said, 'Hatch, Georgia!' and opened the door to the saloon again.

The timber was alight now. The extinguisher's white loops plunged into the fire and it retreated for a moment. Then big ugly flames jumped back. I slammed the door. Georgia had the forehatch open – thank God I had left it unbolted. Scotto was making pedalling movements with his legs. I guided them onto a bunk and he crawled on deck, followed by Georgia.

The air was suddenly icy cold. I slammed the hatch.

194

Scotto was saying in a low voice, 'What the hell? What the hell?'

I said, 'Someone put a plastic bag of petrol down the stove-pipe,' as much to myself as him.

Georgia had her knife out, cutting the clothing off him. It was nearly dark now, and the coach-roof windows were full of a jumping red glow.

'Get him ashore!' I yelled. 'Get help!' And I ran for the bucket forrard of the mast, scooped up a pailful of harbour water and went for the afterhatch. As I went down the deck, I heard a sound from below. My mind was scarcely working. *Nautilus*, my last solid tie with Hugo, was slipping away. The sound was a foreign one, nothing to do with *Nautilus*. I opened the door. The flames whooshed out at me, and I flung in my bucket of water, and the sound shrieked out at me. The cabin was a furnace. There was no chance. None at all.

And with the realisation that *Nautilus* was doomed came another. The alien sound suddenly took on meaning. It was the siren of *Sorcerer*'s intruder alarm.

I stood still for a moment. The siren cut off abruptly. In the silence, I could hear the roar of the flames, the clatter of Scotto and Georgia stumbling along the jetty, the slap of *Nautilus*' halyards, high and serene above the hull. And I knew what I had to do.

I refilled the bucket with water and tipped it over my head. I went and grabbed an axe from its clips on the bulkhead. Then I returned on deck and dived down the forehatch. The heat was terrible and I felt the skin of my hand stick to the brass handle of the head door. But what was driving me was stronger than pain. The head was like a pitch black oven, but I had installed it myself, so I knew it backwards.

I laid about me with the axe, heard the smash of the lavatory pan, felt the resistance as the blade met copper. And I kept chopping for what felt like an hour as the heat grew. I knew I was trapped in a little box besieged by fire, but I kept hacking, hacking. At last I hit the spot, and felt the jet of seawater from the severed plumbing splash on my legs. If I sank her, I might at least save her hull. Then I burst out into the fore-cabin. The bunks were already burning fiercely and the smoke was terrible. I went through the hatch like a jack-in-the-box and spent a moment on all fours, coughing a cough that tasted of incinerators.

When I looked up, I saw that Scotto and Georgia were only a hundred yards away. To my amazement, I found I could only have been below for a couple of minutes at most. So I got onto my feet and lurched across the deck and onto the jetty.

Suddenly a starter motor whinnied in the car park. I looked up sharply. Besides mine and Scotto's, it was the only one on the lot. It was too far away for me to see anything but a dim outline: a saloon.

'That's who's been on *Sorcerer*,' I said to myself, and began to run.

Running was agony. But the anger was stronger than the pain, and I kept my legs pumping even though my throat was raw and my face felt as if it had been skinned. I heard the whinny of the starter motor again; trouble with the engine, you bastard, I thought, as my shoes hit the grit of the car park. Don't start.

But it did start. The sweat was pouring into my eyes, and I saw the dark shape of it slew violently, wheels spinning, and scream away for the gates without lights. I wrenched open the door of the BMW. It started first turn of the key and I put my foot to the floor as the other car turned onto the main road. Turned left.

I was thirty seconds behind it, still too far behind to get my lights on its number plate. I saw the rear lights flick on. Then it was round the bend and into Pulteney. When I glanced in my rear-view mirror, I could see another light. This one was red and smoky, down on the jetties of the marina. I settled grimly in my seat and followed the other car round the bend.

It was fast, the other car. I had my foot flat down and

196

the old BMW was juddering with effort, but I was still making no ground. Two fire-engines flashed by; Georgia had got to a telephone.

Just before Pulteney, the other car turned right after a thatched cottage. I followed, tyres shrieking as I drifted. The lane was narrow, but I knew it well. It twisted and turned like an eel, but I drove it almost unconsciously, thinking of the car ahead that contained whoever had killed Hugo and wrecked *Aesthete* and caused the death of wretched little Hector Pollitt, and had tonight dropped a plastic bag full of petrol down *Nautilus'* stove-pipe to create a diversion while he mangled *Sorcerer*.

The lane turned onto a straight. I went round the corner sideways, banged the bank, and the wheel wrenched at my burned hands. I shouted with pain and let go, and the BMW rammed the verge. Cursing, I wrestled it into reverse, backed off, and stamped on the gas.

At the far end of the straight, slightly uphill, two rear lights vanished abruptly. I drove up to the brow of the hill. The lights of Pulteney were spread below. I knew of old that the lane swept down the side of the hill, in plain view, to join the top of Fore Street. The lights of the car in front made yellow cones down the hill into Pulteney. On Fore Street, I gained a little, but he turned right onto Quay Street, ignoring the 'Unsuitable for Motor Vehicles' sign, and I clattered after him. A white-faced man flattened himself in a doorway. My own house flashed by. Then we were at the top of Naylor's Hill, turning left onto the Plymouth road.

As I hit the straight, I glanced down at the petrol gauge. Empty. I had about three miles in the tank. Cursing, I put my foot down again and went past the last petrol station for twenty miles. The car in front drew ahead. I switched off my lights; the moon was out, and I knew the road well enough to navigate by the white line.

After a couple of miles, the car in front slowed down. I thought: he thinks he's lost me. And I hung back as he turned right, down the road to Brundage.

197

The Brundage road is a dead end. The kind of people who live in Brundage are retired or work on the land, and have very little to do with the kind of people who live in Pulteney – except for one. Amy.

It was a pretty safe bet that Amy and the fire-bomb artist could be left to get on with each other for a bit. I turned around, went back to the petrol station and filled up. The girl at the till looked at me, took in my smoke-blackened clothes and blistered face and looked away. I got in and drove to Brundage.

The lights were on in Amy's house, and there was a car parked in the drive. It was a car I recognized. A Mercedes, blue, gleaming in the hall lamp, except where it was splashed with mud. Archer's car. When I felt the bonnet, it was hot.

I stood by it for a minute. Then I walked softly across the lawn to the front door, which was open.

Inside the door, a woman screamed. I broke into a run, went through the door, and arrived in a parquet-floored hall with a red Bokhara carpet.

I had been wrong about it being safe to leave Amy to get on with the fire-bomber.

She was lying face down on the rug, arms and legs spread out like a starfish. She was wearing a white silk shirt and a black velvet skirt with a deep slit up the side, to show off her good legs. There was blood on the collar of the shirt.

This much I took in as I went through the door. Then I caught a glimpse of something moving out of the corner of my eye and I ducked, too late to avoid something big and heavy that slammed into my shoulders and knocked me flat on the floor beside Amy.

I lay there with a headful of bees and the wool of the Bokhara under my nose. Then I heard the car starting in the drive. I crawled to the door, but all I saw were his tail lights disappearing down the lane. I tottered back to look at Amy.

She was breathing, all right. Some of the blood was

198

coming from a cut in the back of her head. I didn't want to move her. I went to the telephone, dialled 999, and asked for the ambulance.

When I put the receiver down, I went back to see what I could do, and for the first time I looked at her face.

I took a big breath, then another, and said something very ugly under my breath. Amy's face, pretty, foxy Amy's face, looked as if it had been hit by a small truck. She had two black eyes, and her nose was flat. There was blood everywhere, more than I had at first thought. The Bokhara rug was a marsh of it.

I ran to the kitchen and got towels and a bowl of water and ice from the refrigerator. Then I went back and knelt beside her and gently, very gently, began to clean away the blood on her face. When the worst of it was off, I wrapped the ice in a towel and made a cold pad and laid it over the ruins of her nose.

Her lips moved. Blood oozed from the corners of her mouth. She mumbled something between teeth that were probably broken.

'Don't talk,' I said.

'He hit me.'

'Who hit you?' Her eyes were puffing up and narrowing. 'Was it Archer?' I said.

She said, 'Sally.'

'What about Sally?'

'Gone to Sally.' Her head rolled sideways and her eyes closed.

I ran to the telephone and dialled Sally's number. It rang for a long time, with a suspicion of echo, as if in an empty hall. Archer, or whoever was driving his car, would not have had time to get there yet. So Sally must be away from home.

After fifteen rings, I dialled Ed Beith's number. Ed answered quickly.

'Sally?' he said. 'She was helping clear up here. She left ten minutes ago.'

'Where was she heading?'

'Home,' said Ed. As usual, he radiated calm. But then why shouldn't he? He had no idea of what was going on at the other end of the line.

I could hear the distant bray of the ambulance siren. I ran for the door. The marble front doorstep flared white. In the middle, a patch of red caught my eye. Blood. There was blood everywhere tonight, and unless I hurried there would be more. But this blood was different. I stopped in mid-stride. It was a footprint, heading outwards towards the drive.

I put my foot alongside it. My shoes are size nine. This footprint was a good two inches longer. The sole belonged to a Topsider, offshore racing's favourite deck-shoe.

The scream of the ambulance was in the lane now. I ran into the drive and crouched behind a rhododendron as it came through the gate. The attendants jumped down and went into the house. I heard one of them say, 'Blimey.' Then I sidled out of the gate, got into my car, and drove with squealing tyres up the lane and onto the main road.

In the driver's seat, a wave of exhaustion hit me. The whole of me hurt like hell. I turned off the main road, into the lane that led past Sally's house. My heart started to beat faster; what if she was there already? Would he deal with her the same way as he had dealt with Amy? My foot grew heavier on the accelerator. The tyres screamed round a bend, and I over-corrected.

A pair of tail lights came up ahead. I drew out to overtake and I was halfway past before I realised that the car I was overtaking was Archer's Mercedes. I glanced across the wall and through the wood at her house. Lights were on. He must have been waiting out here, and now he was moving in.

I could not see the driver. But he recognised my car as I had recognised his, because he swerved across the road at me, and I swerved at him, and the cars collided with a crash, flank to flank. We screamed along beside the stand of oaks that sheltered Sally's house. I accelerated. So did he. I twisted the wheel at him. Locked side by side, we careered down the narrow lane.

I saw it coming long before it happened. Sally's gates were flanked by massive granite posts, one on each side. I was heading straight for the right-hand one. I braked hard. Then I tried to power out of it, but the Mercedes held me fast. The gatepost hurtled towards me at fifty miles an hour. I changed down into second, tramped on the accelerator. The pair of us slewed sideways, but the forward movement was too much. Tyres yelling, I slid at thirty miles an hour into the gatepost.

The seatbelt held. The passenger door came in to meet me. There was a smell of spilt petrol. The Merc's engine roared. It reversed into the lane and headed back towards the main road. I turned the BMW's key. Nothing.

The door would not open. Groaning at the pain from my burns, I crawled out of the window. In the drive, the wind soughed in the trees. Sally's Peugeot was there, and lights shone from the kitchen window.

I staggered across the gravel and hammered on the front door.

Chapter Twenty-Six

The wind was up. It hissed in the oaks and made them toss their heads like lunatics. My eyes would hardly stay open. When the door opened. I fell inwards and for the second time that night tasted Persian rug. The house seemed to be singing like a mad choir, timbers creaking, windows rattling, doors slamming, pipes ticking. I lay there for a moment, confused by it all. Gradually, I became aware that Sally was calling my name. I got up on my hands and knees.

'Your face,' she said.

I sat down in one of the hard hall chairs.

'What have you been doing?' she said.

I focused my eyes on her with difficulty. They felt burnt. My face felt burnt, too, and my hand was in agony and my body was full of aches, with a sharper ache where the fire-raiser had whacked me with a chair, and where I had hit the gatepost in the car.

'Driving,' I said.

'Tell me.'

'Later. Telephone.'

I rang the hospital and got Hilda Hicks.

'Ooh, Mr Agutter,' she said. 'We've hàd that Scotto chap in again, nasty burns.'

'How bad?' I said, my brain conjuring up a flayed Scotto, dying.

'He's gone home,' said Hilda. 'With that nice Georgia.'

'Someone said you had Amy Charlton in,' I said. 'Is she all right?'

202

'Poorly,' said Hilda. 'She's asleep. Georgia said if you rang to give you a number.' She gave me the number. When I rang, Georgia answered.

'Scotto's okay,' she said. 'Hard to believe, but he had the clothes burned off him and just about nothing else, except his eyelashes. You might have left me the eyelashes,' she said, aggrieved.

'*Nautilus*?'

'Sunk. Burned out. But you saved the hull. I'm sorry, Charlie.'

'So am I,' I said. 'Can Scotto sail?'

'Ask him,' she said.

Scotto came on the line. They must be in bed together. Bed. What a beautiful word.

'Are you hurt?' I said.

'Not a lot,' said Scotto.

'Can you sail tomorrow?'

'Of course,' said Scotto.

'Can you get down early and go over *Sorcerer* from top to bottom? Get the others out to help.'

'Yeah. Dike's sleeping aboard tonight, just in case.'

'I'll get down when I can. Scotto, that guy was aboard *Sorcerer* after he torched *Nautilus*. The alarm went.'

'It did?' Scotto sounded less than his usual confident self.

If you want to stop a boat, there are a lot of ways of doing it and very few ways of finding out how it has been done, until the boat stops. Which was not what we wished to happen, in a Captain's Cup trial.

'Pardon my asking,' said Scotto. 'But you left the marina chasing the guy. Did you catch him?'

'He caught me,' I said. 'And that was the other thing I meant to tell you. Do not have any communication with Frank Millstone, or Archer, or any other *Crystal* crew.'

'Okay,' said Scotto. 'Er . . . nice work with the fire extinguisher.'

'Not at all. Sorry if you were . . . er . . . put out.' I rang off. Sally was staring at me.

203

'Children's games,' I said.

'Shut up,' she said. I was pleased to notice that she remembered our conversation. In my present state, the strangest things were giving me pleasure.

'What happened?' said Sally.

I explained as I dialled another number.

'He was coming here?' she said.

'He was.'

'But why?'

'I was hoping you could straighten me out,' I said.

The telephone was ringing, and a voice said, 'Police.'

I got through to Nelligan, and said, 'Do you want the bloke who's been fixing all those rudders?'

'Nobody's fixed any rudders that I've seen proved,' he said.

'All right. Try arson and attempted murder.'

'Oh.' He sounded impressed. 'Who do I go and see?'

'You could start with Jack Archer. He'll be staying with Frank Millstone. Try asking him who's been driving his car tonight. And you could go and visit Mrs Charlton in hospital. She's got concussion. Try asking her how she got concussed.'

I heard the scrape of a match as he lit a John Player Special. 'Millstone and Mrs Charlton aren't exactly pals of yours, are they, Mr Agutter? Sure you're not being a little bit mischievous? Tell you what, we'll send a man round to Mr Millstone in the morning.'

I was too tired to argue. 'Bit influential, is he?' I said.

'Good night,' said Nelligan, and put the telephone down.

Sally helped me into the kitchen, and said, '*Nautilus* is burnt. *Sorcerer* has been interfered with. Amy's been beaten up. Your car's a write-off. What is it, Charlie?' As she spoke, she was dabbing at my face with a wet cloth. The cloth was coming away dirty. 'What's going on?'

Her Egyptian face was moving in and out of focus, the long, green eyes serious as she did something painful to my left cheek.

204

'Someone wants me out of the trials,' I said. 'What size would you say Archer's feet were?'

She frowned. 'No idea. Eight? Nine?'

'Not twelve?'

'Not twelve.'

'No.' It was getting harder and harder to make my mind work. 'What I think is going on is that someone started out to try and get me out of the Cup, and found he enjoyed the work, and now he's a raving psycho.'

'Why beat up Amy?'

'He could have been screwing her. Just about everyone else has. Jealous, maybe.'

'But why come after me?'

'There,' I said, 'you have me.'

'Millstone?' she said.

'Not impossible,' I said. 'He's got big feet, all right. And he hates Agutters. But then again . . .'

Suddenly I could not breathe sitting down, so I stood up from the kitchen table. And all the pain, the burns and the aches and the misery of losing a brother and a boat and the worst misery of being this close to whoever had done it all but not being certain, came smashing down on me. And I saw the wooden table and the chairs and the paintings on the walls tilt, shrink and flee. And I fainted.

I was having a bloody awful dream. In the dream, I was back in *Nautilus*' cabin. The flames were pouring over me like lava, and I was struggling with the hatch. But the hatches would not open. The pain was horrible, and I yelled.

I yelled myself awake.

I was lying in a big bed onto which green light poured, filtered by young oak leaves on the trees outside. Sally's bed. My right hand was bandaged with nice white bandages. My face was covered with something greasy.

'Good morning,' said Sally. She was sitting at a desk in the window, writing.

205

'Good morning,' I said, and lay there soaking up the light. Everything was very bright and calm. Because, as I lay there in the bed, the facts had sorted themselves and the jigsaw was complete. And I knew what was going on, and why, and who was responsible for it. And now that I knew, I could handle it in a way Hugo would have appreciated.

I tried to sit up. Pain drove away my self-satisfaction.

'Yes,' said Sally, watching me coolly. 'The doctor said you ought to be in hospital. But I said we'd look after you here.'

'What's wrong with me?' I said.

'Burns to face and hands. Bruised ribs. Contusions on neck and shoulders. Possible concussion.'

'Great.' I sat up, despite the noisy protests of my back muscles. I could still taste *Nautilus*' smoke in my throat. 'What's the time?'

'Eleven o'clock. The quack thought you were in a coma, except for the snoring.'

'Eleven o'clock.' I looked around the room. 'Where are my clothes?'

'I threw them away.' She grinned at me. 'You won't need any for a couple of days.'

'I've got a race,' I said. 'The Duke's Bowl. I've got to go.'

'Nobody's indispensable,' she said.

'I am. Today I am.' I swung my feet onto the floor. Except for a few bandages, I was in a state of nature. 'Clothes. Please, Sally. Or I'll have to go like this.'

She sighed. The happiness went out of her eyes, and she went into another room and returned with a bundle that she threw on the bed. The she went back to her chair and watched me as I dressed, taking in my winces and grunts of agony, and making no effort to help.

'I'll make some breakfast,' she said at last.

'Could you ring the hospital?' I said. 'Find out how Amy is, if she can remember anything?'

She nodded and went downstairs.

206

It took me five minutes to tie the shoes she gave me. They had been Hugo's. When I tried to walk to the door, it was even worse. I sat on the bed and wondered how the hell I was going to survive a race from Pulteney to Cherbourg and back, starting in four hours. That led me on to Breen, and the fact that he was arriving in an hour and a half. I hooked a chair, and managed to get across the room by hanging on to its back and shoving it in front of me. I got out of the door and to the stairs, where I clung to the banisters and inched downstairs.

By the time I had reached the bottom, my muscles had warmed up to the point where I could shuffle along unsupported. I staggered to the kitchen. She was frying eggs at the Aga.

'How's Amy?' I said.

'Sedated,' said Sally. 'She came round confused, hysterical, incoherent, and as far as I could gather from Hilda not mentioning names.' She put the bacon and eggs and toast in front of me, and I washed it down with the strong coffee. 'Hugo used to eat all that stuff before he went off,' said Sally. Her eyes were far away. 'It's funny, the little things that get you.' We both sat in silence for a moment. 'Charlie, you are going to catch whoever did this, aren't you?'

'Yes,' I said, and I could feel the certainty in my voice. 'How's my car?'

'The neighbour towed it into the side with his tractor,' she said. 'You might as well ring up the scrapper.'

I rang the scrapper. Then I made another call, this time to Neville Spearman. We had harsh words, Neville and I. But finally, he told me what I wanted to know.

Then I hobbled back to Sally and said, 'Could you possibly give me a lift down?'

As we turned into Fore Street, she said, 'What happens if that . . . person comes again?'

I said, with complete certainty, 'He won't.'

The jetties were lined with yachts. People with trolleys of gear and provisions moved along them like ants on

207

blades of grass, lit by a watery sun. I saw *Sorcerer*'s triple spreaders; and, at one of the outermost berths, *Crystal*'s fractional rig and four spreaders, and her big green-and-orange battle flag on the forestay.

'Are you sure?' she said.

'Quite sure.'

A Transit van had drawn up to the end of the jetty. It had *Crystal* painted on its side. Archer and Johnny Forsyth got out and carried a big sailbag down to the jetty between them.

'Good luck,' said Sally, and leaned over and kissed me on the mouth. She might have done it to avoid kissing me on the cheek, and getting tannic acid jelly over her face.

Then again, she might not.

Using a walking stick I had scooped from her hall stand on the way out, I hobbled down the jetty. The wind wailed in the rigging of the moored yachts. I was feeling better; so much better that I could almost walk.

They helped me aboard *Sorcerer* with a certain tenderness.

'Blimey,' Scotto said when he saw me. 'You look terrible.'

'You don't look so good, yourself,' I said. He had no eyebrows and his hair was all burned off at the front and he was wearing a long-sleeved sweatshirt, motor-cycle gauntlets, shorts and heavy leg bandages.

He slapped *Sorcerer*'s side with his gauntlet, and winced with pain. 'We went over her,' he said.

'What did you find?'

'Nothing,' he said. 'She's just fine.'

'So we're going out there and waiting for her to fall to bits.'

'The bastard may have left her alone after all,' said Scotto.

I tilted my head back and looked up at the taut spider's web of steel and aluminium wailing among the scudding grey clouds. 'What if it's something up in the rig?'

208

'We checked that, too.' Scotto looked less happy. 'I brought some spares.'

I grunted. Short of re-rigging, there was no way of checking. And spares tended not to be much use when you had the stick over the side.

'Good day, gentlemen,' said a voice from the jetty.

I turned. It was Breen, small, chubby and businesslike, his wavy hair crisp, cigar jutting from his pink face above an immaculately-creased blazer and canvas trousers. He stepped lightly aboard, accepted his seabag from his chauffeur, and went below. I had a nasty moment of déjà vu. Last time I had seen him on a boat had been in Kinsale.

This was not the kind of thinking that won races. Stiffly, I clambered below and climbed into my dry-suit. Breen's cigar was polluting the air. I said, 'On deck only, if you wouldn't mind.'

Breen looked at me sharply, then took the cigar out of his mouth and pitched it out of the hatch.

'Sorry,' I said.

'You're the skipper,' he said. 'I'll stay out of the way.' His hand strayed to the pocket where he kept the cigars, then snatched itself away again. 'Have you been in a fight?'

'Protecting your interests,' I said, and grinned at him in a way that hurt my face. 'Now, if you wouldn't mind, we'd better get a move on. I'll tell you later.'

'Certainly,' he said. This time he actually had a cigar out before he remembered. I had the feeling that he was out of his element, as he looked around at the stark, white interior, sailbags, space frames, cooking stove, cots and radio.

He scuttled up the companionway. I followed, more laboriously, and began to concentrate on what Doug had on his clipboard. Scotto, moving stiffly because of the bandages inside his coat and gloves, let go the shore lines and stuck *Sorcerer*'s nose into the wind that was bowling across the short grey seas from the direction of France.

209

Chapter Twenty-Seven

The Duke's Bowl is the first long race of the National Ocean Racing Club's season of offshore races. Yachts of all ratings compete and the results are adjusted according to their ratings, so it has been known for antiques which arrive hours after the leaders to win on corrected time.

We sailed out through a jostling throng of yachts, from wooden pensioners via every shape and size of cruiser-racer, to giant maxis built of state-of-the-art materials, tuned like Stradivariuses and eighty feet overall. Captain's Cup hopefuls were out in force. I waved to a couple of friends. Then the first gun went and the waving stopped, and we started trying, hard.

I saw *Crystal* plugging out beyond the red, white and blue hull of *Flag*, a big American maxi the Sound Yacht Club was entering for the Lancaster Great Circle Race later in the year. There was no denying that she looked extremely businesslike. I watched her tack and come back under *Flag*'s nose, Archer playing his favourite trick. When I brought my eyes back inboard, Breen was watching me.

I knew why. I beckoned him aft, and said, 'Did you know that someone on *Crystal* tried to fix your boat?'

The two eyes and the cigar focused right between my eyes. 'When?' he said.

'Last night.'

He gave no visible sign of emotion. 'What did they do?' he said.

210

'We were going over her all morning. Couldn't find anything. Must be in the rig.'

The eyes and the cigar tilted back. As he looked up, I noticed for the first time that under the chubby pink flesh of his face he had a lower jaw like the ram of a battleship. He studied the taut web of the rig for perhaps thirty seconds. Then he said, 'So something's going to break.'

'One has to assume it's possible.'

'What are you proposing to do about it?'

'Start the race, and drive her till she pops, if she's going to.'

Breen's eyes were deep and remote. He was still as an Easter Island head against the pale sun which was painting the sea cold blue and giving a hectic glitter to the white wakes of racing-boats.

'Charlie,' said Doug, at my elbow.

'Excuse me,' I said to Breen, politely.

Then I went into race mode and the world shrank until it was made of the close-hauled indicator and the flutter of the tell-tales, the lift of the deck and the intricate lacework of other boats' tracks, and Doug's steady mutter in my ear as the seconds on the readout clicked down, ten by ten. The five-minute gun went. The horde of white triangles converged on the invisible line between the two committee boats.

A puff of white smoke drifted from the right-hand boat, followed a split second later by the sound of a gun. We ramped over the line in echelon with three other boats, towards the right-hand end. *Crystal* was somewhere in the tangle far down to the left. I did not have much time to think about her, because we were engaged in a ding-dong tacking duel with our co-starters all the way down to the western end of the Teeth. We were fifth round the buoy. I eased the wheel with my good hand until the compass settled on 118 degrees. The wind was freshening, and the foredeck men had changed down to the number three genoa. Ahead, grey waves marched out of a cold grey

211

horizon. The wind was cold, but I was sweating with the concentration of the first beat.

'Crispin,' I said. 'Take over.'

All this time, I had been dimly aware that Breen was not behaving like an owner. Normally, owners fall into two types. One is the exaggeratedly helpful, who gets in the way hurling himself after loose sheets. The other is the Big Smiler, who sits as far back as he can, out of the way, and grins like a Cheshire Cat at anyone whose eye he can catch. Breen was sitting still, but he was not smiling.

He pulled me back and said, 'Did you re-rig the mast after the last race?'

'No,' I said.

'I got a bill for a backstay.'

'Yes,' I said. 'We bust one. So we made a modification, put on a single instead of a double.'

Breen said, 'Well, if I was going to sabotage a boat, I'd go for some brand-new equipment. How would you sabotage a backstay?'

The bow plunged into a wave, and spray flew aft. It caught Breen full in the face, but he didn't even blink.

'I'd slack it off,' I said. 'Then I'd put a kink in. Then I'd crank up the purchase till it straightened. That way you'd have a stay about as strong as button-thread. It'd take about five minutes.'

'Well?' said Breen.

'Well,' I said, tracing with my eye the taut wire that ran from the transom, through the high, rushing air, to the masthead casting seventy feet above us. 'And why the hell not?'

I beckoned Scotto. 'We need a volunteer,' I said. 'And some of your spares.' Scotto went to fetch. I said to Breen, 'It's not necessarily the backstay. Are you sure you don't want to retire?'

'Balls,' said Breen, with sudden and terrifying vigour. 'This is the first time I've been away from a telephone in five years. Fix that stay, and if we lose the mast we lose the damn mast.'

'All right,' I said, slightly awed. 'You're the owner.'

Sorcerer's crew might not have been together long, but they showed no signs of it now. Within three minutes, Dike the foredeck man was walking up the mast like an orang-outang, while Al the mastman applied his gigantic shoulders to the halyard winch.

'If you needed proof that man was descended from apes, you'd have it right here,' said Doug. Breen turned and glared at him. Then, surprisingly, he laughed.

It was the first time I had heard Breen laugh. It seemed likely that it was the first time anybody had heard him laugh. It made me like him, a lot; after all, it was his money at risk, and there was even a certain amount of danger about the situation – though the danger was mostly for Dike.

Dike did not, however, seem to mind. He sang noisily as he shackled the jury backstay to the masthead casting. He yelled insults at Scotto as Scotto effected a temporary junction between jury backstay and chainplate, and took the strain. And he sang again, obscenely, as he lowered the old backstay to the deck. On the way down the mast, *Sorcerer* hit a seventh wave and stopped dead. He looped out into space like a spider on its web, and crashed into the sail. Al the mastman lowered him with a run, and he unclipped and shambled aft on his prehensile Docksiders.

'Nice work,' said Breen.

Dike grinned at him, showing more gaps than teeth.

'Let's have a look at the stay,' he said. He ran the black coil through his square, calloused hands. Halfway, he stopped. 'Oi, oi,' he said. 'There you are.' It was a tiny bump in the cable. Dike looked down at it thoughtfully. 'What's it blowing?' he said.

'Force six, gusting seven.'

Dike twisted his head on his non-existent neck. 'Shit,' he said. Then, evidently thinking deeply, he returned forward.

'He was lucky,' said Scotto. 'Could have gone any time.'

213

'Thank you,' I said to Breen.

'Not at all,' said Breen. His eyes were glittering with excitement, and I realised that for ten minutes he had not had a cigar in his face. Now he cut off the end of a new one, and lit it, bending down into the trench to shield the flame. When he came up again, his eyes were dull once more.

'Now then,' he said. 'Maybe you'd better tell me what's going on.'

So we went and sat on the weather deck, feet out through the rail, staring at the rest of the fleet reaching out across the growing seas for the far-off coast of France. And I told him everything, omitting nothing. Except the fact that I had twisted *Sorcerer*'s rudder myself.

When I was finished, he said, 'So he threatened you with bankruptcy when you wouldn't sell your house. Upon which he intimidated your old and feeble father. And in order to further his own interests he is employing some bloke who you say has been responsible for murder, arson, and intimidation, and grievous bodily harm, and you reckon that Millstone knows it, but as long as this bloke's useful, he's not turning him in. So why the hell haven't you turned him in yourself, Charlie?'

I waited while a wave broke over *Sorcerer*'s bow and the deck swam clear.

'I'll do it after we've won this race,' I said. 'By fair means. I felt I owed it to my brother, and some other people.' Like my father, and Sally, and my old friend Ed Beith, and all the other people in Pulteney who had woken from the sleep of centuries to find Millstone standing on their faces.

'Fair enough,' said Breen. 'I don't much like vendettas on my time, but as long as you beat them, we'll make an exception, this once.'

'Yes,' I said.

'Beat who?' said Doug, who had come to sit beside us.

'*Crystal*.'

214

'She's a fast boat,' said Doug. 'And it's her kind of breeze.'

But that did not stop us trying.

The wind veered westerly soon after dark, and we pulled out the kite. *Sorcerer* began to fly. It was very dangerous sailing, over-canvassed in a confused sea, and Crispin and I had to change often – not only to keep alert, but because of the sheer physical strain of cranking the wheel. *Sorcerer* carved through the waves with her lee rail feet under and the vees of spray whizzing back from her stanchions. She creaked and she groaned and the wind screamed a horrible chord in her drum-tight rigging. It was exciting at first. Then the wet and the cold and the screaming wind blew away the thrill of doing something very fast and very dangerous, leaving only the dogged determination to hang on through the next twenty hours.

This time, there was an extra edge to the determination, and its name was *Crystal*.

We rounded the buoy at four a.m. with a force eight kicking up the sea and Cap de la Hague flashing white to the southeast. The maxis were already round. We were lying third of the Captain's Cup trialists. Ahead were *Ariel*, a Joe Grimaldi boat; and *Crystal*. *Crystal* had come round the buoy twenty minutes before us.

I handed the helm to Crispin, who had come up from below. 'I'm going for a kip,' I said. 'Sir Alec, why don't you get your head down?'

He had been sitting on the stern, visible only by the glow of his cigar. Now the glow moved left and right, once, precisely, as he shook his head. 'I'll stay up,' he said. 'Don't want to miss the fun.'

It had started to rain. Fun, I thought, as I went into the wet cabin and rolled my aching limbs into a wet bunk. That was one way of putting it.

I woke for the early morning shipping forecast. Force seven, gusting eight, they said.

On deck, a dirty grey morning had developed, with horizontal rain from the sou'west. I took the wheel from Crispin, and Crispin went gratefully below.

Sorcerer was giving of her best, under main and tri-radial. She was flying along the seas on gossamer wings of spray, and the log needle spent most of its time hovering between twelve and fourteen knots.

'Are we catching *Crystal*?' I said to Doug.

'Hard to tell,' he said. 'Have to wait till we see her.'

He was joking, of course, because visibility was down to five hundred yards in the rain. *Sorcerer* might have been on a solo cruise, for all the competition that was visible.

Breen was still crouched on the stern. 'Had enough?' I said.

He grinned at me. The cigar was soaking wet. 'Catch 'em,' he said.

I did my best. The rain stopped, and Dike brought up sausage, beans, eggs and porridge mixed together in tin pint mugs. The wind held. The cloud cover lifted gradually. VHF said that *Ariel* had lost her mast, and had retired. At six minutes to noon, Dike shouted from the foredeck, 'There she is!'

A mile away and on the starboard bow was a white sail and a green-and-orange spinnaker. Breen rose to his feet and winced at the pain in his stiff joints.

'Take 'em,' he snarled.

'It might not be as easy as that,' I muttered.

Through glasses, it was apparent that *Crystal* was going well, with a heavy kite powering her across the water. There were eight figures visible in her cockpit, with Archer, small and stubby, at the helm.

'She's moving,' said Breen.

'Yes,' I said. The clouds parted, and a long beam of sun lanced across the heaving grey, drawing after it a stripe of turquoise flecked with white. *Crystal* suddenly gleamed, and the wet-gear of her crew was piercing yellow. But I was not looking at her crew. I was looking at the boat's

216

side, abaft the shroud chainplates, where a tiny gleam of silver ticked like a pulse in the sun's brilliance – a jet of water.

'She's pumping,' I said.

Doug and Scotto trained their glasses. 'She's got two blokes at it down there,' said Scotto. 'Must be making water.'

'Here we go, here we go, here we go,' said Doug.

It is hard to describe the fierce up-welling of power that you get when you see the competition after a long time out of view. This time, it was more than ever like champagne in the blood.

Sorcerer seemed to feel it, too. She came up and out of the water and set herself to hurdle the big swells like a steeplechaser, fast up to the crests and then breaking loose into the troughs with that marvellous lift under the feet that was more like flying than sailing, landing between the sheets of water hissing from the flare of her bow. It must have been a noble sight from *Crystal*'s cockpit. Or a terrifying one.

Because yard by yard, we were hauling her down.

After ten minutes, even Breen had noticed. His thick shock of grey hair was plastered to his head, and the spray streamed down his face, and he was thumping the deck with his fist, and muttering, 'Go *on*, go *on*.'

'Land,' said Doug.

The clouds were clearing, though the wind had not abated; if anything, it was up a knot or two. Across the white-streaked sea lay the low, green land. Between us and it were four sails canted – *Crystal* and three late maxis. And a shimmer of white water that rose like reversed rain, and drifted at the sky.

'The Teeth,' said Scotto to Breen, and pointed.

During the next half-hour, we narrowed the distance to half a mile. Through the glasses I could see *Crystal* clearly. They were still pumping. I could see the faces too: Archer at the wheel; next to him, Millstone and Johnny Forsyth. I could see their heads in profile. They were

217

making jerky, emphatic movements. I saw Archer shrug his shoulders, and raise his hands in the air, away from the wheel. And I saw Johnny Forsyth step up and take his place. Then Archer vanished from the picture.

'Go *on*. Go *on*. Go *on*,' said Breen behind me, drumming.

Figures scrambled onto *Crystal*'s foredeck. A ribbon of sail went up, and burst into a fat balloon of orange and gold.

'Stone me,' said Scotto. 'That's his big kite. In force eight?'

It lifted *Crystal* for a moment. The water under her bow made a rainbow in the sun.

'He'll blow it out for sure,' said Scotto. 'He must be crazy.'

A gust hit us, then swept on across the water towards *Crystal*, darkening the waves.

'Either that or he'll go over,' said Scotto. 'That'll slow him a bit.'

Another gust shivered us. The first one had reached *Crystal*. She took it with a heavy roll, came back and rolled far to leeward again.

'Bloody death roll,' said Scotto.

But she came back, her mast sweeping across the sky like an inverted pendulum bob.

Then the next gust hit her. I saw Forsyth's face, at the wheel, turn white. The chute rippled and filled tight. The roll, when it came, was slow and leisurely.

But it was all the way over.

A green wave came between us. We stood on tiptoe, shouting with horror, trying to see over the top. When we rose on the next crest, we saw her, or what was left of her.

She was lying well over on her side, with her mast on the water. Scotto said, 'She's not righting.'

She was not. The mast fought clear a moment, wavering skyward, trailing its wet rags of sails. Then it lay down again, wearily, as if defeated.

Scotto said, 'She's sinking.'

218

There was a moment of complete silence. Then I shouted, 'Down spinnaker!' and spun the wheel.

Five minutes later, a life raft was bobbing on the starboard bow. There were ten men in, on and around it. We pulled them in one by one. Millstone was streaming water, his face blue-black with stubble, menacingly silent. Johnny Forsyth was very pale, shivering, with greenish shadows under his eyes that spread onto his cratered cheeks. The rest of the crew was subdued and cold and shocked. The only one who was still talking was Archer, who insisted on coming last. I gave him my hand and he stuck his foot in the loop and heaved himself aboard.

'Below,' I said. 'Warm up.'

Archer was white as the foam on the waves and his eyes were scorching with anger.

'Charlie,' he said. Breen came up to listen. From below, we could hear Scotto's voice on the radio, reporting the wreck and the rescue. 'I want to tell you that that boat just bloody well fell apart.'

'We saw,' I said.

I looked across the water at *Crystal*. She was far down in the water now. As I watched, she rose on a wave, and the silver wand of her mast came up as if this time she was going to right herself. Then there was an explosion of bubbles, and the mast plunged down, and there was no more yacht.

But Archer gazed at the little patch of flotsam that was all that remained of her. He continued talking, to himself, not us.

'The bloody deck came off the hull. We've been pumping since Cherbourg. Then that bastard Millstone tells me to put up the big 'chute because you're catching us. And I said don't be a silly bastard but he said he was the owner and he pulled the bloody deck right off her. Thank the Lord I had time to get the lads on the pumps up from below and launch the bloody life raft.' He laughed, a harsh bark. 'I had the life raft out while the sail was going up.'

219

I said, 'Easy, Archer. Let's get you warm,' and fed him down the companionway. I gave the helm to Crispin, and said to Breen, 'Would you mind coming below a minute? It won't take long.'

Below decks, *Sorcerer* was like a steam bath with the heating broken. *Crystal*'s crew crouched in survival blankets and shuddered. Dike was handing out coffee.

Sorcerer lurched under my feet, heeled and steadied. The boys on deck had her sailing again. There was the squawk of Scotto reporting to shore by VHF. I waited until he had finished. Then I went forward and sat down on the cabin sole, with my back against the mast.

Chapter Twenty-Eight

'All right,' I said. 'This is the end. Nearly two months ago, somebody sabotaged my boat *Aesthete* and killed my brother.'

'Oh, for God's sake,' said Millstone.

'Shut up,' I said quietly. 'And listen. There have been two boats wrecked, and one boat burnt, and this boat interfered with before the race.' I found Millstone's eye. He was staring at me, his face a blank, furious mask. 'There are three men dead who should not be dead: my brother Hugo, Henry Charlton, and poor bloody Hector Pollitt, who went for a ride on a tiger.' They were still watching me.

In the faces of the crew there was incomprehension. But Archer knew what I was talking about, and Millstone, and Forsyth.

'Someone has been running a campaign against me and people connected with me,' I said. 'At first, I thought the idea was to bankrupt me by making everyone think I couldn't design a boat for a boating lake, so Frank Millstone could buy my house. Then I thought that the idea was to stop me competing in the Cup. But finally, after I had been whacked on the head and Amy Charlton had gone to hospital when someone pushed her face in last night – '

'What?' said Millstone. 'Amy?'

'Broken nose,' I said. 'Flattened. Might have been worse, but I happened to go through her front door at the

221

psychological moment so our man laid off. Anyway, when I saw Amy I knew that the reason all these things had been happening might have started with me and races and my house. But now, whoever was doing it was strictly working for himself, and he had his own reasons. Reasons that nobody understood but him, because he was mad as a hatter – look out!'

Johnny Forsyth was on his feet. 'Agutter!' he shouted. 'I should have killed you years ago!'

I had a clear impression of his face, green and ivory-white, the lipless mouth stretched back from his teeth in a terrible crescent grin. His arm went back. I dived sideways, but not quite fast enough, because something caught me on the shoulder and I went over onto the cabin sole. There was shouting and a smell of gas. I could see his feet go up the companion ladder and out of the hatch. The galley stove lay at my side, where it had landed.

'Turn the gas off!' I yelled. Archer, who was sitting by the companionway, turned it off at the bottle. By the time he had done it, I was at the companionway. Feet were thundering on deck. I went up the ladder and out.

It was very bright on deck. For a moment I was dazzled. When I could see again I saw Scotto and Forsyth by the lee rail. Scotto was holding Forsyth's coat. As I watched, Forsyth's fist flicked out, into Scotto's stomach. His other hand was held back, tensed like a spring, ready to break Scotto's neck. There was no time to think. I kicked Forsyth as hard as I could, on the inside of his left knee. His face came round, surprised. *Sorcerer* gave a lurch and he staggered backwards. The lifeline caught him in the back of the legs and he did a reverse somersault over the side.

Overhead, sails roared and flogged as Crispin came head to wind. Forsyth's head came up, vanished again. Fifty feet away, the western end of the Teeth mangled the waves. The head came up again, rose on a wave until its eyes were level with mine.

He was staring at me. I could see the whites all the way round the pupils. I could see into his mind as if into clear

222

water. He took one stroke back towards the boat. Then he seemed to change his mind and trod water. Then finally, he shook his head and turned away.

I lost him in a trough. I scrambled to the wheel. My thumb went for the engine start button. A hand grabbed my wrist.

It was Frank Millstone's. 'It's better this way,' he said.

'Better for whom?' I said, and shoved him out of the way, hard. But Johnny Forsyth's head was a black speck in the waves, now. He was too far away to come back unless we went after him, and I knew now that he wouldn't come back on his own.

Johnny Forsyth was swimming for the Teeth.

As I watched, a wave came under him and he disappeared in the trough on its far side. He rose on the crest, still swimming. At the moment he reached the top, the wave broke. It took him with it. There was one final, spidery cartwheel of arms and legs. Then the wave rose, whitened and collapsed into the black Teeth. The spray of it lifted fifty feet before the wind caught it, and drifted it away until it thinned to a shining fog, and faded from the face of the sea.

They gave us the race. Nelligan sat with the Committee and heard the evidence. Afterwards, they let me go and I wandered, dazed, into the soft evening light that filled the streets of Pulteney. Sally was waiting, and Ed Beith. And Scotto and Georgia, Sir Alec Breen and Archer.

Archer manoeuvred himself alongside me. He said, 'Look, Charlie, it goes without saying that your contract's all right again.'

'Thanks,' I said.

He smiled at me, the public relations smile, full of charm but without remorse. 'I'll pop off and write you a letter, then.'

'Fine,' I said.

He faded away, back into his round of cocktail parties

223

and polite smiles and saying the correct thing to the Press.

We went up to the house, and I brought the Famous Grouse out to the wrought-iron table in the garden. The smoke from Breen's cigar rose in blue coils towards the swallows hawking in the deep blue sky. There was a great sense of peace; a calm, with no impending storm.

'All right,' said Sir Alec. 'What's been happening?'

I said, 'It's quite simple. Johnny Forsyth reckoned that I got too much work, and he got too little. He had it in his head that if he wrecked my reputation, he'd be able to get the contracts I lost.'

'Does that follow?' said Breen.

'Nope. But you have to remember he wasn't quite the full shilling. Did you know Archer asked him to submit designs for a cruiser-racer? Perfectly legitimate, of course. Archer wasn't to know. But it encouraged Johnny in his fantasies.'

'Begin at the beginning,' said Scotto. He drained his glass and poured a new one.

'Me, too,' said Georgia, and held out her glass.

'Forsyth switched the bolts in *Aesthete*'s rudder. It killed Hugo and Henry but it also effectively lost me my contracts. When I took you all on our PR trip on *Ae*, he couldn't risk all his good efforts being undone, so he fixed *Ae*'s rudder, too.'

'How?' said Breen.

'Very devious, that. He'd worked at Hegarty's before, converting a trawler. He knew a bloke called Lenny Dennis, and knew he was an unsuccessful punter. Our Johnny did a lot of jobs for Millstone, as you know. Well, just after the *Aesthete* wreck Millstone went on his annual visit to a company he owns in Ireland, called Curran Electric. Johnny went along to paint a picture for the reception area of the factory. While he was there, he sent Dennis a bribe, with instructions to poison the dog at Hegarty's yard.'

'So you have a sleeping dog,' said Ed Beith. 'Did this Dennis cove do the dirty work with the rudder?'

'Nope,' I said. 'Forsyth did. Which is where Amy gets tangled up in this. Because Amy was having an affair with Forsyth – '

'Among others,' said Sally.

'Among, as you say, others. The weekend we were in Ireland, Amy and Forsyth were there too, staying in a coastguard cottage just down the beach from Crosshaven. Forsyth fixed *Ae*'s rudder on the Thursday night. Presumably Amy joined him on the Friday. On the Saturday, Amy had dinner with Hector Pollitt in Kinsale, and while they were dining and doing whatever they did afterwards, Forsyth went back to the yard and switched broken titanium bolts for the broken aluminium bolts.'

'And that should have been the end of Charlie Agutter, boat designer,' said Ed.

'Quite. But now Frank Millstone was on my case. Frank has never liked me, and he was obsessed with getting this house. Probably still is. He thought my rudders were cracking up because they were badly designed. He put Pollitt, who had been his tame pressman for some time, onto me. At first, I thought it might be Pollitt or Frank who were fixing the rudders. But then I decided it was a bit bold for Pollitt, and a bit basic for Frank, and I knew I had to look further. Then Sir Alec fixed us up with *Sorcerer*, and we pulled up *Aesthete*, and I went looking in Spearman's yard in the middle of the night. But unfortunately, Johnny had heard me talking to Chiefy about sabotage on the barge, and he came looking for me. By this time, I think Pollitt suspected that he was up to no good. But Pollitt was frightened of Forsyth. Johnny was having car trouble, so he made Pollitt wait in the lay-by by the marina while Johnny bopped me and set me adrift.'

'He must have been crazy,' said Scotto.

'He was,' I said. 'He had a theory that he was a full-time victim, oppressed by the forces of reaction in Pulteney and me in particular. He hated Sally because she went around with me, and me because I was supposedly stealing work from him, and Ed Beith because he went around with both of us, and Amy because she went around with anybody who wore trousers. Pollitt woke up the next morning, and discovered he was party to attempted murder, which was not at all what he wanted. So he took a little time to get his courage up, and then he came to see me because he thought I was aboard *Sorcerer* at the marina. But Scotto was there instead, and Scotto bopped him, thinking he'd come to nobble the boat. Forsyth must have been delivering some pretty heavy threats, because when I mentioned to Pollitt that I'd seen his car by the marina the night I got hit, he panicked and fell off his drainpipe.'

I took a gulp of whisky. I should have been feeling tired. Instead I felt free. Breen looked at the end of his cigar and said, 'Go on.'

'So by now, Forsyth was overheating badly,' I said. 'He'd started out with what he thought was going to be a little sabotage but now he'd cracked me on the head and set me adrift, and the principal witness was dead, he must have thought he could get away with just about anything. And at the same time, Millstone is beginning to overheat, because I have told him what I think of his methods of trying to make me sell my house. Forsyth knows he's negotiating for *Crystal*. Forsyth's been working on *Crystal*, and Forsyth sees a chance of showing what a good boat-doctor he is to a man whose objectives coincide with his – viz., to obliterate Agutter from the scheme of things. Also, Forsyth has been sending you some big bills for boat repairs, Ed, and you have been finding difficulty in paying them. Correct?'

'Correct,' said Ed. 'The little bleeder. He wasn't even doing the boat any good.'

'So in order to clinch the thing, Forsyth creeps over and lights your turkey sheds, so you have to sell to Millstone. And Millstone is then racing *Crystal*, and going very nicely, and in fact wanting to win so badly he can taste it. Except that in the first race, we beat her. Which annoys

226

Millstone, and you can imagine what it does to Forsyth. Well, I don't know who suggested it, but they decide to nobble *Sorcerer*, which is out of the water with a twisted rudder stock.'

I looked across at Breen, then at Scotto. Scotto's right eyelid drooped in the suspicion of a wink.

'So Forsyth borrows Archer's car and puts a kink in the backstay. But he makes a bad mistake. He has heard from his close associate Spearman that I have got *Sorcerer* wired for sound. So to divert attention, he puts a fire-bomb aboard *Nautilus*. I'm sure Millstone didn't suspect he'd do anything of the kind; after all, he knew Johnny as a general freelancer who'd do anything for a quid, not as a roaring psycho. But now he'd connived with Johnny in fixing *Sorcerer* he couldn't then turn Johnny in, in case Johnny blew the gaff. Realising this, Johnny began to feel somewhat invincible. After all, you can't get much more powerful in Pulteney than having Frank Millstone under your thumb. So he went to Amy, to chastise her for playing fast and loose. And he was proceeding towards Sally, to chastise her for having married an Agutter and being a friend of Agutters, when I bumped into him. The rest we know about.'

There was a silence. Then Sally said, in a small, quiet voice, 'How did you find all this out?'

'Asking questions. The one who clinched it was Neville Spearman. I was wondering why Forsyth should bother to burn *Nautilus* as well as nobbling *Sorcerer*. After all, he didn't know we had *Sorcerer* wired. The only people who knew were me, Scotto, Neville Spearman and the man who installed the alarms. Well, yesterday morning before the race, I rang Neville. And he admitted that he'd told Johnny. Couldn't see the problem, he said, Johnny was his right hand, good as a partner.'

'Was,' said Scotto.

Breen blew a cloud of smoke. 'It strikes me that you were very lucky,' he said. '*Sorcerer*'s rudder getting twisted at such an opportune moment, I mean.'

There was a crash. 'Sod it,' said Scotto. 'Whoops, sorry, I seem to have dropped a glass.'

'I'll get you a new one,' I said, and went into the house. When I returned, they were talking about Millstone.

'We can't touch him,' Sally was saying. 'It's infuriating.'

'In a way,' said Breen. 'But I believe there's been a meeting of the Pulteney Yacht Club Committee, today, and I think I know what they're talking about.'

'Oh?' said Ed Beith. 'How?'

'I arranged it, through some chaps I know,' said Breen, his chubby face inscrutable behind the smoke. 'I told them I'd seen Millstone prevent Charlie from going after Forsyth to render assistance out there by the rocks. And I gave them some . . . background.' He looked at his watch. 'Why don't we go for a bit of a walk?'

We walked down Quay Street, through my office and onto the quay. It was a beautiful evening. The clouds over Beggarman's Point were tinged with gold, and gulls shrieked over the boats in the harbour. Breen turned left, towards the squat wooden bulk of the Yacht Club. There were people drinking on the balcony; the breeze had died until there was barely enough to flap the Red Ensign on the mast. High on the cliff, the church clock was striking eight. A red Jaguar rolled along the quay. At its wheel, staring straight ahead, was Frank Millstone.

He parked by the Yacht Club door, and went in. I saw him push the inner glass door, and stand in the hall, talking to someone I couldn't see properly. Then he came out again, and I saw. It was the Club Secretary, looking grim and shaking his head. His voice floated down the quay.

'Out,' he was saying. 'Or I'll call the police.'

Millstone's fists clenched. He raised a hand. Then he dropped it again, and yanked open the Jaguar's door. The tyres screamed, and the car shot past and into Fore Street.

'Hmm,' said Breen. 'My friends thought something like that might happen. Barred by the Committee.'

I sat down on a bollard. Sally looked down at me, the

228

dark hair swinging on either side of her cheekbones, her eyes full of secret amusement. She was holding Ed Beith's hand, which was as it should be. I knew that what she was thinking was the same as what I was thinking. We did not give a monkey's for yacht clubs. Pulteney was home, and that was that.

'Would you like a drink at the Club?' said Breen.

'No, thank you,' I said. 'Let's go to the Mermaid. The beer's better.'